this changes
everything

BOOKS BY GRETCHEN GALWAY

THE OAKLAND HILLS SERIES

Book 1: Love Handles
Book 2: This Time Next Door
Book 3: Not Quite Perfect
Book 4: This Changes Everything

RESORT TO LOVE SERIES:

Book 1: The Supermodel's Best Friend
Book 2: Diving In

this changes

everything

Oakland Hills: Book Four

gretchen galway

ETON FIELD

For Joseph.

1

"IT'S A POODLEDOODLE," the little girl said, kicking Sylvester Minguez in the shins.

The sudden pain knocked the smile off Sly's face. He'd been thinking how cute the girl was, a five-year-old holding the leash of a curly brown mop of a dog that was as tall as she was. "I beg your pardon," he said, moving out of the range of her short legs. "I've never heard of a poodledoodle before."

"It's a new word," the girl said. "It means he's all poodle and nothing else."

Sly scratched the dog behind one fluffy brown ear. "Good name."

The girl gave him a look that was grudgingly apologetic. "My mom hates it when people call Charlie a labradoodle."

Sly brushed off the dirt she'd left on his best pair of dark jeans. "Then I'm glad she isn't around." One little girl's kick had been bad enough.

His uncle, fondly called Doctor Hugo at his decades-old veterinary clinic in El Cerrito, California, strode over from the front desk, took the leash, and escorted the girl and her poodledoodle to a man staring at his phone at the far end of the waiting room.

When Hugo returned to Sly, his eyebrows were raised in mock concern. "Will you need surgery?" Like Sly's father, he had a square, handsome face with short black hair, caramel-colored skin, and brown eyes as sad as those of a hungry basset hound.

Sly smiled and handed his uncle the gift bag he'd brought. "Possibly an amputation. That was a hell of a kick."

Hugo frowned at the bag. "What's this?"

"It's a birthday present." Sly looked around the busy clinic, saw several people and their companion animals waiting, and patted his uncle on the shoulder. "You look busy. I won't keep you."

Hugo nodded at the bottle of Laphroaig, his favorite whiskey, inside the bag. "I would've forgotten it myself if your dad hadn't called me first thing this morning."

"Maybe you can get off early, enjoy yourself."

Hugging the bottle under his arm, Hugo looked at his busy clinic. "I'm already enjoying myself. Nothing for me at home. You know that."

Sly shook his head. "You need to get married again."

"Me? You're what, thirty-five? I thought you would've gotten married a long time ago."

"I work too much for any woman to put up with me." Sly's own parents were proof of how sour a marriage could become when one or both of the participants were obsessed with a career. It was only fair to choose one or the other.

One of the vet techs behind the desk cleared her throat. Hugo patted the desk, waved at the group who was waiting, and gave Sly an apologetic shrug. "The Minguez men always have been workaholics. Sorry Sly, but I really have to get back—"

At that moment the front door burst open to a distraught woman holding a tiny dog. Both she and the animal were covered with blood.

"Help, Dr. Hugo," the woman gasped. "It's Luna. Luna's been run over."

The atmosphere in the clinic changed instantly. The technicians jumped out of their chairs, the other people and their pets stiffened with alarm, and Hugo strode over in a flash and put his arm around the woman, guiding her around the desk to the back.

"Easy, Trixie. Let's not move her any more than we have to," he said.

In those first few seconds, Sly had been too distracted by the sight of all that blood to recognize Trixie Johnson. Now his stomach took another lurch. Trixie was the mother of one of his best friends and had fostered dozens of rescue dogs over the years, although now only had a few. She loved her dogs almost as much as she loved her children, and that was saying something.

He followed them into the back, driven to help if he could. "Trixie, it's me, Sylly." He used his nickname—it sounded like "silly"—one that had amused him more when he was twenty-five than in recent years.

"She got away from me," Trixie was saying, not looking at him. "It's all my fault. Doctor Hugo told me to get a harness or a martingale so she couldn't wiggle out of the collar, but I didn't listen. She knew I was going to clip her nails when we got home, and she hates the clippers. Oh boy, does she hate the clippers." Her shoulders trembled.

Gently, his uncle examined the dog in Trixie's arms while a nurse and a technician hovered behind him. "We have to get her into the back, Trixie. Can you walk with me? I don't want to pick her up just to put her down again."

Trixie nodded and walked with them through another doorway. Sly waited behind and took out his phone to call Mark, his friend and Trixie's son, before remembering that he was out of town. Putting the phone back in his pocket, he paced around the small room, hoping for the best but dismayed by the memory of all that blood. It was a very little dog. His uncle would probably have to put it out of its misery. Poor Trixie. Damn unfair, life was.

His friend Cleo was expecting him, but he couldn't leave Trixie now. He sent her a quick text message and returned to pacing.

In a few minutes, the door opened. A young technician led Trixie, looking dazed but calm, into the room, before disappearing again.

Trixie walked over to the sink in the corner and began washing her hands very slowly. She went still, staring down into the pink water, her lip trembling. Sly walked over and put an arm around her.

"I'm so sorry," he said.

Trixie leaned against him for a moment, then drew away and went back to washing up more vigorously, squirting a mountain of liquid soap into her palm and sudsing up her forearms. "Don't be sorry. Hugo says she'll pull through. She's a fighter like her sister."

"That's great." He squeezed her shoulder. "What a relief."

"I'm all right now. There was a lot of blood, but it's not as bad as it looks. It was just the shock."

"Luna, her name is?"

Trixie nodded. "Luna."

He handed her a paper towel.

"There's nothing I can do." Roughly, she dried her hands and forearms with the towel. "They're doing everything they can." There was still a faint quiver in her voice.

"Let me bring you home. I'll make sure Hugo calls you as soon as they know how she's doing."

"I hate to leave her here all alone." She turned away and dabbed at her cheeks with the towel.

"She won't be alone. Hugo's here. And all the animal-loving minions he's hired are running around the place."

"But then my car will be here and I won't be able to come back in the morning."

"I'll give you a ride."

"You have to go to work. You're always working. Even worse than my own children."

"Not anymore," Sly said. "I quit this morning."

"Really?"

"Really."

"You don't have any new business you're starting up to take its place?"

"Not yet," he said. The thought of being idle and directionless terrified him. But maybe it would be good for him.

Trixie threw away the paper towel and looked down at her stained sweatshirt. She sighed. "All right. I'll take you up on that. I need to feed Zeus and Europa. They'll sense what's going on, and I don't want them to worry."

That settled, he led her out to his Audi on a side street behind the clinic and opened the door for her.

"No, you don't want me in that fancy car with Luna's guts all over me—"

He gave her a gentle push, and in several minutes they were heading south through Berkeley to her house in the hills of Oakland.

"Is there anyone I can call for you?" he asked. "I know Mark and Rose are out of town, but maybe—"

"I'll be fine. It's Luna I'm worried about. But your uncle is a wonderful vet. Expensive, but they're all like that now, aren't they?"

He was trying to think of a polite way of offering to pay for Luna's care when a call came through on his car's speakers.

"Hi, Sly," Cleo said cheerfully. "What's your ETA?"

"Less than an hour." He hadn't explained in his text why he was going to be late, just that something had come up at his uncle's. "I'm in the car."

"With a hot chick, right?" Cleo laughed that unexpectedly throaty, sexy laugh of hers, and he knew she suspected exactly that and was trying to embarrass him.

"Hello," Trixie called out. "I'm a chick but not very hot. At least, not at the moment. My dog just got run over by a bicycle."

Cleo's swift inhalation of breath made the speakers crackle. "Oh, I'm so sorry." She fell silent, no doubt wondering whom the hell she was talking to.

"Can I call you back?" Sly asked. "I'm bringing Trixie home. She's up in the hills."

"Just come over whenever you're done. No hurry," Cleo said, then raised her voice. "Sorry about your dog."

"Thanks," Trixie said. After Sly hit the hang up button on the steering wheel, she said, "I'm so glad you've found someone. She sounds wonderful."

"Oh, that's just Cleo. A friend."

"Oh?" The word spanned an octave and expressed deep skepticism.

He chuckled. "Take it easy. I know how you like to set people up."

"She called you Sly. Not Sylly."

"Yeah, she insisted on that when we met."

"Sly is much sexier."

He snorted. "Cleo's not like that."

"Not like what?"

"You know what I mean. We're friends. Great friends. We talk to each other, hang out, just relax."

"And what did you do with your girlfriends?" Trixie asked. "When you weren't having sex? Or were you always going at it?"

Another laugh tumbled out of him. Trixie was one of the most plainspoken people he'd ever met. "What's the fastest way to your house from here, do you think?"

She sighed. "Sorry. I was trying to distract myself. Do you think your uncle would've called me if something serious had happened?"

"Absolutely. Right away."

Silence settled between them. He felt guilty for not staying on the topic that had brought her a little relief from worrying about the dog, but he knew that if she made a project out of his love life, he'd be in trouble. Hitched within the week, probably. All three of her children had settled down recently, and since Chihuahuas didn't date, she needed fresh victims for her schemes.

"What does she do?" Trixie asked. "Your *friend*."

"She's a musician."

"Like a rock star?"

He shot her a smile as he turned left on a steep street up into the hills. "Like a piano teacher."

Trixie's face melted into ecstatic approval. "Really? Oh, she sounds so nice."

"She's not. She's a pain in the ass." He cleared his throat. "Pardon my French."

"Cleo the piano teacher," she said thoughtfully. "I can't wait to meet her."

Warning bells ringing, Sly was careful to say nothing more about Cleo for the remainder of the journey. When they reached the house, Trixie became preoccupied with the other dogs waiting for her and didn't say another word about Cleo except that Sly should hurry along and see her.

"Are you sure I can't call anyone for you?" he asked, lingering at the front door.

Hugging two tiny dogs up to her chin, one of them remarkably ugly, she said, "No, I can do that myself. But I will hold you to that ride in the morning if that's all right."

"More than all right." He took a business card—the job title was now obsolete, but the phone number was good—out of his wallet and handed it to her. "Call me anytime."

She took the card and studied it. "Because you won't be worn out from just being with a friend."

Smiling, he shook his head. "I'm never worn out."

The door was already closing between them, but she stopped it and peeked out at him. "Don't be so sure about that, Sly. Oh well, thanks again." The door banged shut.

He wondered what she meant. You thought you knew with Trixie, and then you learned you were about half-right. Half-right and sideways, inside out, or in reverse. You just didn't know how exactly until it was too late.

When he got back in the car, he closed his eyes, leaned back on the headrest, and yawned. Maybe he was worn out. He wasn't as young as he used to be.

With that depressing thought, he started the car and headed for Cleo's. Good old Cleo. There was no sideways or inside out with *her*.

2

CLEOPATRA HOLT, CALLED Cleo by everyone except her parents and telemarketers, answered the door in her pajamas. She'd put them on the moment she got home in spite of the evening's plans. It was only Sly, after all.

"How's the dog?" she asked him, taking the six-pack of IPA and hugging him stiff-armed bro-style over the pizza box he carried. Her heart squeezed to see how tired he looked. Nobody could work as hard as he had for so many years and not fall apart eventually.

"She's doing OK, actually. It was a bike, not a pickup. Hugo thinks she'll pull through. He just called me."

"Awesome." She took the pizza and strode through her tiny living room to the kitchen.

"Listen, you got a pair of sweats I can borrow? I didn't have a chance to go home, and I can't really chill in these clothes."

"You know where they are." She stole an early slice and shoved it in her mouth. Her apartment was so small she only had one small walk-in closet for all her things—clothes, old sheet music, books, copies of tax returns, signed divorce papers…

A few minutes later, he appeared in an old San Francisco State sweatshirt and his own tattered jeans, which he'd forgotten there a month ago after helping her paint the bathroom. She'd washed them, but they were spattered with Zen-green acrylic paint.

"That's better," she said. "It's like Superman in reverse. Always a relief to see you take off the business casual."

Wiggling his eyebrows, he ran a hand up and down his chest in mock lust. "I know what you're after, you wench."

"You have no idea. Do you realize how long it's been since I got laid?"

"Maybe you should, you know, wear something other than—what the hell is that, old men's underwear from Goodwill?"

She sniffed. "You know I have sensitive skin. The fabrics from the store make me itch. Second-hand clothes have all the chemicals washed out of them already." She opened one of the beers, poured it carefully into a pint glass, and handed it to him with her tongue sticking out. "And I wear men's because it's comfortable and well-made. I'm not one of those skinny chicks you like to date. I've got big thighs and broad shoulders and huge —"

"Old men are shaped nothing like you, Cleo." His dark eyes danced over her. "Trust me on that one. Under all that ugly, there's a hot babe lurking."

"You're so full of shit." She finished the first slice of pizza before grabbing a plate for her second and Sly's first. "I have some bagged spring mix, but it smells like ass. Want some?"

"You need to work on your marketing. Take it from the tech guru." He gulped down half his pint glass, looked at it, then tipped it back for another swallow. Then a belch. "Ex-tech guru, that is."

She smiled. "You quit!"

"You can't quit when the company doesn't exist yet."

"Sure you can," she said. "Congratulations."

"Yeah, OK. I quit." He drained the glass. "I'm unemployed."

"I'm so happy for you."

He shook his head, looking miserable. "I feel like throwing up."

"That's because of the IPA. Let me get you a lager."

But he didn't play along. "I'm serious. I think I made a mistake."

She took pity on him, in part because she'd been the one to persuade him to take time off from his relentless professional life. "You weren't into the concept. You didn't like that guy on the team. You hated commuting to New Jersey."

His only answer was to get another beer, load up his plate with pizza, and pad into the living room, where she'd already set up their bimonthly binge of TV. Lately it had been *Battlestar Galactica*. They'd been doing this now for four years. This whatever it was. This friendship based on pizza and immersive serial television. It was much better now that he didn't pretend to be learning to play the piano. The first two months of their acquaintance, he'd sat at the bench of her upright piano and failed to play the simple tune any better than he had the week before. Finally she'd suggested they have a beer. The lesson had been much more enjoyable for both of them after that. Another month or two later, they'd ditched the piano altogether and added pizza.

It was the most perfect friendship she'd ever had.

"I owe you for the pizza," she said, "but there's no way I'm handing over hard-earned cash for that bitter swill you pretend to like because it's trendy."

"This again? I refuse to take any of your tiny dollars. Do I need to make another graph comparing our net worths?" He saluted her with his second beer. "And you'd love ale if you'd let your taste buds evolve. How can a woman with so much personality be so damn bland about everything she puts in her mouth?"

She grinned. Even when he was complaining about her, he snuck in a compliment. "You sweet talker," she said. "How was Hugo?"

"Didn't get a chance to talk. Trixie came in with her dog." He flinched. "It was horrifying, actually. All that blood. And I've never seen Trixie upset like that."

"After I hung up, I remembered who she was." Sly often talked about his brilliant friend, Mark, and his family. "After all, how many Trixies can there be?"

"This is the only one I know, and that's enough." He sank onto her old sofa and closed his eyes. "She has a romantic frame of mind."

Ooh, this sounded good. "She hit on you?"

He looked at her without turning his head. "Oh yeah. Sucked me off right there in the car."

She hit him. And not as hard as he deserved. "The poor lady."

"The poor lady thinks you're in love with me."

"Maybe I am," she said, burping into her hand.

"Obviously."

"Everyone thinks that. I mean, look at you. Seriously hot. Dark, smoldering eyes. Broad shoulders, tight ass, flat abs. Wavy hair that probably feels really good to slide your hands through." Still holding her beer, she got up on her knees and patted his head. "You're like a cologne commercial."

He snorted and swatted her hands away. "Settle down. Are we going to watch this thing or not?"

Laughing, she flopped back down and reached for the remote on her coffee table. Well, it wasn't really a table—just a shipping box with a blanket thrown over it—but it did have coffee on it occasionally.

Sly dimmed the lights. They gingerly put their feet up on the box, eating their pizza and drinking their beer, and fell into their typically relaxed, comfortable, happy coexistence.

When the show was over, Cleo frowned at the screen, unhappy with the ending because it left her hanging, wondering if she'd be able to wait until two weeks from now or if she'd sneak-watch the next episode by herself, like she sometimes did, and then have to pretend to be surprised when they watched it together.

She flicked on the lights and saw that Sly had fallen asleep. Dark head tilted back, handsome nose in the air, strong jaw slightly less strong.

He really was a good-looking devil. And fairly rich by now with a few successful start-ups under his Gucci belt. Trixie wasn't the only person to assume she was in love with him. Her mother the ex-therapist was also a tiresome believer.

Few, however, ever suggested *he* must be in love with *her*. She knew she was perfectly adorable in a geeky-tomboy, curvy-real-woman kind of way, but her type and his type seldom paired up in life or the imagination. Not even hers.

And could she ever love a man who couldn't even carry a tune?

But she enjoyed his company and regretted the day he'd finally find a woman to spend his life with, because that would certainly mean the end of sharing their TV marathons and talking about their lives with uncritical ears and having a few hours every month where they could just *be*.

Given how scarred he was about his parents' cold war of a marriage, however, that day wasn't going to be anytime soon. He'd never said it out loud, but Cleo knew he was afraid of making the same mistakes his parents—and his father in particular—had.

Smiling, she lifted the empty plate out of his lap and set it on the cardboard table. "Sly?" she asked softly, leaning close. She hated to wake him. The past few months, he'd worked hundred-hour weeks, flying back and forth to the East Coast as he tried to make another new business a success. Yet he'd always made time for her, always kept their every-other-Thursday night date in front of the TV.

But the strain had been too much. His eyes were sunken and shadowed, the lines around his full lips deeper than they should've been. The price of being a successful tech mogul was too high, in her opinion, no matter how many millions rained down upon you. As her incorrigibly idealistic parents would say, you can't take it with you.

His eyes opened and found her face close to his. "Am I dead?"

"Almost. What's the last thing you remember?"

"The sexy blond robot chick," he said.

"That doesn't give us much to work with. She was in every scene."

"Actually, the last thing I remember is you," he said, smiling. "You sneezed. Woke me up for a second."

"Sorry." She patted him on the knee. "Well? Are you leaving?"

His hand came down over hers. He stared at her, heavy-lidded, half-asleep. "You're awesome, you know that?"

"How much did you drink? Maybe you should sleep on the couch."

He squeezed her hand. "No, listen. I mean it."

Then the funniest thing happened. She *blushed*. "You're embarrassing me," she said, rolling her eyes.

The perfect grin that disarmed employees, competitors, investors, strangers, and, yes, women, lit up his face. Seeing the Sly she knew so well, she couldn't help but relax and smile back at him.

But he continued to stare, his strong, warm hand over hers. She fought the urge to pull her hand away. And maybe pour a beer on his head.

Then his gaze dropped to her mouth.

Her breath caught in her throat. What was the matter with him?

He blinked, shook his head, and pulled away. "Man, I'm exhausted." Yawning, he massaged his face with both hands, then jumped to his feet and pulled out his phone. "What time is it? Wow, only eleven?"

She got up and busied herself picking up the plates, used napkins, empty glasses. For a second there, she'd thought he'd forgotten where he was. Who *she* was. "I bet you'll sleep around the clock. Want some coffee before you go home? You're close, but it's never safe to drive when you're half-asleep." She didn't repeat the offer to stay over.

"I promised Trixie a ride in the morning." He tried to take the glasses from her, but she shook her head and fled to the kitchen, leaving him alone in the living room. "I'll pass on the coffee. The sooner I get going, the sooner I can be sleeping." His loud laugh sounded a little forced.

"Let me know about her little dog, OK?" she called out to him. She heard the front door open. Waiting a little longer than she would've any other time, she strode out to say good-bye, catching him when he'd already stepped out into the hallway.

"I'll text you," he said, reaching down as if to button his jacket, then seeing he was wearing her sweatshirt. "Oh. Forgot what I was wearing."

"Don't worry about it. Give it to me later. I'll go get your clothes—"

"No, don't bother. I won't be needing them for a while. I'll get them next time."

They stared at each other through the doorway.

"Sure, of course," she said.

"Well, see you." He turned on the grin again. "Boy, I'm wiped out." Shaking his head, he pulled the door shut between them.

Cleo stood in place, listening for the sound of his departing footsteps but not hearing anything other than the hum of her cheap refrigerator. Her apartment building's hallways were carpeted. She wouldn't be able to hear anybody's footsteps. Nevertheless, she walked to the door and, feeling ridiculous, looked out the peephole.

He was gone.

Of course he was.

Laughing at herself, she finished the cleaning up and got ready for bed, wondering if she'd imagined it but knowing she hadn't.

Thank God he was finally taking a vacation. The strain of working too hard had obviously gotten to him.

3

CLEO WOKE EARLY most mornings to work on her own compositions. She hooked up her laptop to her keyboard and lost herself in her music, with noise-canceling earphones embracing her head in a cocoon of sound. Her latest work was just for fun, mostly Europop with a hint of her new ukulele. It probably wouldn't be her biggest seller—she had a small income from selling her work online—but she didn't care. Teaching was her day job. This was for her.

She hadn't talked to Sly since he'd been over to her place the previous Thursday. She hoped he was feeling better. Stress could break the strongest of men.

Her thoughts didn't linger on him for long, however, preferring the stimulation and satisfaction of music. Knowing this about herself, she'd set three timers on her computer to go off in sequence to remind her she had lessons scheduled all afternoon, mostly with elementary school kids at their own homes. One timer wouldn't be enough to break through her state of hyperfocus. Past experience had proven that she could ignore one, even two alerts. A third, however, artfully timed to go off ten minutes after the first two, usually broke through her fixation.

In fact, one of them seemed to be beeping right now. She'd

been ignoring it for several rings already.

She looked up from her laptop and took off her headphones. It wasn't a timer. It was her phone.

The number was unfamiliar. "Hello?"

"Is this Cleopatra Holt?"

Telemarketer. "Sorry, I'm not int—"

"My name is Trixie Johnson. I got your number from Sly."

"Sly?"

"Sylvester Minguez? Some people call him Sylly, but I think he's grown tired of that, don't you?"

Cleo had no idea why Trixie would be calling her. Her head was still wrapped up in her work, and she hated being taken away from it. But something about the woman made her smile. "I think he has too," she said. "By the way, how's your dog?"

"Pitiful. She's milking her cone of shame for all it's worth. Thank you so much for asking."

"I've been thinking about her. I'm glad to hear she's home."

"Didn't Sly tell you? He played doggie ambulance for us. I sat in the back and made a fool of myself blubbering all over her. Sly was so nice not to fuss over the tears on his nice leather seats. Well, and worse. The accident has made Luna a little incontinent, but Hugo thinks that should clear up."

Her concentration on her music completely shattered now, Cleo saved her work and closed her laptop. It was time to get dressed anyway. "He can just buy another car. Don't worry. He'll be glad for the excuse."

Trixie's laughter was light and girlish. "You're just as nice as I thought you'd be. Most people would've hung up on me by now. Or at least demanded to know why I was calling."

"I am a little curious."

"Of course. But it's nothing too surprising for you, I'm sure.

I'm looking for a piano teacher."

"Oh," Cleo said, relaxing. Sly's comment about her being a matchmaker had made her worried about the woman's motives. "Great."

"You do teach piano?"

"I do. Usually to kids, but I love working with adults. Have you ever played before?"

"Here and there. I have a piano in the house, but I'd love to get better. Do you think you have time for me?"

"Sure, of course," Cleo said. "I even make house calls."

"Wonderful. I was hoping you could come right now."

"Now?"

"Is that a problem?"

Cleo looked down at her men's boxer shorts and T-shirt. She was free until one, but... "How about in an hour?"

"Perfect. Got a pencil? I'll give you my address."

Why not? She jotted down the street and her phone number and hung up, tempted to call Sly and ask him what he thought of Trixie Johnson asking her for music lessons. But he must know already since she'd called her. Just sending her new clients. Helping her scrape out her humble living.

And so an hour later, she pulled her burnt-orange Honda Fit into the shallow driveway up in the Oakland Hills, checked the number on the old house, and went up to the door. Nice view. Between the trees she could see the Golden Gate Bridge and parts of Marin. Expensive neighborhoods up in the hills. Sly owned a house or two up here, although he lived in an apartment in Rockridge, squirreling away the rental income from the larger properties.

Trixie threw the door open. "You made it. Come in, come in." She held a bug-eyed Chihuahua swaddled in a pink sweater and wearing a plastic cone around her neck. Two other pint-sized dogs trotted around her feet. One of them was missing most of its hair and had a tongue that nearly reached the floor.

"The piano's nothing fancy, but it's in tune," Trixie said, sizing her up with a big smile. If she'd expected her to look like one of Sly's girlfriends, fashionably coiffed and athletic, she didn't show it. Many people who knew the dashing, acclaimed Sylvester Minguez seemed surprised when they met this great friend of his and saw she was just a normal person.

"I'm sure it's great," Cleo said, following Trixie to an upright in the living room. "I brought you my brochure. It's got my rates, my philosophy, other instruments I teach—"

"Other instruments? Like what?" Trixie sat on the bench and looked up at her over her shoulder. She had short white hair and shrewd eyes.

"I'm a big fan of the ukulele, especially for kids."

"I don't think I want to learn the ukulele. I'm a piano girl."

"No problem. Why don't you play a song for me so I get a sense of where you are, what I might be able to help you with?"

Trixie nodded with enthusiasm, turned, and launched into an enthusiastic, passionate, and brilliant recital of "Ode to Joy."

When she was done, Cleo waited a long moment before asking, "So, how long have you been playing?"

"About fifty-two years."

Smiling, Cleo sat on the bench next to her. "I think you should be the one teaching me."

"Don't be ridiculous. I missed several notes just now."

"You did that on purpose so I wouldn't get suspicious."

Trixie bit her lip, eyes dancing. "Suspicious of what?"

"I'm not sure, but I think it has something to do with a certain tall, dark, and handsome businessman we both know."

"He is handsome, isn't he?" Trixie asked.

"Yeah, he is. Not actually that tall, but the ego fools you. Makes him seem bigger."

Trixie looked down at her hands and caressed the keys. "It was harder to flub that one than I'd expected. I should've picked a different piece. That one's an old favorite."

"You played it beautifully."

Trixie sighed. "I don't suppose you work with very young children?"

"How young?"

"She'll be one next month," Trixie said.

"One? As in a baby?"

Trixie nodded.

"That's a little too young. Just a little."

"Even for the ukulele?"

"For another year, at least," Cleo said.

"OK, you got me." Trixie got to her feet and turned to her. "I'll learn the ukulele."

Smiling, Cleo stood. "I don't think your heart is in it." She glanced at a large antique wall clock. Her first real lesson was in two hours.

She was curious. What had Trixie's long-term plan been? What had she really been trying to do? "Trixie, pardon me for asking, but..."

"He's lonely. You sounded so nice." Trixie picked up the funny-looking dog and nuzzled him. "But you're not interested, are you?"

"No. I'm not."

"Just friends?"

"Just friends."

"Then you must see how lonely he is," Trixie said. "Don't you think it's time he found someone special and settled down?"

As much as Cleo didn't want to lose him, she had to admit Trixie was right. "He'd never admit it."

"But you agree?"

"I think it's why he was willing to walk away from that start-up. He knows he's unhappy. But he's been single for so long, he thinks that's his natural state. Other people get married. Sylvester Minguez doesn't."

"How about you?"

"Hey, leave me out of this." Cleo softened the words with a grin.

Trixie smiled back. "You're younger, aren't you? Not even thirty?"

"In a few months." Cleo had no intention of telling her that, in spite of her young age, she already had a failed marriage in her past. It had been over four years since the divorce.

She'd dated since, but nothing serious. Whenever she liked a guy enough to see him two or three times, she panicked and ended it. Maybe if she'd had more experience before Dylan, her ex, she might have more confidence now managing a relationship. But she and Dylan had married right out of college. And the way it had ended...

No wonder she was pessimistic about her romantic future.

Trixie set the dog on the floor. He danced around Cleo's legs, panting up at her with love in his lopsided eyes. "You're not as desperate as he is," Trixie said.

"Desperate enough to be interested in me, is that what you were hoping?"

"Do you have such a poor opinion of yourself?"

This was entirely too personal coming from a woman she'd just met. Turning, she pulled out her phone. "It's been nice talking to you, Trixie, but I've got another lesson—"

"I'm so sorry. I didn't mean Sly would be desperate to love you. I mean he's desperate enough to love *anybody*." She smiled, happy with this explanation. "Finally."

It would take more than a vacation to wipe away Sly's fear of following his parents' bad example. Although they still ran their accounting business together, his parents hadn't been happy for decades, only avoiding divorce by avoiding each other. When his dad was at their house near San Diego, his mom would go to their condo in Hawaii and vice versa. Family gatherings were strained and chilly.

Sly blamed his father for most of the trouble, pointing to his long hours at the office and inability to take a vacation longer than three hours. Even before cell phones, his father had always found a way to make business calls from anywhere, anytime.

And Sly knew he was a lot like his father.

"Well, no matter how desperate he is," Cleo said, "I'm not the one."

"If you say so," Trixie said. "Can you think of anyone who might be?"

She laughed. "Afraid not. He and I run in entirely different circles. The women he usually dates are high-powered, fashionable Stanford types who run marathons with perfect hair and then go out and set up water filtration in a developing country, all before their gluten-free paleo breakfast."

"He dropped out of Stanford himself, you know."

"I know. What a slacker."

Trixie picked up the dog in the cone, Luna, and cradled her in her arms. "I wish I knew more young women. The ones I know are all married. I'd thought April might be the apple in Sly's eye, but she met Zack, so of course Sly was out of the question. I wonder if he'd be interested in an older woman?"

"Great idea," Cleo said. "You're single, right? When's the last time you had a date?"

Trixie's face turned a deep rosy red. "That's just what Sly's uncle said when I asked for his help. I wish people would focus. It's Sly who's never been married, Sly who needs a companion and a home and children."

"You talk to Uncle Hugo about Sly?"

She waved her hand in the air dismissively. "I've known Hugo for a long time. Quite a fortune he's made off me over the years. I used to foster a lot of dogs for the Chihuahua societies in the area."

"Uncle Hugo's looking pretty lonely himself," Cleo said. "Sly has tried setting him up a few times, but it never works out."

Trixie's eyes lit up. "There's an idea."

"I don't think I like your idea. Whatever it is."

"I feel like we're old friends, you and me, don't you?" Trixie asked, squeezing her upper arm. "We both want Sly to be happy. So does Hugo. There's a solution in there somewhere. We just have to work together."

"I don't meddle, I really don't. It never ends well."

Trixie's eyes widened in amazement. "Really? That hasn't been my experience at all."

4

ON SUNDAY MORNING, for the first time Sly could remember, picking up his phone to call Cleo made him nervous. There had been that strange moment the other night. Just stress, booze, and exhaustion, and he was sure she hadn't noticed anything, but it made it a little more difficult to ask for the favor he needed.

She didn't pick up until the fifth ring. "What's up?" Her voice was as cheerfully, comfortably teasing as always.

Taking a sip of his coffee, he said, "What are you up to today?"

"Funny you should ask. It just so happens I could use some company," she said. "A friend of mine just canceled our date to walk over the Golden Gate Bridge. Given the great weather—the fog's already burned off—I can't stay home. It's going to be a perfect day."

With some uneasiness, he wondered whom the "date" had been with. A new boyfriend might interfere with his own plans. "Fall is a great time to walk over the bridge." And a great place to put a woman in the mood for travel.

"Exactly," she said.

"When should I pick you up?" he asked.

"No way. I'm taking the bus."

He groaned. "Come on, it'll take forever."

"Driving takes forever. And it's bad for the world. And there's nowhere to park."

"There's always parking if you're willing to pay for it. Which I am."

"I'm taking BART to the city and then catching the bus. That's what I'm doing. Are you going to join me or are you going to be a high-maintenance, spoiled weenie?"

"Can't I do both?"

The sound of her laughter always made him smile. Everything was going to be fine. Nothing had changed. He'd put up with her fetish for public transportation to make her happy, plus it would give him more time to work up to asking his favor.

"I'll meet you at Rockridge BART," he said.

"Think you can figure out how to operate the ticket machines by yourself?"

"I'll text you if I get confused."

An hour later he found her on the open-air, raised train platform in Rockridge, the North Oakland city streets beneath them, wearing a duplicate SF State sweatshirt of the one he'd borrowed two weeks earlier and a lime-green daypack. Her pale blond hair was pulled into its usual ponytail and stuffed under an aggressively pink, sequined baseball cap that he'd given to her for her last birthday as a joke. Her baggy jeans were probably from the men's side of the Gap store, and he suspected that if she were to take off her sweatshirt, an equally voluminous T-shirt would be unearthed, probably advertising a sports team she didn't follow or a school she'd never attended.

Squinting at the sun, he handed her a bag holding a peach scone from her favorite café. "Nice hat."

"I love this hat. It lets me wear whatever I want and still be just a little bit girly-girl."

"Just a little bit."

"Oh! You're awesome. It's still warm." She reached in and withdrew a morsel of the pastry. "How apropos. A peach from a peach." She winked at him.

Tension that had clung to his deepest thoughts finally faded away. He looked around the platform with distaste. "What's that smell?"

"Humanity," she said, her mouth full.

"We're outside. It's windy. It shouldn't smell so bad."

"Urine odor really clings."

"I'm so glad I left the A4 at home."

"God, you're such a princess." She took off her hat and put it on him, dragging pink sequins across his forehead just as the train honked its arrival into the station from the east. "There. That's better."

Because he liked seeing her without the hat, he left it on his own head. He followed her into the car, wrinkling his nose at the stale, sour smell of its carpeted interior. But he didn't mind that as much as the lack of any empty seats. Pink hat on head, he shimmied between the Sunday morning crush of bodies to a small open space near a pole they could cling to when the car lurched forward.

She watched him with narrowed eyes. Even under low-wattage lighting, they were a stunning blue. "Don't say anything," she said.

"What's that smell?" he asked loudly. People around them turned their heads slightly, frowning, and he grinned at the pink spots that bloomed on her cheeks. For all her jokes and sarcasm, she was ridiculously easy to embarrass.

She turned away from him, casting him into the ranks of other crazy, unwanted subway creeps, and didn't talk to him until they were under the streets of downtown Oakland. "Where were you Thursday anyway?" she asked.

The horde now pressed them closer together. He lowered his head closer to hers so he didn't have to shout over the rumble of the train. "Later."

"Why, was it illegal?"

"You'll give me a hard time."

Her mouth dropped. "You were working."

He'd expected her to see right through him, and she had. He hung his head in only partially mock shame. "I was."

She didn't make a joke, just stared at him with those bright blue eyes of hers. "I can't believe you."

"I'm too young to retire," he said.

"But to go back to work after only two weeks? Not even two weeks!"

"I was going crazy," he said.

"You were already crazy." She rolled her eyes. "I knew it wouldn't last forever, but I thought it might last the month at least."

Shooting an eavesdropping lumbersexual a dirty look, he pulled her a few cramped inches away. "I'm not working yet. Just setting something up for later."

"Right. Like Monday morning, I bet."

"Not at all. You were right. I do need a vacation."

"Tuesday?"

He smiled and gave up for now. He'd ask for his favor when they were out in the sun, breathing fresh air, and had more than three inches of space around them.

The train lumbered through the Transbay tunnel between

Oakland and San Francisco. He tried not to think about the cold, shark-infested waters swirling over their heads and was glad when they reached downtown San Francisco. They got off the train at the Montgomery station and went up to the street.

"Ah, how beautiful," he said, looking around at the tumbleweeds of garbage bouncing along the financial-district sidewalks. "No wonder this Golden Gate Bridge thing is so famous."

"Very funny. Follow me. The bus stop isn't far." She already had her phone out and was scrolling through the screens. "My excellent and free transit app tells me it'll be here in six minutes."

"We could just walk down to the Ferry Building," he said. "Grab some lunch. Walk through the farmer's market and relax."

"No way. It's pushing seventy degrees, and it's sunny, and it's not even noon yet. We're going to the Golden Gate Bridge, buster."

"Watch your language."

"Watch your step. There's some humanity clinging to the sidewalk down there."

He dodged the dark puddle she was pointing at, biting his lip to restrain his reasonable complaints about the six-minute wait that turned into twenty. And then, when the bus finally did arrive, they were forced to stand again with several people between them during the slow journey up Sutter and Van Ness Avenue. Eventually they were able to grab seats together, watching the cobalt-blue water of the bay to their right dotted with sailboats, ships, and ferries, and the blood-orange span of the bridge that had inspired the color of Cleo's new car.

And then they were there. As she stepped off the bus, the ocean breeze whipped her ponytail into her face. Smiling into the wind, she reached back, retrieved her pink hat—he was still wearing it, though he'd turned the brim around—and replaced it on her head.

"Do you realize what time it is?" He tucked a loose strand under the cap behind her ear. Her eyes were a brighter, lighter blue than the sea behind her, more like the cloudless sky above. "That took almost two hours. We could be in LA by now."

"Why would we want to be?" She stretched her arms wide to take in the cliffs of the Marin Headlands, the famous bridge, and the sparkling sea. "I never get tired of this." With a deep breath, she spun around and headed for the walking side of the bridge.

Even in October, the area was overrun with people, tourists and locals alike. He considered putting off asking her for the favor until they were done, but they'd already wasted hours getting here, and the hike over and back would take at least an hour more, and then the snail-mail return pace home...

No, he'd just have to talk to her here.

"So, I've got a favor to ask," he said. Had to shout it, actually, because a family with thirteen million children and a dog, all on scooters (including the corgi), cut between them.

Cleo waved at him over her shoulder, not looking as if she'd heard him. If she had, she'd probably be rolling her eyes and walking faster.

"Did you see the dog on wheels?" she asked him when they were finally reunited.

"This is the walking side. Wheels should be over there."

"Yeah, because Lassie is totally about to win the Tour de France."

"Lassie was a collie, not a corgi."

She elbowed him. "Come on, Sly. Try to enjoy the moment. Real life. No screens, no Internet, just reality."

Nodding, he fell silent, walking with her in the stream of

people, breathing in the cold, salty air, trying to be patient. But when she stopped to tie her shoe, he seized the moment. "Cleo, I need to ask you a favor. It's making me kind of tense."

"You? Tense? That's not like you."

"I know you're going to mock."

"As if I would ever mock," she said mockingly.

"But I'm going to press on."

"Of course you are. I bet I'm on your to-do list and you want to check it off." A blast of wind hit her from behind, blowing the ponytail into her face again. She hugged her arms around herself. "I wish I'd brought my jacket. You'd think I'd know better by now."

He reached for the zipper at his throat. "You can borrow mine."

"It wouldn't fit. But thanks."

"Sure it would. It's at least a large."

"Please, Sly. I'm fine." She put her hands over his and tugged the zipper back up to his throat. "I just like to complain."

"I'm going to ask my favor now, all right? Brace yourself."

She lowered her hands, eyeing him warily. "You're making *me* nervous."

"First of all—your date today," he began. "Was it a *date* date or just a friend thing?"

"Why?"

"Just curious."

She continued to stare for a moment. "Just a friend thing."

"Great, then you can help me," he said.

"Don't get carried away. I've already got a bad feeling about this."

He smiled in an attempt to soften her up. "So, there's this charity auction. In Carmel next weekend."

"Oh God, they're auctioning you off again," she said, clapping her hands together.

He'd once participated in a win-a-date function for charity, and she loved to tease him about it. "No, nothing like that. This will have trips to the Riviera, rare tech prototypes, butt lifts—"

"The really classy stuff for rich people."

"Exactly." Here we go. "I want you to go with me."

Her eyes widened. "Me? Why?"

"Please, Cleo. I can't go to this one alone."

"So don't. Ask one of your girlfriends."

"You make it sound like I have a harem," he said.

"You know what I mean. One of the women you've dated in the past."

"I don't want to start..." Resting his elbows on the railing, he looked over at Alcatraz on its famous rock out in the middle of the bay. "I wouldn't want her, whoever, to get the wrong idea. The auction is on a Saturday. We'd drive down Friday night, spend the weekend there. It's... a nice place. Expensive and..." He trailed off.

"Yes?"

"Romantic. There's a woman there I want to meet—"

"Oh, I get it." She threw her head back and laughed. "You know *I* won't get in your way."

"It's nothing like that. She's a business contact. Or I'd like her to be."

"Ah. Work again."

"It's not for me. It's for Mark. I think he might like to hire her in my place." He rubbed his eyes. "I left him in the lurch when I quit his start-up. It was his idea, you know? And I know the guys I left behind can't do it without help. This is the best way I can think to meet her."

"But you said the idea wasn't going to fly. What can a new

person do?"

"I don't know. Maybe something I couldn't. I want to walk away, but this bad feeling is keeping me up at night. I owe Mark. Don't let him hear me say that, but I do."

"Why can't you go to the auction by yourself?"

This was the part he'd rather not get into. "I'd rather not get into it," he said.

"Which is why I probably don't want to go."

"Yeah, probably. But I hope you will anyway." He gave her his most toothy, charming smile, which made her roll her eyes. "Teresa's going to be there," he said.

"*Teresa* Teresa?"

He nodded grimly.

"You can't show up alone if Teresa's going to be there," she said.

"Exactly." His ex-girlfriend periodically attempted to reignite their former relationship.

"But you can't show up without a serious girlfriend if Teresa's going to be there," she continued. "Maybe even a wife. And full-body armor."

"Since I don't have any of those things, I thought of you." He gestured at the crowded path, and they resumed walking. "It's a really nice place. A resort overlooking the ocean. Some of the best views on the entire coast. I'd pay for everything, of course. Two nights, two days. Spa treatments. Food. Whatever you want."

"I work on Saturdays, Sly."

"I know, but sometimes you make special arrangements if you have to."

She crossed her arms over her chest, gazing up at the suspension cables, and didn't say anything for a minute.

"Other than joining me at the auction," he continued, "which is only a few hours, you'll be free to do whatever you want. Bill everything to the room."

"Room, singular?"

"I'll sleep in the bathtub."

She shook her head. "I'd be willing to do it—"

"Excellent! I'll make sure—"

"If it weren't for the Teresa thing. She's never going to buy it that I'm your girlfriend. Nobody will. You might as well go by yourself or find a new female sacrifice who's willing to sleep with you right away."

"People will believe it if you wear something other than men's pajamas."

"I'm not doing a *Pretty Woman* makeover just for a weekend with a bunch of rich Silicon Valley geeks."

"I'm not asking you to. Wear whatever you want other than pajamas."

"Nobody will believe it."

"You're mental. They will."

"I bet you they won't," she said.

"I bet you they will."

"How much?"

"What?"

"If I'm right," she said, "and nobody thinks I'm your girlfriend, what do I get?"

"That's not fair. You'll have too much incentive to wear old-man boxer shorts and scratch yourself inappropriately."

Her eyes glowed with dangerous enthusiasm, the way they did when she beat him at poker. "We'll have ground rules. I hold up my end, you hold up yours. If people don't believe I'm your hot babe, which they won't, then I get the jackpot. Which will be what, I wonder?"

"Can't be cash. You're impoverished. I'm loaded."

"I'm not impoverished. You have a distorted view of reality. And besides, I'm going to win." She slapped him on the back. "Let's say a thousand."

"That's nothing to me and a fortune to you."

"Please. It won't kill me."

He knew she couldn't have much more than that in her checking account. "I can't do money. I'd try to lose. It has to be something else." He hadn't intended on making a game out of this, but if it got her to go to the auction, he would play along. "If I lose, I give you a thousand. If you lose, you play the ukulele at my wedding, which will probably never happen, so all the more reason for you to go for it."

She regarded a gull swooping beneath them under the bridge, then turned to him. "Teresa will never ever believe I'm your girlfriend. I'm warning you right now."

Watching Cleo lose this bet was going to be a pleasure. It was past time she ventured outside her comfort zone. "We have a deal?"

She held out her hand. "Deal." Then she added with a grin that lit up her eyes, "Let's hope Teresa likes ukulele music."

5

THE FRIDAY EVENING of their journey south to Carmel was cold and misty, threatening rain. October on the coast usually alternated between hot, summery days and the first taste of rain since April. This weekend was forecast to have a little of both.

Cleo glanced at Sly behind the wheel. "You didn't say anything about my outfit."

"I didn't want to encourage you."

Smiling, she turned her head to look out at the rocky cliffs tumbling down to the inky waters of the Pacific. Her jeans and sweatshirt were the same she'd worn on their hike over the bridge. "You can't say this isn't what I normally wear, since I was wearing it when you invited me."

He didn't say anything.

"If you're hoping I packed cream silk pantsuits and designer evening gowns," she continued, "you're going to be disappointed."

"You never disappoint me, Cleo."

She bit her lip to stifle a laugh. Only two hours into their bet and she was already having fun. "This is going to be a blast."

"I'm glad. I want you to enjoy yourself. You're doing me a favor."

His sincerity almost made her feel guilty about how easily she was going to win. "Have you talked to Mark lately? Maybe he wouldn't want you to be reaching out to this woman for him and his new company."

"He was psyched, actually," Sly said. "He's a recluse. Hates to network. If I can do this for him, my debt to him will be paid, at least enough for me to sleep at night."

"What's her name?"

"Poppy Lee."

Cleo whistled. "I've heard of her."

"Yeah, she's pretty high profile."

"Why would someone like that want to work on Mark's little project?"

"Because Mark is a genius who makes millions by accident," he said.

"Millions, sure. But not billions."

"I like how you say that so casually, as if making millions is no biggie."

"Doesn't seem to impress these people anymore," she said.

"It does. Especially now. It's crazy time again, money pouring in from Wall Street, Main Street, all over the world, companies with six people on staff getting bought for a billion overnight."

She strummed the ukulele in her lap. She'd been playing for the past hour, the soft high notes tinkling into the leather interior to his murmurs of appreciation. Did she really want to make his life difficult? They were friends. He wasn't asking a lot. "Sly, if you want to drop the bet, it's fine with me. I'll dress up and do my best."

"Dress however you like. Just be yourself. You're the one who thinks that won't be enough."

Both flattered and annoyed, she said, "You don't realize how different you and I appear to most people."

"This isn't Hollywood. These are Silicon Valley people. They won't notice your clothes or mine. If you don't outright argue with me when I tell people you're my girlfriend, they'll believe me. Even Teresa."

"So basically, the bet is on. That's what you're saying?"

"Looks like."

The hotel perched on the highlands above the coast, its sloped entrance enclosed by the tall, horizontal branches of Monterey cypress trees. Cleo carried her ukulele and backpack herself, amused at how naturally Sly accepted the assistance of the valet and bellhops and desk staff as they checked in.

The resort was made up of multiple short wood buildings connected by exterior walkways, all surrounded by more cypress and pine, giving it the feel of a vast, luxurious tree house on the edge of a cliff. Sly strode down a set of stairs and up another as if he knew exactly where they were going, which he probably did.

"Here we are," he said, opening the door of a building at the far north end of the resort. The rocks dropped directly below the planks under their feet, sloping gradually to the coast. The wind had picked up, and the surf roared. "Feels like rain."

She followed him inside, wiping mist off her cheeks. "Will that interfere with the auction? People might not come if they can't golf?"

"They'll come. These people don't usually golf."

"Unless it's a video game," she said.

"Even then. No time. Most are workaholics."

"Like you."

"No," he said. "I'm much worse."

The bellhop arrived and brought in the bags, asked if he could do anything, then cheerfully accepted Sly's folded bill and departed. With a start, Cleo noticed the champagne and chocolate-covered strawberries waiting for them on a tray on the bed.

The only bed in a room bigger than her apartment.

A fireplace crackled from the corner. The bathroom held a walk-in tub and a shower stall with several heads, so that everyone inside—and there was room for quite an orgy in there—had a constant stream of hot water.

"Hope that bathtub's comfortable," she said, picking up the strawberry by its GMO stem and dangling it over his mouth.

He bit off the berry and smiled at her, cheeks bulging.

"Shall I pop open the bubbly?" she asked.

He held up a finger as he swallowed, then said, "Wine reception in an hour."

"That should be fun," she said. "For you."

"You'll be joining me, I hope."

"You said I only had to go to the auction."

"This doesn't really count. It's free food and drink. Aren't you hungry?"

She crossed her arms over her chest. "What else is there going on this weekend you need me to attend?"

"Don't you want to win your bet? A few hours at a busy auction aren't going to give you much opportunity."

"You're dastardly."

He grinned. "I like the sound of that. It goes really well with 'tech mogul.' I bet it would be great for business."

"You're hopeless. Fine, I'll go. But I want to walk around first. I saw hiking paths."

"There are many. Go past the pool. There's a vineyard, but otherwise they've left it fairly wild."

"Except for the miles of golf courses."

"Except for that." He flung his garment bag on the bed, rattling the champagne flutes on the tray. "Go take your hike, hug your tree. I'm going to get pretty."

She pinched his chin. "Already did." Grabbing her parka, she walked to the door. "I'll meet you there. Where is it?"

"The Cypress Room. Six thirty. But…"

"Yes?"

"Aren't you…" He pressed his fingers into his forehead. "Never mind."

Smiling, she closed the door, knowing he'd almost asked her if she was going to change what she was wearing.

In spite of all his business smarts, he really didn't have a clue about some things. They were great friends, but nobody would have paired them together, not even them. Only chance—and a passing interest in piano lessons—had done that. The band geek didn't go to prom with the Most Likely To Succeed. In fact, she'd refused to go at all, hanging out at the twenty-four-hour diner with her similarly geeky friends, sharing a plate of garlic fries with extra garlic and arguing about superheroes.

During her marriage, she'd made an effort to "grow up," as Dylan had called it, wearing more fashionable women's clothing and giving up the flip-flops. She'd followed his advice—choosing pink instead of green, tight instead of comfortable, dressy instead of casual—and look where it had gotten her. Divorced at twenty-five. When he hadn't been able to transform her into what he'd wanted, he'd found an off-the-shelf model that was ready to go.

She looked off to the west and inhaled the cold salt air, trying to banish the image of her ex-husband with her best friend—now her ex-best-friend—together. Not that she'd ever admit it to Sly, but she hadn't slept with anyone since her marriage. If Dylan had chosen a stranger, maybe it would've been easier to move on and get serious about somebody else. But he hadn't chosen a stranger. The two people she loved and trusted most, other than her parents, had ripped her heart out of her chest and diced it into pieces.

But she was over it now. She was. Four years was more than enough time to stop punching the empty pillow next to her in bed while she imagined a certain handsome, self-satisfied face.

Cleo unclenched her hands and bounded down the steps to the garden below, whistling a new melody she'd been working on for over a week.

It had been *at least* a year since she'd punched the pillow imagining Dylan's face, and she'd only lost her temper then because a mutual acquaintance had accidentally copied her on the email loop about his first anniversary party with Ashley—in Tahiti. When he'd been with Cleo, he'd refused to leave the county for their honeymoon, let alone the hemisphere. But with Ashley, the lovely, perfect Ashley...

She whistled louder to cleanse away the unwelcome thoughts. Some lessons were painful to learn, but worth the hurt in the long term. The world would have to accept her as she was. And if that meant Sly had to hand over a few bucks, all the better.

6

SLY FINISHED HIS second plate of food from the gourmet buffet, eyeing the corridor to the vineyard hike with growing impatience. He set down his plate and got another glass of wine at the bar. About two dozen people had come to the reception. A few familiar faces, most unfamiliar. He'd had a little success in his career, but it was a big industry and he was a relative nobody.

Teresa liked to arrive a little late so she could make an entrance.

Making a face, he sipped his wine. She didn't love him; that wasn't why she chased him now. Five years ago, she'd been the one to break it off after six months together. Her next boyfriends had all been high-profile, newly minted millionaires. When WellyNelly survived the recession and started attracting big corporate interest and then looked like it would make him a fortune, she called him up, sweet as an In-N-Out Burger chocolate milkshake.

He had no interest in seeing her now. Even if he had sold WellyNelly to big pharma and cashed in eight figures, which he hadn't. Maybe it was the write-up in *Businessweek*, when he'd gone into business with Mark, that had renewed her interest.

Speak of the devil. There she was now, gliding into the room.

Stepping behind a potted palm, he took another mouthful of wine and watched her accept a glass from the host and then begin to work the crowd. Long dark hair, smooth as glass, framed her delicate face. Petite, with elfin features that made her seem harmless, Teresa wore a clingy, shimmery gold dress that showed off her slim shape. Her shoes, as usual, increased her height by at least three inches.

She didn't *look* dangerous. He glanced at the beach entrance again, wishing he hadn't let Cleo out of his sight. This was the moment he'd need her most, before the auction was underway as a distraction.

"Hi, honey," Cleo said loudly behind him, a mischievous grin on her face. She lifted a beer bottle to her lips, then leaned closer to him, lowering her voice. "How was that? I called you honey."

He'd never been so glad to see her in his life, even if she was wearing a ski parka over a bright orange Giant's T-shirt and mud-caked Chaco sandals. Curving an arm around her shoulders, he pulled her against him and kissed her hair. Something scratchy brushed his lips. "Fantastic, darling."

Uneasiness flickered in her eyes. Her body went tense under his arm. "Don't overdo it."

"You're the one with plants in your hair," he whispered. "Lichen, I think."

A dimple flashed in her left cheek. "Pull it out for me? That would be very romantic."

"My pleasure." Gazing deeply into her eyes, he stroked her cheek and caressed the crispy green strands out of her hair as if touching her hair was the greatest privilege of his life.

"Oh, you're good," she said, batting her eyelashes.

"You have no idea."

"She's right behind you."

He brushed his lips across her temple to her ear. "I know." Beneath the plant matter and the beer, he smelled the sweetness of her hair. And he couldn't help but feel her soft curves pressing against his pelvis. In response, his body began pumping blood a little harder, a little faster, to key locations.

Not again. He released her and lifted the wineglass to his lips, looking away, concentrating on cooling down.

Teresa was flirting with a guy he didn't know, those big green eyes of hers pinning the helpless geek where he stood.

Sly reminded himself that he didn't want to be that guy again. The breakup had thrown him for a long time. He'd convinced himself he'd been in love with her, and maybe he had.

Cleo jabbed him in the ribs with her index finger, as if pressing the button on a candy machine. "You promised me food."

Plastering a seductive smile on his face to cover the pain, he looked down at her. "Yes, sweetums. Let's go find it together."

Her eyes twinkled. "Are you going to feel me up while we eat?"

"Only if you stab me again."

With a throaty chortle, she took his arm and tugged him toward the buffet table. He tried to walk with her the way he would walk with a girlfriend, but she made it impossible. Giving up on being the manly, dominant one, he let her drag him along.

At the table, he drained his glass and held it out to a passing waiter for a refill. Might as well enjoy himself.

Which is what Cleo was obviously doing as she filled her plate with beet salad, cheese cubes, crab cakes, chicken satays, canapés, and two chocolate chip cookies. Based on the sideways looks she kept giving him, she was trying to get a rise out of him. Did she really think the women he usually dated didn't eat? Or that he'd be offended if they did?

Of course, eating a beet with her fingers was just asking for it. As was dropping it down the V-neck her orange T-shirt.

In growing alarm, he watched her stick her hand between her breasts, extract the beet between two red-stained fingers, and bring it to her parted lips.

He slung an arm around her shoulders and confiscated her plate. "I warned you," he whispered in her ear, sliding his hand down her back to the curve of her waist, hauling her against his side. "Honey."

The wide-eyed innocent looked up at him, then pushed the fallen beet past his lips into his mouth.

He had no choice but to swallow it.

"It's like a wedding," she said brightly. "We can feed each other."

"I'm going to feed you to the sharks in Monterey Bay if you keep this up."

He was afraid if she kept laughing so hard, beet juice was going to shoot out of her nose. But after a moment she nodded, took a deep breath, and looked down at the plate in his hands. "Fine, I'll stop. Can I have my food back? I really am hungry."

"Sylvester?"

Teresa's voice. Right behind him.

He handed Cleo her plate as gracefully as he could, then glanced at the woman he'd been avoiding. "Hello, Teresa."

Either because she was busy chewing or because she took some pity on him, Cleo didn't do anything embarrassing for a few seconds. He helped himself to the cookie on her plate, gave her a seductive wink, and clamped it between his teeth as he reached for an empty plate.

"It's so nice to see you," Teresa said. "Hui Zhong mentioned you were invited."

He took a massive bite of the cookie and nodded as he chewed. Balancing the fine line between rude and indifferent was going to be a challenge.

Which was why he hadn't come to this shindig alone. Swallowing the cookie, he moved closer to his outdoorsy girlfriend and smiled politely at Teresa. "Have you met Cleo?"

"Your younger sister, right?" Teresa asked.

Cleo tapped his foot with hers, but Sly knew it hadn't been an honest question. Unless his sisters were adopted, which Teresa knew they were not, there was no way he and Cleo could be siblings. His mixed DNA—from Mexico, Africa, Scotland, the Philippines, and beyond—was written all over his face, whereas the tiny Scandinavian village from whence all Cleo's ancestors had no doubt lived for millennia was written all over hers.

He guffawed as if they all knew it was a hilarious joke. "Cleo, this is Teresa Lapham. Teresa, Cleo Holt." He put down his plate so he could stroke Cleo's back in a sufficiently intimate manner. She stiffened but didn't knee him in the balls, for which he was grateful.

Teresa, eyebrows raised, shook Cleo's hand. "How long have you two been together?"

During the drive down, they'd agreed on a few basic details to their story. Cleo trotted them out now. "We've been friends for a long time, but started dating last year."

"Really." Teresa didn't release Cleo's hand. "How romantic."

"Yes," Cleo said. "Very."

"After being friends, it must be hard finding new things to talk about." Finally dropping Cleo's hand, Teresa reached up and fiddled with a tiny pendant at her throat. "You'd be like an old married couple."

Sly tightened his grip on Cleo's shoulder, drawing her away.

"Not quite. Well, have a nice—"

"And what do you do, Cleo?" Teresa asked. "Were you at WellyNelly too?"

"Teresa," he said, giving her a hard look. She'd always accused him of sleeping around at work, which he never had.

"I'm a musician," Cleo said.

"Oh, really?" Teresa's gaze flickered over Cleo's body, resting momentarily on her muddy sandals. "How interesting." Her tone was sincerely curious.

"Lately I've been especially interested in the ukulele." Cleo popped a green canapé into her mouth. Mouth full, she said, "Oh, these are great. Have you had any yet?"

"I've already eaten."

"So?" Cleo shoved another one in her mouth. "I never pass up free food. Isn't that right, honey?" Resting her head on his shoulder, she gazed up and made calf eyes at him. "Honey bunny?"

Sly tried to hide his annoyance. She wasn't even trying to be convincing. The most socially obtuse guy in the room—and that was a high bar—could tell she was being sarcastic. Cupping her cheek, he lowered his head and kissed her lightly on the lips. "I love that about you."

Freezing under his touch, Cleo's smile fell.

Ha. Not laughing now, are you? he thought. He rubbed his thumb along her lower lip and felt her cheeks get warmer. "You had a little avocado there." He bent down and licked the corner of her mouth. "Right there," he whispered.

If he were being honest with himself, he'd admit that he'd had to whisper because his throat had tightened with a rush of adrenaline.

"Let's talk later, Sylly," Teresa said, patting his arm. "Perhaps when you haven't had a few glasses of wine already. Tomorrow?"

He dropped his hand, heart pounding, and nodded at Teresa. "Sure. Tomorrow."

When she walked away, Cleo set down her plate and walked to the bar at the opposite side of the room. He watched her ponytail sway, afraid he'd gone too far.

But she'd pushed him. Sure, they had a bet, but she was cheating. He was doing everything he could to make this enjoyable for her, even booked a deep-tissue massage for her in the morning.

The thought of her soft, deep tissues made his heart pound harder.

Don't go there.

But his thoughts didn't listen. They went there.

What would it be like? The last guy she'd dated had been a guitar-playing, big-bearded hipster without a car. Rode his bike everywhere. Very sensible and eco-friendly, and not unusual in Berkeley, but Sly thought he was just trying to spin his true nature as an underemployed loser into something datable.

Watching Cleo at the bar, he noticed her switch to hard liquor. Not a good sign.

He'd upset her. Hell, he'd upset himself.

Inhaling deeply, he turned away and picked up her abandoned plate. Other than the beet and the canapés, she hadn't eaten. That drink was going to go right to her head. He added a second cookie to replace the one he'd eaten, then rejoined her in a quiet corner behind an eight-foot-wide aquarium where she'd gone to hide.

He handed her the plate. "I'm sorry I got so physical."

Her face was blocked by her cocktail glass, which now seemed to hold only ice. "It's OK. I pushed you."

"If I forfeit the bet right now," he said, "will you try a little harder? Or a little less hard?"

"She did ask if I was your sister. Bet won right there."

"Yes, she did." He picked up a cheese puff and tried to put it in her mouth. "Even if she was just yanking my chain."

Cleo lifted a hand to block the cheese puff. "Maybe because it's still shackled to your ankle."

"What do you mean?"

"Come on," she said. "You know."

"She knew you're not my sister. She was just trying to annoy me. And you."

"And she succeeded, which makes me think you might still have a little teeny weeny thing for her."

He shuddered. "No. Unless that thing is like salmonella."

"Then why do you care what she thinks? Tell her to screw off."

"Not my style."

"No, your style is to stick your tongue in my mouth." She took the glass out of his hands and strode away.

Well, that clarified that situation. She was angry. She wasn't curious the way he was curious.

God, was he really admitting that's what was going on? Couldn't his body's reaction simply be basic biology? The instinctive reflex of a heterosexual male who hadn't been with a woman in a while?

He stared at the colorful fish in the aquarium darting around their plastic seaweed.

It had to be that.

Of course it was that.

Almost two hours later, Cleo paused at the hotel room door, key card in hand, her stomach tightening.

How had it come to this? She was nervous to go in. Afraid of a good friend.

She'd left the reception and wandered outside around the resort, climbing over rocks between the cedar and gardens. At one point she tripped over a stone and stubbed her toe, bare in her sandals, and it was bleeding. She had to go into the hotel room to wash and bandage her wound.

Something deeper was stinging too.

It was all a joke. Just fun. She was stupid.

Sliding the card into the door, she limped across the threshold. "Honey, I'm home!" She kept her voice cheerful and light. Not worried and heavy. Or hot and heavy.

Oh, for God's sake, Cleo, get a grip.

One glance told her the room was empty. She was so relieved she laughed as she walked into the bathroom to tend to her wounds. But then she saw herself in the mirror, and the laughter died.

She looked terrible. Ponytail askew, nose red, dirt on her cheek, jacket frayed, faded, and stained. Was it worth a thousand dollars to embarrass herself like this? No. Well, it would've been if he hadn't been such a formidable opponent. She'd nearly choked when he'd kissed her hair, but when he'd *licked* her...

She was strong, but she wasn't made of stone. No wonder he was a mogul. He played to win. She played piano. Time to call a truce and enjoy the resort for its own sake. One of the pools overlooking the beach was steaming, obviously well heated. There was that hour-and-a-half massage in the morning. And she still hadn't eaten a real meal.

Her rumpled, hoboesque image frowned back at her.

The joke was on her. She hadn't dressed down because she wanted to win the bet; she'd done it to protect her pride. If she'd put on a sexy dress and her expensive makeup and had her hair done—and *then* nobody had believed she was his girlfriend—she would've been hurt. For all the progress she'd made since the divorce, she'd feared she couldn't handle that kind of blow. In other words, she'd been a coward.

Enough. She turned on one of the many showerheads and got under the hot spray, letting it sting, washing away the evening.

After she finished and dried herself off with those thick resort towels you could never find at the store, she bandaged her foot and swaddled herself in pajamas and a terry robe, then took the time to blow out her hair, glad she'd had the time and privacy to screw her head back on straight. Now she'd get something to eat and be good as new.

She was standing in front of the entertainment cabinet, looking through the room service menu, when he stumbled into the room.

Within seconds, she realized he was as drunk as she'd ever seen him.

"Cleo," he said. He strode past the bed and fell to his knees at her feet, dark head slumping forward. "You win." Slowly, with the pained movements of the intoxicated, he pulled a stack of dollar bills out of a paper bag and began counting them out, setting them down around her feet like a faded green patio.

"Where did you get a bag of money like that this time of night?"

He shushed her noisily. "I'm counting. Don't interrupt. Twenty-seven, twenty-four, thirty..." He began to laugh. "Just kidding. Kidding I don't know how to count. Twenty—shit. I forget. Let's start over."

She reached down and hauled him upright. "I hope you didn't knock over a convenience store."

"It's not as much as it looks. Not *quite* a thousand. Mostly twenties at the bottom. ATM units. Not as funny though."

"Not as funny but easier to put in my purse."

"Right. Purse. Because you're a girl." He grinned. "Cleo."

"Yeah, that's me. You aren't going to get sick, are you?"

"Hope not." His smile faded. "I gave you my germs earlier. Sorry about that."

"It's not your germs I'm worried about. It's your undigested stomach contents." She grabbed his arm to stop him from swaying. "You need to sleep this off. Big day tomorrow."

"So true. Thanks." He patted her on the shoulder and lurched away, sticking his hands in his jacket pockets. "Did I bring a toothbrush? Oh, right. I already unpacked. I'm a very organized man. I take pride in my"—he burped—"powers of organization." He went into the bathroom and slammed the door.

She set down the menu and glanced at the clock. Past eleven. Too late to eat anyway. After scooping up the cash, which she stuck back in the paper bag, she stripped off the robe, climbed into bed, and pulled the covers up to her chin. As soon as she closed her eyes, memories of the way her body had reacted to a little hugging and kissing, all done in jest, washed over her.

How embarrassing. She wasn't fifteen. She'd been married, for God's sake. She should be immune to a little playing around.

It's just that it had been so long. So very, very long. Years of living as a cautious recluse had made her as needy as a dried-out houseplant in front of a watering can.

The bathroom door opened. "Cleo?"

"Yes?"

"I'm going to have to sleep with you."

Her heart lost a beat. "Excuse me?"

"I don't fit in the bathtub."

She wondered if it was too late to call a cab. Laughing silently, she rolled onto her side and curled into a protective ball. "All right, then. You can use the bed. Just don't hog the covers."

"Don't hog. Got it."

The lights went out. As he climbed into bed, he made a funny sound she realized was supposed to be the oink of a pig.

"You poor man," she said. "You're going to be so hungover tomorrow."

The snoring began instantly.

Poor him? she thought. *Poor me.*

7

WHEN SLY WOKE, furry-tongued and cotton-brained, the bed was empty. He rolled out onto the floor and staggered over to his pants, lumped in a pile by the TV. He pulled out his phone, glad he hadn't forgotten it at the bar last night, and squinted at the screen. Looking at his phone always helped wake him up, no matter how much he wanted to slip back into unconsciousness. His calendar scrolled past with today's agenda, his list of longer projects flickered at the top of the screen, and unanswered text messages popped up one by one.

As he plugged back in to his life, he remembered Cleo. She must be at the spa, getting her massage. And as his mind cleared, he had the sense to see her clothes were still in the dresser, and her muddy sandals parked next to her empty backpack in the closet.

She hadn't bailed. Grunting with relief, he went into the bathroom to wash up and rehydrate. Touching her had crossed a line, a line he'd been trying not to think about. Perhaps before that moment at her apartment a couple of weeks ago, he could've kissed her for fun and it wouldn't have meant anything. Now it meant something. He just didn't know what.

Instead of taking a shower, he got dressed for running and went out, hoping to sweat out the rest of the poisons he'd poured into his body the night before. It was already past nine, late for him, and kids were already swimming in the pool. It still looked like rain, although none had fallen. Perfect for running.

An hour later, sweaty but refreshed, he was limping past the pool on his return when he heard his name. He scanned the few bodies stretched out on the deck chairs, all but the children wearing long-sleeved shirts and pants on the overcast autumn morning, but didn't see who had called him.

"Sylvester!" It was Teresa, waving to him from the water. She jumped out at the edge and strode over. "Back from a run?"

He nodded, careful to keep his gaze above her chin. For a second he'd glimpsed erect nipples pressing against her sheer white one-piece, and she wasn't making any moves toward one of the fluffy towels stacked nearby.

"I saw you at the bar last night," she said.

That wasn't good. He'd been hammered and alone, like a wounded baby deer just begging for the she-wolf to eat him. "I bet that wasn't a pretty sight."

"Oh, I don't know." She gave him a naughty smile. "Even at your worst, you're not bad. Not bad at all."

He made a show of wiping the sweat off his forehead. Maybe his ripe odor would drive her off. "I should get going."

"I didn't see Cleo last night." She looked around. "She doesn't run with you?"

He wasn't going to explain anything; it only encouraged her. "She's expecting me now. Excuse me." Returning his neon-green earbuds to their conversation-blocking location on his head, he began to leave.

"Hope everything's OK," she called after him. "She looked a little upset at breakfast."

In spite of the danger, he turned and removed the earbuds.

"Breakfast?"

"I was surprised you weren't there."

Cleo was going to kill him. She'd endured breakfast with Teresa by herself. "I'm full of surprises. You hated that about me, remember?"

"Maybe I've learned to appreciate spontaneity in my old age." She looked down at her glistening, toned, picture-perfect body and shook her head. "Not getting any younger."

"So true," he said, happy to leave that bait on the hook. If she wanted to hear him say she was as lithe and lovely as a nineteen-year-old swimsuit model, she was going to be disappointed. "See you later."

This time he managed to escape, wondering as he ran up the stairs why he'd thought he couldn't resist Teresa on his own. Whatever appeal she'd had for him was long gone. Bringing Cleo had been unnecessary and potentially dangerous.

Dangerous? He strode down the walkway to their room, wondering at his choice of words. What's the worst thing that could happen? She'd tell him she wouldn't be his friend anymore? No. They weren't first graders. Their relationship could handle a little ambiguity. A little excitement.

A little danger. The thought spread through him like a warm breeze.

Mumbling repressive curses under his breath, he went into the room, saw it was empty, and got into the shower. To distract himself, he used three of the four showerheads in the cavernous stall. After he'd lathered and rinsed, he got out to shave and brush, and eventually he began to feel like his old self again. He walked out of the bathroom with his mind on a late meal and Poppy Lee, whom he hoped would be at the preview for the silent auction at two.

"Jeez, Sly," Cleo cried, slapping her hands over her eyes. She stood right outside the bathroom door in a pink sundress. "Have some consideration for my nerves."

"I'm decent." He readjusted the towel slung around his hips, wishing that were true. "I just need to get my clothes."

She turned her face to the wall. "For a mogul, you aren't very good at planning ahead. You should bring the clothes with you into the bathroom before you get naked."

Thoughts of danger made him linger. He studied the dress she was wearing, liking the way it showed off her body. "You're wearing pink."

"It's all they had."

"All who had?"

"The store last week. The gray was sold out. They call this dusty rose. It's all they had."

He didn't know why she was shopping for a dress last week or why she sounded insecure about it. "It's pretty." Clearing his throat, he walked past her to get his clothes out of the closet and the dresser, strode back into the bathroom, and put them on, checking himself out in the mirror on the door as he did.

Not getting any younger.

Cleo loved to tease him about his looks. He knew he wasn't bad, but she talked about him as if Hollywood would've been a reasonable alternative to Silicon Valley. As he buttoned his shirt, he struck poses in the mirror, just to prove to himself she was full of crazy.

He caught himself staring too long and slapped himself. He was the one full of crazy. Jesus.

"How was the spa?" he asked as he walked out. Very cool and casual. Not crazy at all.

Slumping against the wall, she sighed. "Fantastic. I felt so relaxed when it was over."

"But not anymore?"

"It always wears off. I'd have to—" She rolled her eyes. "Never mind. How are you feeling, by the way?"

He noticed her face had turned as pink as her dress. "You'd have to what?"

"I'd need more than a professional massage. You know what I'm saying?" She offered an exaggerated wink, but he could tell her mirth was forced.

This new weirdness between them was all his fault. "Sorry about last night," he said. "For everything. For fondling you, for drinking too much, for anything else I did that I don't remember."

"You snore like a congested elephant seal."

Smiling, he gathered his wallet and phone. "Teresa said you ate breakfast with her, another thing I'm sorry about. Are you hungry for lunch?"

She hesitated. "Not really. It was quite a buffet."

"That's good. I'm glad you finally got to eat." He went to the door. "The dinner's at six thirty. Then the auction. Should we meet here?"

"Sure. Here's good," she said. "I have another dress I'm going to wear."

"Another one?" In all the years he'd known her, he'd never once seen her in a dress. Now he was going to see her in two different ones, all in one day. "You'd do that for me?"

"I decided not to embarrass you anymore. For both of our sakes. Since I already won the bet, right?"

"Right." He couldn't bring himself to leave. "Look, Teresa noticed we've been alone a lot. Are you sure you won't join me?"

"You really are scared of that tiny little woman, aren't you?"

"Terrified."

She smiled. "Well, that's what I'm here for, isn't it? All right, I'll hang out with you. To help you out."

As she walked past him into the hallway, he caught a hint of perfume. Not just shampoo. Perfume.

And he liked it. A lot.

"That's what friends are for," he said.

Watching Sly eat his farm-to-table lunch didn't help Cleo maintain the state of relaxation she'd achieved at the spa. How many meals had she watched him shovel in over the years? Why had *this* one suddenly made her think about what else he could be doing with those lips, that tongue, and those long, lean fingers?

The erotic turn to her thoughts depressed her. Sly was a friend. Perhaps her best friend, one she couldn't afford to lose. Any lines they were stupid enough to cross would lead them into momentary pleasure and nowhere else.

"Want to look at the silent auction stuff with me?" he asked as they walked out of the restaurant.

"OK," she said. "Let's see what the butt lifts are going for."

"Doing some early Christmas shopping?"

"Totally. You're impossible to shop for." She slapped him on the ass.

Which was a mistake. Now her palm was all tingly as it remembered the feel of his muscled cheek while they walked along the deck to the conference rooms. The ocean crashed against the rocks below them, gray and white water sending mist up in the cypress trees around the hotel.

It was one of the most romantic places she'd ever seen. Maybe that was the problem. She was too sensitive to her environment. It muddled the obvious: Sylvester Minguez was a workaholic who thought he was a slacker if he took a few hours to read a book for fun, whereas she lived life at half the pace he did, composing music that made her pennies, giving lessons to pay the rent, and intended to keep doing it. His parents were wealthy, hardworking accountants with a thriving business. Hers were clinical therapists who had retired to Oregon to grow organic vegetables. She and Sly could be friends who saw each other twice a month, but more than that?

Impossible.

They walked together into the room for the silent auction, which had panoramic windows of the sea and a harpist playing in the corner. The gentle notes added a heavenly quality to the foggy view. A man in a black shirt and pants handed her a glass of champagne, and another offered tiny plates of grapes.

"From our own vines," he said.

She smiled and followed Sly to the far end of the longest table, near a grand piano that had a giant red satin bow on top, like a TV commercial for a luxury car during the holidays. But instead of imagining the beautiful wife running outside in the snow, crying with joy next to her beaming, proud husband, she imagined how nice the grand would look next to her couch. Well, she'd have to remove the couch to make room for it. But if she had that piano, she'd always be sitting at it anyway. No couch needed.

She'd probably have to take out the dining table too. And maybe a wall.

"That must be a nice piano," Sly said. "You're drooling."

"That's because I'm with you, sweetie," she said absently. Oh, it had been a long time since she played a decent piano. She'd bought the best one she could afford, but... well, that wasn't much. It had good tone but wasn't the kind you'd want to roll around on top of in the nude.

Like that one.

"Seriously, Cleo, you're flushed," Sly said. "Do you need a few minutes alone?"

She shook her head to break the spell. "Let's find the butt lifts."

He picked up a brochure on the table. "How about a weekend in Vegas?"

"That's practical. Because when you have too much money, you need to find new homes for some of it." She sipped her drink, raising her eyebrows in appreciation. Not the cheap stuff she was used to. "This is good. Didn't you want any?"

"Staying sober today. Thanks."

"Suit yourself." She took another mouthful and searched the table for something Sly could waste his money on. A poster advertising a trip to the Sierra Nevada for "your adventurous canine companion" caught her eye. An all-expense-paid vacation for your dog. Bath upon return included.

Sly caught her arm. "That's Poppy over there. Mind if I...?"

"Go ahead. I'm going to call the one eight hundred number for this place near Yosemite and see if they'll take humans."

Flashing her his trademarked grin, he left her to shake the hand of the gray-haired woman surrounded by a cluster of men in T-shirts and jeans. Cleo had seen pictures of Poppy Lee, fondly nicknamed the "Silver Helmet" because of her hair. She watched Sly join the group, offer Poppy his hand, and draw her away from the other men with speedy grace.

He really had that rare charm that made life look easy. A mere mortal like herself would've felt uncomfortable barging in like that. Not Sly. He got what he wanted, and people thanked him for letting them give it to him.

She set her empty glass down and applied herself to reading

the other auction items. Some of them were up into the thousands, and she was tempted to put down Sly's name. Although he was generous with her, he could be cheap, always looking for a bargain, and not likely to treat himself to any luxuries, even small ones. The trip to the Patagonian Andes looked pretty good. She was just picking up the pen when he tapped her on the shoulder.

"I hope that's not for me."

"You can bring one of those solar panel chargers and your laptop," she said. "Work on the trail."

"You make it sound like I don't know how to take a vacation."

"You don't."

He put his arm around her and led her away from Poppy, who had returned to the cluster of jeans and T-shirts. "We can go whenever you're ready. I've set the stage for tonight."

"Stage for what?"

"Talking to Poppy about Mark's start-up."

"Didn't you do that just now?"

"You don't rush these things." His hand slid down her arm and squeezed her elbow.

Her body was rushing to divert blood to her erogenous zones. The dress covered her upper arms, but now he was touching bare skin, and she was having trouble concentrating on the poster advertising dog sledding in Vail.

It wasn't her imagination. He was touching her differently. His fingers lingered, made tiny circles on her skin, explored neighborhoods they'd never visited before.

"You know," she said, "I think I'd like to walk a little more. Get some fresh air. Should I meet you at—"

"I'll join you."

"Are you sure you don't want to set more stages or whatever

you do for—"

"Don't want to come on too strong," he said. "I know there's a lavender farm in Carmel Valley. I'd love to see that. We could drive there. Interested?"

Was she? Her rapid pulse suggested that something was interesting her. "It's probably too late in the year to see much. And I don't feel like getting in the car."

"So we'll walk." His hand moved down to her hand and clasped it.

Walking. Not as easy as it sounded. Her attention was so distracted by the touch that she tripped over the threshold on the way out the door.

She pulled her hand away and pretended to adjust her ponytail.

They could walk, but just for a little while. And then she was going to have a headache.

It was almost true.

8

SLY DRANK HIS third mineral water in the bar, watching the lobby for Cleo. They'd only walked for a little while that afternoon before she'd come down with a headache. They'd returned to the room, but when she made it clear there was nothing he could do for her, he'd quickly dressed for dinner and left her there with a pillow over her eyes.

Maybe she did have a headache. But he knew he'd sent a few mixed signals, testing her out, and her running away with a headache was one of the results.

He was done mixing any signals with Cleo. Weeks of no work had messed up his head. He got twitchy if he wasn't conquering something—climbing a mountain, closing a sale, seducing a woman. He had the sinking feeling he'd fixed his sights on Cleo out of pure leisure intolerance.

Tonight he'd do what he could to interest Poppy Lee in Mark's company, and then he'd do some networking himself. The sooner he got back into the workforce, the better.

"Evening, Sylvester."

He spun around on his seat to see Teresa standing behind him with a silver vase of sunflowers in her arms. "Hi."

"Help me out? They screwed up the arrangements, and I'm

trying to fix them before everyone gets into the room."

He hesitated.

"Come on. I can see you've finished your drink. I just need help carrying the last few vases." She thrust the sunflowers at him and turned. "Follow me."

Sly had never liked wishy-washy women. Being a man prone to domineering behavior himself, he liked being with someone who could hold her own. Teresa, however, had a pathological need to control everything at all times, even a charity auction at which she was the guest.

"Come on, come on," Teresa said. "People are arriving."

He looked around one last time for Cleo before following Teresa through the lobby to the banquet hall, figuring that carrying flowers was better than brooding at the bar.

Just as he passed the sitting area, he noticed a woman standing there with her back to him. Her snug emerald-green dress showed off an ass that could stop traffic. It had certainly stopped him.

And then his peripheral vision registered the color, length, and texture of her blond hair, and his heart began to pound harder.

When Cleo turned, he was holding the vase so tightly he was glad it wasn't glass because he might've shattered it. "Hi." He cleared his throat. "I'm helping out with the flowers."

She smiled. "I can see that." The dress was modest, with long sleeves and simple lines, but it clung to parts of her he'd never known she had. "Like my work clothes?"

He imagined the work she could do in it. "Excuse me?"

"You know, when I play at events."

"Right." Slowly, the gears in his brain began to turn again. "How's your headache?"

"Better, thanks. But seriously, is the dress all right? I didn't know if it would be too cheesy. It's good for weddings and anniversaries, but at those I'm just the chick playing the piano, not a mogul's hot date." She waved her hand up and down in his general direction.

"It's very all right."

Smile faltering, she reached for the flowers. "Can I help?"

He hugged the vase against his chest, suddenly needing to squeeze something. "I've got it. Teresa drafted me. You might want to hide before she catches you too."

"It's not me she wants to catch."

With a grim nod, he gestured to the banquet hall, and the two of them made their way through the growing crowd. Teresa was at the far end of the room near the stage, placing another vase of sunflowers on a round table. Immediately, as if she'd been watching the door, which she probably had, she waved him over.

Sly paused.

"I'll take them," Cleo said. "You can find us a table."

"Are you sure? That would be above and beyond the call of duty."

"It's what a jealous girlfriend would do."

Their eyes met. He handed her the vase. "Thanks."

Because it's what an admiring boyfriend would do, he watched her walk across the room, her generous hips swaying, her hair shimmering under the chandeliers, then back to her hips...

Teresa seemed to be staring past Cleo at him, watching him watch Cleo. He couldn't read her expression, but it wasn't happy.

He tore his gaze away and found a table in the middle near the side doors. Picking up an auction booklet as he sat, he returned his attention to Cleo, who was already walking back to him. For a woman who loved men's pajamas, she certainly looked comfortable in a dress. The soft, clingy fabric draped around her curves like the toga of a Greek goddess.

"You're laying it on a bit thick, aren't you?" she asked him as she sat down next to him. "I think she got the idea. She told me I was a lucky woman."

Forcing a smile, he put an arm around the back of her chair and lowered his mouth to her ear. Her perfume struck him again. "I'm the lucky one."

She didn't move, didn't say anything. Her hair, loose and glossy around her shoulders, was brushing his cheek.

I want her.

He jerked away and reached for a glass of ice water. His palms were sweating.

"There's Poppy," Cleo said.

Keep your eye on the prize, Minguez. He got to his feet and waved to Poppy, then held out his hand, palm up, to invite her to share their empty table. If he could talk to Poppy all evening, he might stop trying to check out his good friend's body. Or taste it.

Thank God, she was coming over. Except instead of taking the seat next to him, she took the one next to Cleo. Her husband, a quiet man whose name he couldn't remember, sat on the other side.

Sly stood for a moment. "Great to see you again." He introduced Cleo, the three of them shook hands, took their seats, and then Poppy got her husband's attention. He had buried his face in the auction booklet.

"Bob," Poppy said. "This is Sylly."

"Totally agree," Bob said, throwing down the booklet. "We could just write a check directly instead of going through all this hassle."

"Sylly's an old nickname." Sly was able to smile at the misunderstanding, although he didn't enjoy it as much as he used to. "Short for Sylvester. People also call me Sly." Out of the corner of his eye, he saw Cleo smiling around her wineglass.

"Sorry," Bob said. "This is why I try to let Poppy do all the talking."

Poppy kissed him on the cheek. "Bob hates these things. He's sweet to put up with so many of them."

"It's not the charity. It's the crowd." Bob's gaze darted uneasily around the table. "I'll shut up now. I don't know why she doesn't leave me at home where I can't cause any trouble."

Poppy kissed him again. "You need to get out every once in a while, pumpkin. Besides, the food here should be fantastic."

"The food everywhere is fantastic these days," Bob said. "And I'm not picky."

Lips pressed together, Poppy gave Sly and Cleo a discreet eye roll.

"I've never been to one of these," Cleo said. "At least not as a guest."

Poppy held up her glass in a toast. "I was a waitress all through graduate school. Hardest work I've ever done."

"Oh, I'm sure it was," Cleo said. "I was lucky enough to just be the pianist."

"A pianist," Poppy said. "How wonderful."

Sly put his hand on hers. "Cleo's very talented."

"You know," Cleo said, withdrawing her hand, "I bet the two of you have a lot to talk about. How about we switch places, Sly?"

"No, no. Don't do that," Poppy said. "Then you'll end up with nobody to talk to."

"Maybe that's the idea," Bob said, lifting the booklet again. "We're not all extroverts like you, dear."

"And few are as reclusive as you, honey," Poppy said.

This comment gave Sly an opening, and he wasn't one to miss

an opportunity. "Have you ever met Mark Johnson, Poppy?"

She threw her head back and laughed. The famous silver hair barely changed shape, even with the shift in gravity. "Speaking of recluses, you mean?"

Sly grinned. "Exactly."

"I haven't had the pleasure," Poppy said. "You're an old friend of his, aren't you?"

"I am. In fact..." Sly launched into a brief history of his work at WellyNelly, his relationship with Mark, and the start-up he'd just left. Cleo seemed to relax, sinking back into her chair with a smile as he talked with Poppy. In his element, he was able to shove aside thoughts of curves in emerald-green satin and lose himself in the conversation.

At least for a while. Salads appeared before them, other people at the table caught Poppy's attention, and Sly let the business conversation fade away. He'd gotten her personal email and the impression she was interested in something new, especially with Mark.

While Poppy was looking the other way, Cleo leaned against him. "You're good," she whispered in his ear.

Inhaling her perfume, heat rushed through him, obliterating the calm he'd regained while talking shop for a few minutes.

This attraction wasn't going to go away. He was going to have to deal with it.

He looked into her eyes, searching for any sign of what he himself was feeling. "You have no idea," he said in a low voice.

The live auction would've been a lot more fun to watch if Cleo had been able to pay the smallest bit of attention to any of it. Everyone seemed to enjoy themselves, and the various educational foundations raked in a fortune thanks to the professional auctioneer who lathered up the privileged crowd and inspired higher bids for each item, praising their generosity, their social consciousness, and their obscene wealth (that last one was a running joke that always got a laugh.)

Cleo was glad when the meal was over. Sly's romantic playacting—whispering in her ear, touching her hand, holding her gaze—had lathered her up in an entirely different way.

But finally she could relax. Sly reignited his professional rapport with Poppy over the cheesecake, and when loud dance music started playing, the four of them escaped to the lobby. Sly and Poppy walked shoulder to shoulder, talking business, while Poppy's grumpy husband and Sly's fake girlfriend trailed in their wake.

His grumpy fake girlfriend.

"Nice guy," Bob said to her. "Your boyfriend."

"He is a nice guy," Cleo said.

"You can tell a lot about a person by who their friends are. Or girlfriends."

Afraid shy Bob was about to get too personal, she glanced over his shoulder for the exit.

"You're a nice woman," Bob went on, confirming her fears. "That tells me Sly is a nice guy. He could be with somebody like that lady over there." Bob nodded at a woman in a sleeveless black dress that ended just low enough to cover the bottom curve of her ass.

Cleo couldn't resist. She smirked. "He likes that type too."

"Of course he does. But he's here with you, isn't he?" Bob seemed to realize he'd used up his daily allotment of words, because he shook his head, pressed his lips together, and walked faster, patting her on the shoulder as he left her behind.

Poppy took her husband's arm, waved a business card at Sly,

and walked out a side door. Cleo saw Bob cop a feel just as they were turning the corner.

"Nice guy," Sly said, unwittingly echoing Bob's words.

The thought of going up to their room for the night filled her with dread.

OK, not nearly enough dread.

"So, who won the piano?" she asked.

"Let's go see."

"Where?"

"They mark the winners and the highest bids on the sheet. It's fun to see what they went for." He bumped his shoulder against hers, a platonic gesture that shouldn't have made her shiver.

They returned to the space where they'd seen the silent auction, but the door was closed and all the tables with the winning bids were lined up outside with a dozen or so people looking at the results.

"Checkout is in the lobby," a woman in a dove-gray dress said, looking them over. "If you're a winner, bring the tag to the register and we'll give you a receipt."

"Thanks, but I'm not a winner," Cleo said.

"Sure you are," Sly said in her ear.

Shaking off another shiver, she searched the posters and tablet displays, but didn't see one for the piano. "The last bid I saw was way over what it was worth. I'm curious to see how high it went."

"I bet it's still in the room." Sly gave her a meaningful look and moved toward the door. When the woman in the gray dress was looking the other way, he turned the handle, pushed, and signaled for Cleo to follow.

"You rebel," she said, hurrying past him into the room. This was what she loved about him. He was fun.

He closed the door, enveloping them in darkness. Only the

moon and the city lights outside illuminated the room. At the far end, the grand piano sat in the shadows, dark and alone.

"It looks lonely," Cleo said. "I think it would rather be at the party."

"Why don't you try it out? Make it feel better?"

"You didn't buy it for me or anything, right?" she asked, suddenly worried he had.

"Cleo, don't say that."

"What do you mean?"

"I would've loved to buy it for you, but I figured you'd never accept it."

She nodded. "Totally true."

"But you thought I might." He ran his hand through his hair. "I should have. Sneak it into your apartment when you aren't looking."

"Don't be ridiculous. Where would it go? It's bigger than my living room."

"That's not saying much."

"Don't insult my home, mogul boy."

Clapping his hands together, he walked deeper into the room. "All right, piano woman. Why don't you play us a song?"

She looked around at the stacked chairs in a ring facing the windows. "It looks like they're getting ready for another event."

"Looks like they're not here."

Why not? It would delay the moment they went back to their room. She walked over, sat down, lifted the lid, and lightly caressed the keys first. "It's not new."

"The poster said it was just a stand-in for the donation. This one is always here."

She played a chord, sending rich notes into the darkness. Then she began to play in earnest, loud enough to feel the vibrations in her chest, her arms, her legs. Tension drained out of her. Whatever was bothering her, music lifted her out, above, and up into that space beyond reality where she could recognize her own insignificance and touch, for just a moment, the vastness of the universe.

Until she felt Sly's presence behind her. Her hands stilled, and her last chord faded away.

She waited for him to say something, joke about her forgetting the rest of the song, but he was silent.

Oh God. Her heart thudded against her ribs, more in step with a disco beat than the dreamy sonata she'd been playing.

Was she imagining this thing between them? Years of nothing, and now...

"Cleo." His voice was rough.

Frozen, she closed her eyes and tried to catch her breath. Frantically she searched her memories for something silly and embarrassing that would return him to his Friend Box. She would stuff him inside, close the lid, lock it, and throw the key over the balcony outside this room and onto the rocky cliffs below.

He touched her hair. Softly, just a graze. "Cleo," he said again.

"What?"

"You know what."

Shaking her head, she closed the lid over the keys, stood, and moved so that the bulk of the piano was between them. Its curved surface felt cold and smooth under her palms. Soothing.

He followed her, his face hidden by the shadows. "You play beautifully."

Her mouth was dry. "Thanks."

He took another step, close enough for the cuff of his jacket to brush against her arm. The perfume she'd worn that evening had been too strong, overwhelming every other smell in her environment. But now his scent was close enough to detect. Familiar but dangerous, like a pampered pet that suddenly bared its fangs.

Her pulse, already racing, shifted into a higher gear. He moved, putting himself between her and the door. A shaft of light from outside reflected in his dark, gorgeous, almond-shaped eyes, pushing her over the edge into mindless wanting. He was actually taller than she'd thought he was, his shoulders broader. And she couldn't see his handsome face at the moment, but she remembered it, not as a friend, but as a—

He caught her face in his hands and kissed her.

He was kissing her.

Fire engulfed her belly and spread throughout her body. Hot, wet fire. His mouth was warm and tender, barely touching her, but she felt as if she would collapse under the shock of it. Explode.

His lips slid across hers, gently nibbling. She tasted wine and something sweet, and was shocked by how good it felt for him to hold her, even just one hand on her cheek, the other digging into her hair. She imagined taking off his shirt and licking her way down his chest to his navel and beyond, she imagined liking it very, very much. And then he would take off her clothes too and treat her to the sexual expertise he'd acquired over his years and years as a handsome, rich, successful bachelor. She would be one of his women, one of the many, and she knew that as long as he was making love to her, she would enjoy it.

But then it would be over, like it was always over.

She breathed his air, her legs wobbling, desiring him so much she hated herself. And she hated him too, for teaching her that all this lust was inside her, just waiting for him to unleash it.

She wrenched herself away and strode to the door, not knowing where she was going to go but needing to be there as soon as possible.

9

"AT LEAST RETURN my calls so you can get your clothes," Sly said, finally leaving a voice mail message after days of Cleo ignoring his text messages. "And I owe you for the hotel room. That was… my fault."

He didn't know what else he could say, but he certainly couldn't say it to a machine that was recording every mistake. After a quick good-bye, he hung up.

Talking in person was the only way they were going to survive this. He'd screwed up; he could admit it. But she had to give him a chance to explain and atone. Grovel.

He put his phone in the console and tapped the steering wheel. Sitting in his car outside her apartment was making him feel like a stalker, and as frustrated as he was, he knew it was time to drive away.

But instead of leaving, he watched a young guy, probably a Berkeley student, lift a bike onto his shoulder and walk into the apartment building. Coming to Cleo's place always made him feel two hundred years old.

He slapped the steering wheel. It was Thursday night. *Their* Thursday.

But what if there was no longer any "their" there?

He dug his knuckles into his forehead and started the car, driving very slowly in case she called him back, then faster when she didn't.

Maybe Uncle Hugo was around. The clinic was open late sometimes, and he often worked after hours anyway. Sly didn't want to go back to his place right now and be reminded of what was missing in his life, that he was jobless, friendless.

Cleo-less.

When he pulled up in front of the vet clinic, Hugo was walking out the front door with the biggest dog he'd ever seen. The thin leash looked about as useful as dental floss would be to lasso a grizzly bear.

Sly rolled down the window. "Tell me his name is Yogi."

"Afraid not," Hugo said, patting the giant black dog's head without bending over. "This is Mouse."

"What is he?"

"Don't be rude. You'll hurt his feelings."

Sly got out of his car and walked over, shivering as a blast of wind came down San Pablo Avenue. Mouse stopped lumbering, looked up at him with enormous, droopy, gentle eyes, and smiled. Sly held out a hand. "Can I pet him?"

"Try not to," Hugo said.

His skull was the size of a soccer ball, and his long fur was soft as velvet. White flecks of drool spotted his jowls. "Newfoundland, right?" Sly asked.

"I couldn't resist. His mommy couldn't bring him to Hong Kong with him. New job."

"Mommy?" Sly shook his hand to dislodge the fur and drool sticking to his fingers.

"The woman who used to own him." Hugo scratched Mouse behind his floppy black ears. In response, the big dog closed his eyes with rapture and sat down on Sly's shoes.

It hurt.

"He's got to weigh two hundred pounds," Sly said, stroking Mouse's soccer ball of a head.

"Oh, no. Only one sixty-three. On the small side for a male. It's selfish of me, but I figure a vet's the best home for a dog like this. He has a few health issues. Can get expensive. Besides, he's great with everybody, other dogs, lies around all day, keeps me company."

"When I said you needed company, I was thinking you might find a woman," Sly said. "A human woman."

"Have plans tonight, actually." Hugo clucked his tongue and began walking, and Mouse immediately hauled himself to his feet and followed. "I told Trixie Johnson I'd come by and see how Luna's doing. That Chihuahua that got run over when you were here."

"And then you have a date? What's her name?"

Raising an eyebrow, Hugo opened the passenger door of his Fiat and shoved the seat forward. "For a smart kid, sometimes you're pretty slow."

Sly's mouth dropped open. He tried to picture his uncle and Mark's mother together. He loved Hugo, but he was a gloomy, difficult old bachelor, and Trixie was a sunny, tirelessly happy grandmother. "Trixie?"

"I think she's ready for a relationship," Hugo said. "Now that her kids are all paired off, she can think about herself."

Mouse stared into the backseat of the tiny Fiat and then up at Hugo, as if thinking, *You've got to be kidding.*

"Go on, you'll be fine," Hugo told the dog.

If a dog could shrug his shoulders, Mouse would have. But he put one paw in, then the other, and after a short struggle he was sitting in the backseat, facing forward with his head brushing the sloped rear window.

Hugo slammed the door. "Hope he's not too afraid of Trixie's Chihuahuas. Barking gets on his nerves."

"If they don't get along, your relationship will be strained from the start."

"Exactly. That's why I'm bringing him now. Lay the groundwork. Get everyone used to each other."

"I had no idea you felt that way about her. Why didn't you say anything?"

"For one thing, she insists she's given up on romance," Hugo said. "Only for herself, obviously—she's always talking to me about setting you up. And you're friends with her son. I thought it might make you uncomfortable."

"But now you're getting me used to the idea," Sly said. "Like the dogs."

Hugo flashed a rare smile. "Laying the groundwork." He walked around the car and opened the driver's side door, suddenly frowning. "Did you need something, or were you just driving by?"

Sly glanced down at Mouse, who was watching him through the window, a string of drool hanging down from the left corner of his mouth. He could fit both Chihuahuas between those jaws and still have room for a ham sandwich.

"Just driving by," Sly said with a wave. "Good luck with Trixie."

Cleo picked up the phone for the third time and stared at the screen, feeling ridiculous about the way her heart was pounding. If she was worried about losing Sly's friendship, refusing to talk to him and then standing him up on their Thursday night was an irrational method of rescuing it.

Biting her lip, she hit the button. He picked up on the second ring.

"Hey," he said. Then a pause. "Thanks for calling back."

"Sorry I didn't earlier."

"Don't apologize. It's all my fault."

"You keep saying that," she said. In his texts, in his phone message.

"It's true."

She moved the phone away from her mouth to let out her breath. Hearing his voice, so familiar, took the edge off her nerves. And whatever lust had driven her wild down in Carmel seemed to have vanished. This was just Sly, her old friend. They could get past this.

"You've probably made other plans for tonight," she said, "but I thought we might get together next week. Or the week after. Pick up where we left off."

No, had she said that? A smoky hot memory of his lips dragging across hers blasted through her mind. That wasn't the leaving-off place she'd meant.

"On TV," she added.

"I know what you meant."

Awkward silence swelled between them. After a moment she strode over to her work area and played a silent song with one hand on the powered-down keyboard. Maybe they couldn't get past this after all.

"I don't think we should wait that long," he said. "I'll come by tonight."

"It's already eight."

"We have time for one episode."

She looked down at what she was wearing. If she didn't change into her usual pajamas, he'd think she was coming on to him. But now, going without a bra and panties carried an entirely different message. Convenient access.

This was stupid. She'd never been his type and wasn't now. Every one of the women he'd dated over the years she'd known him had been tall, thin, and athletic, well suited to their conventional, professional lifestyles. They were also brunettes, for the most part. She was so blond that some people, from a distance, mistook it for white. Sly was in his midthirties, a classic age for a midlife crisis. Because the two of them were so close, he was grasping at anything that would give him comfort as he hurtled toward his inevitable approaching death.

Perhaps she should tell him that. *Then* he'd stop trying to kiss her. In fact, she'd probably never see him again.

"I've already eaten," she said, "but how about you bring the beer? Lager, not that pee you like to drink."

He laughed. "See you soon."

After a moment's hesitation, she compromised on the fashion dilemma by changing into a pair of yoga pants and a sweatshirt but leaving on her undergarments. When he rang the buzzer, she felt almost normal.

When she opened the door and looked into his eyes, she told herself she really did feel normal. And then when he walked in, took off his jacket, and held out a six-pack of Rolling Rock, she knew it was true.

"Went all out, did you?" She took the budget beer from him and hugged it to her chest. "Listen, Sly—"

"You don't have to say anything. I got the message."

"It's not that you're completely disgusting or anything—"

"Thanks."

"You're welcome." She gathered her thoughts. "The thing is, you're... we're..."

"Please, let's not drag this out. I've been trying to understand what happened, and the best I've come up with is that I've been a little confused lately about my life, about the future, who I am, and you were there, it was dark, and you smelled good—"

"I smelled good?" Here she'd been blaming it on the dress. But she'd guessed the life crisis part correctly.

"Not that you usually smell bad," he added.

"Neither do you, sweetie."

He looked startled, then laughed softly. "I'm doing this all wrong."

"You're doing fine." She went into her galley kitchen, opened two bottles, grabbed the bag of popcorn she'd microwaved, and joined him on the sofa—where, she noticed, he'd sat at the far end. A pony could've sat between them.

"You know how goal oriented I am. I couldn't let go of it once I'd gotten the idea into my head," he said.

"Is that where it was?"

Eyes widening, he flushed. Then laughed again. "Go ahead. Mock."

"Unless you hid something from me, it's been over six months since you had a date," she said.

"Eleven."

"No wonder," she said.

"I really am sorry." He held her gaze. "Your friendship means more to me than I can say. I promise to keep my hands to myself from now on."

"And your mouth," she said.

"Oh, all right. That too."

She had to laugh. It was going to be all right. "I'm glad you came," she said, handing him a beer.

Relief showed all over his face. "Me too."

They reached over the wide middle cushion to click their bottles together, then started the show.

10

THE FOLLOWING SATURDAY, Cleo found herself looking up at Trixie Johnson's house again. This time, however, she was ringing the bell next door. Trixie's son Liam lived there with his wife, Bev, who wanted to learn how to play the new piano they had sitting in their living room. Trixie, apparently, had bought it for her first and only grandchild. Since the baby had only recently learned how to walk, Cleo wouldn't be teaching her just yet.

She assumed Trixie had given her number to Bev, and here she was. She hoped the lessons were serious and not just another excuse to interfere in Sly's life. Their relationship was edging back to normal, and she didn't want to rock the boat.

The door swung open to a dark-haired, statuesque woman in yoga pants and a Fite Fitness sweatshirt. Her bright blue eyes crinkled at the sight of Cleo as she drew her inside. "Welcome, I'm Bev. We've got the house to ourselves for an hour. It's so nice for you to make house calls."

"I have such a small apartment, it's nice to get out of it," Cleo said, looking around. "Wow, what a gorgeous view."

Huge windows overlooking the bay spread across the living room. A baby grand piano, littered beneath with stuffed animals and plastic blocks, sat between a sofa and a red-and-yellow nylon play tent.

"I tried to clear some space around it," Bev said. "I'm ashamed to admit it was covered with Merry's unfolded laundry a few minutes before you got here. You wouldn't believe how many garments a baby wears in a single day."

Smiling politely, Cleo studied the piano. "It looks brand-new. Has it been tuned?"

"Yes, Trixie sent somebody over a month ago when she had her own done." Bev rubbed her hands together. "So, what do we do first? Can I get you something to drink?"

"I'm fine." She knew how nervous people got, especially adults, about their first lesson. Small-scale performance anxiety. "Just have a seat and play whatever you remember how to play from when you were a kid. And don't worry about being good or bad or anything. You're doing this for fun, for yourself."

Bev gave her a grateful glance and sat on the bench. "I'm so nervous."

"Don't be. There's nobody here but—"

The front door banged open. "Hi, Bev. Hi, Cleo. Hope I'm not interrupting." Trixie walked into the living room with a garden tub filled with monster-sized squash in her arms. "I can't let anyone escape without taking some of my zucchini. The neighbors won't take any more. That crabby woman down the street sicced her nutty schnauzer on me."

Bev groaned. "I don't think we can eat any more squash, Trixie. Merry cries at the sight of it."

"I know how she feels." Trixie set the tub down and pointed at Cleo. "But I brought it for our lovely pianist. What she doesn't want herself, she can give to her other students. Or Sly." She said this last part as if the idea had just occurred to her.

"I love fresh vegetables," Cleo said. "I don't have any land to grow my own, so sure."

"Hope you really, really like zucchini," Bev said quietly.

Trixie stood there beaming for a moment, watching Bev at the piano and Cleo standing behind her. "Well, that's settled then. Are you supposed to be playing, Bev?"

"To be honest, I'd rather not play in front of you." In spite of her words, Bev's tone was warm. "You're so good, and I haven't played in decades."

"Of course, of course. I'm intruding. But I was wondering..." Trixie flushed. "Cleo, would you have a moment when you're through to come by my house? Just next door?"

With Bev there, Cleo didn't want to get too personal and ask why. "Sure, I'll have a few minutes."

When Trixie was gone, Bev began to play, with effort, "Deck the Halls," cursing at herself as she stumbled over the keys.

Finally, she gave up and looked at Cleo. "I wanted to impress everyone on Christmas Eve. Looks like that's not going to happen."

Cleo assured her she was doing fantastic for a woman who hadn't played since the twentieth century, took out a book of Christmas carols, spread it open at an easier arrangement of the song, and began the instruction in earnest.

An hour later, after setting up the next lesson, then putting the tub of giant vegetables in her car and a few of Bev's homemade oatmeal-raisin cookies in her belly, Cleo went over to the house next door.

Trixie led her into the house, her three little dogs circling her feet. "This is very embarrassing."

"Look, I'd rather not talk about Sly if that's—"

"No, no, not exactly." Trixie picked up one of the dogs for a cuddle, avoiding Cleo's gaze. Her cheeks were pink. "You know what? Never mind. You go on. Thank you. Did you remember the vegetables? I can't ask any more than you taking those off my hands."

Seeing her obvious distress, Cleo was both sympathetic and curious. She hadn't seemed uncomfortable when she'd been trying to set up Sly, so maybe it was something else. "Come on, you can't leave me hanging like that. What is it?"

Trixie closed her eyes. The dog began french kissing her ear. "It's my vet," she whispered.

"Sly's uncle?"

She nodded, turning a brighter shade of red. "I shouldn't call him *my* vet, as if I were a parakeet."

"I knew what you meant."

"I've known him for years. We're friends. Kind of like you and Sly."

Cleo let that one go without comment.

"But now..." Trixie set the dog on the floor and finger combed her short white hair. "Well, you get the idea."

Not exactly, but Cleo didn't know what to say. "What can I do?"

"It's this trip to Las Vegas."

"What trip?"

"The one Sly gave to Hugo. He won it in an auction. I thought you'd been there?"

"Sly bought the Las Vegas trip?" Cleo thought back to the silent auction in Carmel. She'd been too preoccupied with other things to notice if Sly had purchased anything.

In a tiny voice, Trixie said, "Hugo has invited me to join him."

"That sounds nice." Cleo said, trying not to smile too broadly, which might seem like she was being patronizing. "Isn't it?"

Trixie studied her hands. "I've been on my own for a long

time. I'm not sure I want to change that."

"It's just a weekend. You're not agreeing to marry the guy."

"It's Las Vegas. Years ago, that's exactly what it meant."

Cleo squatted down to pet the ugly dog with the floppy tongue. "Not anymore. But if you want to take it slow, maybe you could get separate rooms." Then she bit her lip, afraid she might've offended Trixie by suggesting she *wouldn't* get separate rooms.

Trixie sighed. "Since my husband died, I've only dated a few times. I made it to third base once, but that was it. Do people still say that? You probably don't even know what it means. It's when, well, you—"

Cleo stood quickly. "No need to explain."

Trixie smiled. "You're as prudish as my children. They never want to talk about sex."

"You are their mom."

"But I'm not yours."

Cleo slipped her hands into the front pockets of her jeans. "OK, I admit it. I'm a little uptight." She would never have admitted that to anyone her own age. It was very uncool.

"That's all right. I'm sorry to drag you into this. And here I gave you all those vegetables that look like penises." Trixie smiled.

"I think I can handle a few phallic squash."

"Handle them all you like," Trixie said, breaking out into giggles.

"I think I will. Right before I chop them up into tiny pieces and sauté them. Or bake them into muffins." Cleo peeked at her phone. "I should be going. I've got a lesson at my place soon."

"Of course, of course. But I haven't—oh, I haven't asked my favor yet."

Cleo's grip on her phone tightened. Somehow she knew what was coming. "Oh?"

"I was hoping you and Sly would join us."

"I don't know, Trixie. I work on weekends—"

Trixie clutched her arm. "Please. I know we barely know each other, and I'm much older than you, but I feel a bond. Maybe it's the music. Maybe I'm as crazy as my children think I am. But as soon as I saw you I felt it. Will you come? Will you at least consider it? It would make it so much easier for me."

Cleo was touched. "I'd love to help, but Sly would have to—"

"He's going to invite you," Trixie said, patting her arm and releasing her. "I'm begging you to say yes. I wanted you to know it wasn't his idea so you can accept. It's just to help out two lonely old farts."

"It depends on—"

"Whenever works for you," Trixie said. "We'll work around your schedule."

Cleo was still trying to understand what she meant by *it wasn't his idea so you can accept*. "But I don't—"

"Don't tell me now. Just think about it." And then, with a quick hug, Trixie shoved her out the door.

"Please," Hugo said. "Trixie won't go unless you and your friend come with us. The prize you gave us is good for four."

Sly stroked Mouse's head, distracted for a moment by how huge it was. "I think Mouse is part mastodon," he said. The Berkeley café where they sat had an outdoor area that allowed dogs, at least informally. Mouse had rested his chin on Sly's knee, which required the large dog to slump. It also increased the amount of drool seeping out of his jowls onto Sly's jeans. The wet spot had spread halfway down to his ankle.

"You'd only have to go to dinner with us, maybe a show," Hugo continued. "The rest of the time would be your own. Hit the casinos, whatever."

"I'd like to Hugo, but I don't think she'll do it."

"At least ask her."

Sly wiped his hand on a dry patch of denim before lifting his coffee to his lips. Maybe he should confide in Hugo about the recent complications in his relationship with Cleo. It had been two weeks since Carmel. She'd been as warm and funny as ever, but he thought they were fooling themselves. They couldn't go back to the way they were. He knew *he* couldn't. Maybe women were different, or Cleo was, but now that he'd kissed her once, he frequently thought about kissing her again. He thought about doing all kinds of things with her he hadn't before, not seriously.

Before, if he'd noticed her body and felt a little curious about sleeping with her, he'd dismissed it as mundane heterosexual male lust, nothing deeper than that. Now, however, he'd felt her respond to him. He'd tasted her interest.

And that enticing knowledge was keeping him up at night.

"I'll ask her, but no promises," Sly said. "The last time we spent a weekend together, I got a little too friendly." He held his uncle's gaze over his mug.

"You what?"

"You heard me," Sly said. Mouse's nose prodded his upper thigh, probably looking for scone crumbs again as he dragged drool strings across his lap.

"When was this?"

"When I bought the Las Vegas trip for you. The charity auction in Carmel."

"But that's perfect," Hugo said. "It'll be a real double date then. Me and Trixie, you and—"

"We're just friends."

"I don't understand. You changed your mind?"

Sly scratched Mouse's skull, nudging him away from his balls, a location he'd rather keep drool-free. At least from a dog. "She's not interested."

"Of course she's interested," Hugo said. "She must be."

"Thanks, but there really are women on this earth who don't find me irresistible."

Hugo narrowed his eyes. "Were you drunk? Maybe she didn't think you were serious."

"That wasn't the problem."

"I never did understand why you spent so much time with a woman you weren't sleeping with."

"It's called friendship. We enjoy each other's company. You don't have to want to have sex with somebody to enjoy her company."

"But you do want to have sex with her," Hugo said.

Sly looked past Hugo to the sidewalk where a panhandler was talking on his cell phone. "Yes," he said softly. "It seems I do."

Hugo tapped his foot against Sly's shin. "Weekend after next. Friday flight out of SFO. I'll set it up and email you the itinerary." He stood and snapped his fingers for Mouse, who, after shooting a longing glance at Sly, turned to follow.

"I can't promise anything," Sly said.

"I've known you your whole life. You always get what you want." Shaking his head, he patted Mouse's rump. "Eventually."

11

THE FRIDAY AFTER next, Cleo sat on a plane to Las Vegas.

"It's all a setup to get us together," Sly had told her the week before. "Trixie's not really interested in Hugo. She made that up to get you to say yes."

"Thanks for warning me," she'd replied. "Now I don't have to feel guilty about saying no."

"Sure you do. Think of poor Uncle Hugo."

"But if she's not interested—" Cleo had begun.

"Hugo thinks she could be if he gets her away from home. Here she's got her family and the dogs. In Las Vegas, he thinks he just might have a chance."

"Maybe," she'd said. "But why should I be the sacrificial lamb? Can't you find a date?"

"She thinks you've got the hots for me." Before she could hit him, he'd added quickly, "But since we both know it's not true, that won't be a problem."

No problem. Right.

She'd finally agreed to go, officially for Hugo's sake, and here she was. Privately, she'd had her own reasons for coming. Although they'd smoothed the waters since Carmel and things seemed to be back to normal, she regretted the way she'd run away from him after that kiss. Instead of explaining to him with a lighthearted laugh that she wasn't interested, she'd fled like a coward who had something to hide.

She was grateful for the chance to show him she didn't.

They walked off the plane at the Las Vegas airport into a circular gate area bursting with slot machines and flashing neon lights. Around them, high windows displayed a vista of arid mountains and flat desert. Cleo stopped to gape.

Sly caught up to her and touched her shoulder. "You OK?"

"It's already like a casino. Right here in the airport."

"Haven't you been to Las Vegas before?"

She shook her head. "Never got around to it."

"Why didn't you say so?" he asked.

She hadn't wanted to make a bigger deal out of this trip than it already was. "Didn't I?"

His eyebrows rose. "No, you didn't."

"I felt like I already had," she said. "From movies and TV."

"If you find me parked in front of the slots for too long," Trixie called out behind them, "do an intervention, will you?"

The four of them paused near one of the empty machines while Trixie bent over to tie her hot-pink minimalist running shoes. A sign warned them that the seats around the slots could not be used by tired travelers, only for gamblers.

"If you want to play the slots, play the slots," Hugo said. "Enjoy yourself."

"But it wouldn't be any fun for you," Trixie said.

"Being with you is all the fun I need." With that declaration, Hugo pulled a pink rose out of his jacket and presented it to her.

Sly and Cleo shared a look. "Sweet," she whispered, but he just rolled his eyes.

Cleo stifled a laugh. Romantic, Sly wasn't. Not that way.

It was one of the things she liked about him. Her ex-husband had always put on a show for her birthday, anniversaries, Valentine's Day—candy and flowers, candlelit dinners, love letters (via email), and even, during graduate school, poems. Since the divorce, she hated all that phony sentiment, seeing it as flashy distraction from the lack of solid, steady respect and affection underneath. If Dylan could do all that phony romantic crap while he was sleeping with her best friend, what good was it? She wouldn't mind if she never got flowers again for the rest of her life.

But it was touching to see the surprised pleasure on Trixie's face. Even if she was faking half of it.

They continued on through the airport to the baggage and rental cars, and soon they were driving down the Strip in a massive Buick that had enough room just in the trunk for several dead bodies. Cleo craned her neck out the window to check out the shining black pyramid with its laser beam pointing to the sky, the glimmering fountains, the moat, the roller coaster tracks snaking between glass and steel, and the afternoon crowd of curious families pushing tiny children in strollers between the hollow-eyed adults who looked as if they'd been up for days, either working or playing, for profit or loss or every point between.

When they pulled up in front of their hotel, Cleo and Sly got out of the car long before Trixie and Hugo, who were talking to each other in low, serious voices in the back seat.

"What's the problem?" Cleo asked Sly.

"I think she's trying to decide if she wants to room with you or Hugo," he said. "You know, not sure which would be more likely to result in our happy ending."

"I wouldn't mind sharing a room with her," Cleo said. "You snore like a congested—"

"Yes, yes, so you've said. Don't rub it in."

"I'd be rubbing the pillow into your noisy gob if I had to sleep with you again," she continued.

He didn't laugh. "We're not here for our own comfort though, are we?"

"You're right. Hugo's odds are better if he can get her alone and work his—"

Trixie and Hugo finally joined them on the sidewalk. Putting an arm around Cleo's shoulders, Trixie walked with her down a red carpet through two enormous fake oak gates into reception.

"I wonder if I could ask you a favor," Trixie whispered.

"Is it about the room? Because I wouldn't mind sharing."

"Actually, I was hoping we could be naughty." Trixie gave her an exaggerated wink. "Hugo is so handsome, don't you think? I don't see why I should even try to resist him."

Cleo swerved to avoid a bellhop. "You've really got it bad, huh?"

Trixie bit her lip and stared straight ahead. "Oh, yes. Very bad."

"Sure," Cleo said, trying not to laugh. "I knew I might be stuck with Sly when I agreed to come."

"Is he that terrible?"

"I'll survive."

Trixie hugged her. "Thank you. I'll make you a blackberry pie when we get home."

They checked in and went up to their rooms, which were on different floors, so they separated in the elevator with plans to meet in a few hours for dinner at a restaurant Trixie had read about in *Sunset* magazine. When Cleo and Sly reached the door of their room, a wave of discomfort washed over her as she relived the last time they'd traveled together. Unlike the trip to Carmel, he wasn't trying to impress anyone, so he wore faded jeans, an old leather jacket, and sported two days' worth of stubble.

He'd never looked so appealing. She had to keep mentally slapping herself.

They walked into their room, a luxurious suite decorated in shades of cream, crimson, and black. Everything was glossy or plush—marble, steel, glass, velvet. The bedroom was behind a separate door, and a sunken living room overlooked the mountains. There was enough space for a string quartet and a little dancing.

While they were unpacking, Sly's phone rang. He looked at it and put it to his ear. "Hi, Hugo, what's up?" After a long pause, he looked at Cleo. "I'll ask her, but she says I snore like an elephant seal."

"What is it?" Cleo asked.

"Trixie's getting cold feet," Sly said. "They've only got one bed. Would you be willing to switch rooms?"

"Both of us?"

He nodded. "Should I tell them no?"

Trixie must've overestimated how well she could manipulate this thing with Hugo. "No, I don't mind. I'll have to repack though. Tell them to come up in ten minutes."

Sly smiled at her, told Hugo what she'd said, and hung up. "Thanks, Cleo. That's really nice of you."

"She's a nice lady," Cleo said. "In spite of the scheming."

"You're the nice one. I'm here to help Hugo out, but you don't owe them anything."

"Maybe Hugo has a chance," she said. "I wouldn't want to stand between him and his dream girl."

"Are you being sarcastic?

"Not at all. I'm being romantic," she said.

He snorted. "You? Since when?"

"Hey. I'm as romantic as anybody."

"Oh, really?"

"Don't sound so skeptical," she said.

"You're the least romantic woman I know."

"I've very romantic, actually. You don't know everything about me."

"True enough." Shooting her an unreadable glance, he rolled his suitcase out of the closet and began to pack again.

Less than five minutes later, Trixie and Hugo arrived with their luggage.

"This is so embarrassing," Trixie said, hanging her head in the doorway.

"It's OK, no problem." Cleo pulled her in, waving aside the stream of apologies and gratitude. "No problem at all."

Trixie tugged nervously at her cardigan's buttons. "I'll treat you both to dinner."

"Don't be silly." Cleo reached for her suitcase, but Sly already had it and hers and was moving into the hall.

"You'll change your mind when you see the other room," Hugo said. "This place is much nicer than the one we're sticking you with."

Three minutes later, as they dragged their suitcases into their new room, she saw that Hugo hadn't been kidding.

One bed. No lounge area, no dance floor, no wet bar. And their only view was of a neighboring hotel and a parking lot.

Shooting her worried glances, Sly set his key card on the TV stand. "I can get us an upgrade if this doesn't work for you. Looks like the auction package wasn't much of a prize."

"Why was ours so much better? Wasn't the prize for two rooms?"

He ran a hand through his hair. "Well…"

"Did you pay extra for the suite?"

"It was comped. I travel a lot. I used some of my points." He held up his phone. "I could do it again."

"If Trixie heard we did that, she'd feel bad. No, we'll survive. I'll wear earplugs. And take a horse sedative. No problemo."

He smiled. "Thanks, Cleo. You're a champ."

Champ. Like a ten-year-old on the neighborhood Little League team. Or the family golden retriever. Hardly a femme fatale.

She shoved her suitcase into the closet. Since when had she ever, ever, ever wanted to be a femme fatale? Vegas was already messing with her head.

Sly bumped into her behind, then grabbed her shoulder to steady her before she toppled headfirst into the closet. "Sorry," he said, holding her now with both hands.

She pivoted in his grasp and looked up at him, her face only inches away from his. "No wonder Trixie felt uncomfortable."

His voice dropped. "Do you feel uncomfortable?"

"Of course not."

"Of course not," he repeated, dropping his gaze. "Well, should we go down to the casino?"

"Throw some money away?"

"Sometimes it's worth taking a few risks," he said.

"You go ahead. I've got more to risk than you do."

"I don't know about that," he said.

Instead of going down to the casino, Sly took the stairs up to the suite that had been his and Cleo's less than an hour earlier.

Hugo opened the door wearing the athletic-fit gray polo shirt and designer jeans that Sly had given him secretly on the plane.

He must've just changed into it.

"Hi, Uncle," Sly said. "Don't you look nice?"

"Thank you." Hugo's dark look warned Sly not to say anything more in front of Trixie.

As if Sly would be so clumsy. With a wink, he went inside and stepped down into the living room. Trixie was sitting on the couch, her bare feet propped on the coffee table, peeling a banana.

"How's the campaign going?" she asked.

"Early days, early days." Sly joined her on the couch. "She wants you to know you're welcome to change rooms again at any time."

"She's so nice." She took a bite and smiled at him as she chewed.

"She is," Sly said. "But not too nice to realize you're manipulating her."

Trixie put the hand, the one holding the banana, over her heart. "Me? I don't have that kind of power. I'm just setting the stage for her to do what she wants to do."

"That's a good definition of manipulation, Trixie," Hugo said, coming over. He used his telepathic powers—and a head jerk—to tell Sly to get off the couch.

Sly indulged his favorite uncle by getting up, and Hugo quickly took his place. Although Trixie believed the budding romance with Hugo was a sham to get Cleo to Las Vegas, the lonely vet wasn't going to waste any time to make it real.

"How about we see that comedy show tonight?" Hugo asked. "Sly and Cleo can do something by themselves. Much more romantic."

"Too soon," Trixie said. "If she's alone with Sly, her defenses will be up. We need to be there so she doesn't think too hard."

Sly met Hugo's gaze. He was probably wondering if that

would work with Trixie too.

"Actually, Trixie," Sly said, "I came by to ask you to give us some space."

"Oh, you don't want that. Sharing that little room will force you to spend some intimate time together. After all these years, that's just the push you need." She popped the last bite of banana into her mouth. "The push *she* needs."

"I think he meant a different kind of space," Hugo said.

"I know you mean well—" Sly began.

Trixie shook her head. "This suite looks romantic, but close quarters are much better. If you'd both been in here, she'd get the bedroom to herself and a door to lock you out of it." She patted Hugo's knee. "Like Hugo, you'd end up sleeping on the sofa out here."

Hugo looked up at Sly. *We'll see about that*, his expression said.

"I don't mind the smaller room," Sly said. "We'll be fine. But I'd like you to please not try to help in any other ways."

"Me?"

Sly smiled. "Yes, you. I appreciate that you've got my back—"

"It's a very nice back," she said quickly. "Such broad shoulders."

"They run in the family," Hugo said, stretching to expand his chest.

This wasn't going well. Sly pinched the bridge of his nose. "We'll have dinner together, but I've got it from here, all right? I'll take her to the Bellagio fountains later. And tomorrow I've got reservations at a romantic Italian place. I've let my beard grow out a little because I know she goes in for that."

"And you've dressed down a little bit," Hugo said, nodding. "I noticed the old jeans."

"See?" Sly asked. "Hugo gets it. I know what I'm doing,

Trixie. You can relax."

"Funny you said that about tickets." Hugo turned to Trixie. "As I was saying, I can get tickets for some stand-up comedian from TV. I've never heard of him, but he's supposed to be good."

"We should all go to that," Trixie said. "Laughter is such an aphrodisiac for women. She'll be laughing and feeling happy and relaxed and then look at you and all your sexy stubble and realize she has to get in bed with you as soon as possible. And once you sleep together I'm sure a lot of this fuss will melt away."

Hugo's face lit up. "Comedy does that?"

But for Sly, the thought of having Trixie as his wingman all night, whispering advice as she judged his seductive technique, drove him to harden his tone. "Thank you, Trixie, but no. We won't be joining you for the show." He moved to the door. "But we will see you for dinner very soon."

"Where is she, by the way?" Trixie asked.

"She went to explore. She's never been to Las Vegas before."

Hugo coughed. "And you let her go without you?"

Sly knew his uncle was teasing him. "She wanted to be alone. I don't think she would've appreciated me chaining her to my ankle."

"You never know," Trixie said. "Maybe I should ask her if she goes in for that stuff. Like that book."

"Please," Sly said, holding up his hands. "I know what I'm doing."

"Now that I've met her, I'm not so sure," Trixie said. "She's afraid of something bigger than you. Not that you're a huge guy. In fact, I think you might even be smaller than her, volumewise, but you know what I mean, something emotional. Possibly sexual. I hope you're prepared for that."

Sly wasn't going to discuss the traumas of Cleo's marriage.

What little he knew wasn't his to share—and if Cleo was willing to date unemployed losers, she had to give him a shot. He opened the door, hoping Hugo would keep Trixie too busy to interfere more than she already had. "I'll see you in an hour."

12

ON HER WAY to the hotel's front door, where she'd planned on walking around the Strip, Cleo lost three hundred and fifty-two dollars. One minute she was walking past reception, the next she was downstairs in the casino watching other people play blackjack. Before she realized what she was doing, she was caressing the felt table and praying she didn't go over twenty-one. Ten minutes later, after losing her first fifty, she was sipping a screwdriver to calm her nerves—forgetting she didn't usually drink until nightfall. There wasn't any natural lighting in the casino, giving her the impression of unending night, unending day.

She didn't lose it all at the blackjack table. That would've been stupid. No, she decided to scale back her risk by trying a few slots. Hit the button, lose. Hit the button, lose. Hit the button, win.

The joy was crack. She poured her winnings into the machine to taste it again.

God knows how long she would've sat there or how much of her nest egg she would've poured into the casino's black heart if Sly hadn't rescued her.

His hand covered hers before she could hit the button again. "You haven't been answering your phone."

She pushed his hand away to keep playing. "I will. Just a minute."

"You don't need to answer it now," he said. "I'm here."

"Great, great," she said, not looking at him. She pressed the button. The reels spun. Lights flashed, music tinkled, suspense killed. Cherries, cherries, watermelon. Damn it.

Through the din, she heard a man's voice, faint and amused. "It's time to meet Trixie and Hugo for dinner."

"I'm close. I can tell. I just need a minute."

"They're waiting for us."

She patted the machine. "My ticket still has money on it."

"Good time to go then." His arm came under hers and lifted her off the stool.

"But—"

"Have you been drinking?" He put his hand on her cheek and forced her to look at him. "Oh, you poor lamb. You've been on your own for less than two hours."

"The nice lady gives out free drinks." His hand felt warm and strong. Flashing lights reflected in his dark brown eyes. "I won twenty-three dollars."

"How much did you lose?"

"More than that, but I won twenty-three. You should've heard it. It was the best moment of my life." She laughed, knowing she'd lost her head but not caring.

"Come on, Warren Buffett, you need a chaperone," he said.

Knees wobbly, she let him reclaim her ticket and drag her away from the slot machines—oh, there were more! even bigger ones!—to an escalator. He was holding her hand now, shooting her amused looks. A young couple on the steps above them was arguing about where they'd parked the car between bites of a shared burrito wrapped in aluminum foil. Black beans fell like high-fiber hail at their feet.

The escalator brought them to the lobby, where Sly pulled her around a giant glittering fountain to another escalator. "One more floor."

His hand felt comforting, but she was in control now. The spell was broken. "I'm back," she said, slipping her fingers free as the escalator climbed. "I don't know what came over me."

He leaned close and sniffed. "Booze?"

"I only had two. I wish I could blame the liquor, but I just went crazy."

"It happens."

"Does it happen to you?"

"Me? Of course not," he said. "I've built a career launching tech start-ups. I *hate* gambling."

"You're being sarcastic, right?"

He put his hand over hers. "Yes, Cleo, I'm being sarcastic."

The soft touch and playful look in his eye worried her. The next floor arrived more quickly than she'd expected, and she stumbled backward when the escalator steps disappeared. Sly sprang forward, caught her around the waist, and righted her on the floor.

"The restaurant is on the top floor of a different wing," he said. "We'll need to walk a little, then take an elevator."

Cleo remembered how excited Trixie had been about the article she'd read about the place. It was decorated like an English manor house, with all the servers in authentic costume, manner, and speech. Several of the diners were also dressed for the period, pretending to be nineteenth-century aristocrats spending the weekend in Vegas. It was like character dining at Disneyland, except with a dowager duchess instead of a furry.

She grabbed Sly's arm. "Wait. Let's call and say we can't make it."

"Why?" He smiled. "No, never mind. Good idea."

"I forgot to change. Even I wouldn't wear jeans to dine with a duchess. And this way they'll have some alone time."

"Good point." He got out his phone and began jabbing at it. "I'll tell Hugo you'd rather gamble."

"Hey! No, tell him you're the one who wants to gamble."

"Then they'll blame me," he said.

"I want them to blame you."

He put an arm around her. "Always looking out for me, aren't you?"

His tone was joking, but the muscle flexing under his forearm was serious. She turned her head to tell him to stop manhandling her but got distracted by the sexy five-o'clock shadow that made his jaw stand out. She knew he had a scar on his chin, but the stubble gave it a more exciting dimension. She stared at that for a long second before looking up into his eyes.

Her heart tripped over itself. It was him, but it wasn't him. It was more than him.

It was worse.

"I'm going back to the casino." Twisting out of his embrace, she reached into her purse to fondle her ticket. It was worth a lot less than she'd like. "I think I'd better switch to the nickel slots."

"I think you'd better hand over your money to me. I'm not going to be responsible for you ruining your credit rating."

"I can afford to have a little fun," she said.

"Save it for something good, like hurling it into the fountain. No, don't do that—the house collects that too." He held out his hand. "Give me your wallet. I'll watch your back."

She gaped at him. "No way. If I want to throw my money away, I will. All right, buddy?"

"I'm just trying to help."

"You're trying to dominate. And I know it comes naturally to you and fulfills you in a way normal people can't understand, but back off." She strode past an elderly couple in matching Celine Dion sweatshirts to the escalator down to the casino.

He hurried after her, jumping onto the step behind her. "That's the addiction talking, you know."

"Shut up."

Smiling, he looked at his phone, swiping the screen. "Uh-oh. Trixie won't go to dinner unless you go too."

"What? Why?"

He shrugged. "Hugo says he can't convince her. Now she's talking about going to bed early with a good book."

"That's crazy! She's in Vegas!"

"She is an older lady," he said.

"Pfft. She's half the age of most of the party animals around here. She must be afraid of being alone with Hugo."

Sly looked at his phone again. "I think you're right. Hugo just sent a text saying he's depressed."

"Poor man." When they reached the next floor, she turned away from the tempting casino lights and turned back to the up escalator. "Well, we'll have to join them after all. Did you give Hugo the new clothes?"

"He's already wearing them."

"How'd he look?"

"Good. I hope he remembered to take off the tags."

She looked him up and down. "I'm surprised you didn't change into something more snazzy yourself."

"What's wrong with this?" He held his hands out, forcing her to study the tight T-shirt, the low-slung jeans, the scuffed leather jacket.

Swallowing over the lump in her throat, she said, "You didn't shave, either."

He rubbed his jaw. "Didn't I?"

"No. You should."

"You think?"

"Yeah, you should." The whiskers over the scar on his chin were entirely too distracting. She hurried across the marble reception floor, past the two-story fountain with the palms and the string quartet—not bad at all, she noticed—to the elevator up to their room. "You can shave while I change. And wear something other than a T-shirt. What are you doing, trying to lose a bet?"

He joined her on the elevator, a funny smile teasing his lips.

13

SLY TRIED NOT to stare at Cleo while she walked ahead of him into the restaurant. There were several ornate mirrors around the fake-manor entrance hall. He didn't want her to notice the direction of his gaze.

It wasn't the green dress again. It wasn't even a dress, just a long skirt and a sweater, like a kindergarten teacher might wear. But the fabric was tight and clingy, and she had the curves underneath that filled it out in such an interesting way. A way that wouldn't be interesting to a kindergarten class—unless that class was composed entirely of thirty-five-year-old heterosexual men.

He rubbed his eyes, wondering what was happening to him. If he'd never touched her in Carmel, would he still be living in blissful ignorance of his own feelings? Would he be able to hang out with an old friend without craving more?

She turned and smiled at him over her shoulder, her eyes bright, her cheeks pink, and his body heated.

No. His realization was overdue. There was no going back.

She looked around, smiling with unrepressed pleasure at the ornate decor. "This is fantastic."

"They certainly go all out in Vegas." Just seeing her enjoy herself made him feel good. And he had to admit that hadn't changed. He'd always wanted her to be happy. Now he just wanted to make her extra happy.

A footman—or whatever the thin men with featureless expressions in long-tailed black suits were supposed to be—led them to a small round table beneath a turquoise ceiling adorned with chandeliers. Most of the walls were covered with tapestries, enormous mirrors, and classical paintings, mostly portraits and landscapes, in gilt frames. From the smiles on the faces around him, he gathered that nobody minded it was historically and culturally inconsistent. France, England, Prussia—whatever. Georgian, Elizabethan—same difference.

Several dozen tables flanked the center of the room, which was cleared for dancing. Two costumed couples were waltzing there, gazing into each others' eyes, apparently oblivious to the tourists in modern clothes seated around the room who were staring, pointing, and taking pictures of them.

"This one isn't quite as good as the one in the lobby," Cleo whispered to him as they sat down. Hugo and Trixie had sent him a text that they would arrive in fifteen minutes—time for Sly to set the stage for his seduction, apparently—and to start without them.

"One what?"

She nodded at the musicians sitting behind a column. "The quartet." She paused, listening. "But they're all right. The cellist is excellent. She's carrying the rest of them."

He smiled at her. Music brought him pleasure, but he didn't hear half what she could.

The footman cleared his throat and bowed. "May I start you off with a drink, my lady? My lord?"

"My lady and I will have a bottle of this," Sly said, pointing at a two-hundred-dollar bottle of Chardonnay on the wine list.

Cleo snorted. "Hope she likes it." She turned to the footman. "I'll have a lemonade."

"We'll also have the wine," Sly said.

"Excellent. I'll return shortly." The man bowed and withdrew.

Cleo stared at his departing tails. "I wonder if that's a fake accent."

"Probably," Sly said. "I don't think a real footman would sound like the Prince of Wales."

With an unladylike snort, she touched his leg. "That's it. I knew he reminded me of somebody."

He inhaled deeply, surprised by the way his body jumped at her touch. "Why'd didn't you want the wine?"

"I do. But don't get the idea I like you ordering for me."

He grinned. "The lord always orders."

"Lord Sly. Catchy." She squeezed his leg and released him, then turned away as their drinks arrived.

The man poured out a little wine for him to test. He sipped it, although barely aware of what he tasted, and nodded his acceptance. With uncharacteristic eagerness, he watched his glass being filled. He needed a drink. His hands were unsteady.

"Lord Sly," Cleo repeated. "You sound like a villain in a little kid's board game."

Ignoring her, trying to ignore her, he drank.

"Better than Lord Sylly though," she continued, laughing. "I wonder if anybody has ever called you that behind your back."

"People have called me Mr. Sylly before," he admitted.

Seeing he wasn't sharing her mirth, she bit her lips to contain her laughter. After a moment, she asked seriously, "Do you ever regret it?"

His first thought was that she was referring to the kiss in Carmel, and he wanted to say that his only regret was that it had taken him too long, and that she'd run away from him.

But then he realized she was talking about his name. "It started in college. Everyone was so ambitious and driven."

"Unlike you."

"I did drop out," he said.

"And promptly started a business."

"Yes, but I didn't want to take myself too seriously. The nickname was always there, bringing me back to earth." He poured her a glass of wine, not ashamed to admit his odds would be better if she drank more than lemonade. "My family called me Sly. I didn't want coworkers calling me that. Or people who worked for me."

"I'm flattered you let me call you Sly when I was just your piano teacher."

"You insisted."

"That was because, even though you never practiced, you thought I wouldn't notice."

He looked down at his hands.

"You're blushing!" she cried.

"You're projecting." The warmth in his cheeks couldn't possibly be visible.

"Why didn't you practice?" she asked. "Nobody made you sign up for lessons, you chose it yourself. So why didn't you put any effort into it?"

Back then, he'd thought she was cute, a welcome change from the high-pressure high-tech world he lived in. Teresa had been his girlfriend then, and he hadn't seen Cleo as anything other than a piano teacher. A sexy, funny piano teacher whose company made him unwind and forget the stress of his days.

So why hadn't he practiced the lessons she'd given him every week? "I realized early on that I wasn't very good at it."

"You only do things you're good at?"

"Don't you?" he asked.

"Not at all." Eyes twinkling, she smiled at him as she sipped her wine. "Just a few hours ago, I was happily losing my shirt in the casino, remember?"

Involuntarily, his gaze dropped to her shirt, which was actually a tight raspberry-pink cardigan that was unbuttoned low enough for him to see a bit of lace between her breasts. Was the lace part of her shirt or one of those camisole things? Or her bra?

She elbowed him, rolling her eyes as if he'd been staring at her chest as some kind of joke. "You didn't give me a chance."

"I was—" He stopped himself. He'd been about to remind her that he'd been dating Teresa when they'd met and so hadn't been able to give her a chance back then, before he realized she was talking about the chance to teach him piano. Not the chance of stripping down and rolling around on the floor together.

Heart pounding, he smoothed the napkin on his lap. "I'm sorry. I had a lot going on back then."

"You should give it another shot. Not with me, of course."

"Maybe." He tapped his glass against hers. Having her teach him would be impossible; he'd be too distracted. But someday, maybe after this itch had been scratched...

An image flashed before his eyes: him at the piano, her laughing at his ineptitude, him kissing her to stop the laughing and then pinning her over the keys and taking her right there while the discordant notes accompanied their love.

He realized he'd shredded the corner of the wine list into confetti.

My God, he'd lost it. After surreptitiously brushing the torn paper onto the floor, he poured himself a second glass of wine and buried his face in it. He had to calm the hell down. Seething lust wasn't going to win her over. Slow, he had to go slow. Tender, curious, restrained. It had to feel like a discovery that surprised them both. Her ex-husband had been a promiscuous charmer. Nothing he did could remind her of him.

"There's Hugo and Trixie." Cleo stood and waved wildly. "Wow, she looks incredible."

Sly glanced over at Trixie, who wore a long, sleeveless purple dress and had something in her hair. A feather? Hugo, on her arm, looked happier than Sly had ever seen him. Both corners of his mouth were lifted. Some might even call it a smile.

"Love the dress." Cleo stood to greet them. Hugo helped Trixie into her chair before sitting himself. "Where did you get it?" Cleo asked.

Trixie made a dismissive gesture but looked pleased. "This old thing?"

Cleo peered closer. "Is it vintage?"

"Oh, no. It's not authentic. I had to make it."

"That's incredible," Cleo said. "I couldn't darn a sock. I don't even know what darning is. Unless it's how I swear when I'm around my grandparents."

They all laughed politely and reached for the wine. Trixie and Hugo took in the atmosphere for a few minutes, admiring the dancers and the decor, and the footman came to take drink orders and ask if they were ready for the first course.

Although at first he was grateful for the distraction of Trixie and Hugo's arrival, he soon resented the loss of Cleo's attention, which was now fixed on Trixie—more about the dress, her feather, the costumed dancers and servers.

Conversation on these thrillingly feminine topics continued through the soup and the salad and two entrees.

He met Hugo's gaze over the table. Instead of bored, his uncle seemed excited, alive, happy. Sly remembered Hugo's ex-wife as an aloof, serious kind of woman who kept to herself. Never having had any children, she and Hugo had divorced when Sly was in high school, and he had never seen her again. Last he'd heard, she'd moved to Phoenix and married a banker. Hugo had always told Sly he was as good as a son of his own, and hadn't ever remarried. As far as Sly knew, he'd never been seriously interested in any woman until Trixie.

That was almost twenty years of waiting. Sly felt a renewed burst of motivation to help him out.

When the last of the dishes were cleared, he refilled Hugo's glass from the third bottle of wine he'd ordered for the table. "How's Mouse?" Then he turned to Trixie. "Did you know Hugo adopted a new dog? A Newfoundland. He barely fits in the Fiat. The owner moved out of the country and couldn't take him with her. She was lucky her vet had such a big heart."

"Newfies make great companions," Trixie said. "Nanny in Peter Pan was a Newfie."

Hugo frowned, maybe not liking the comparison of him to a child in the nursery. "He has special needs. Your average person might have trouble meeting them."

Trixie sighed. "We do love to spoil our babies, don't we?"

Having his heroic efforts dismissed made Hugo's shoulders slump a little.

"Mouse is really lucky to have found you, Hugo," Cleo said. "Who's taking care of him over the weekend?"

Hugo gave her a grateful smile. "One of the vet techs at the clinic took him home with her. Bella has cats, but Mouse doesn't mind cats." He lifted his coffee. "Mouse doesn't mind much of anything. Easygoing breed."

"Just because he doesn't complain doesn't mean he isn't

suffering," Trixie frowned into her wineglass, her sunny mood vanishing.

"What's the matter, Trixie?" Cleo asked.

Hugo put a hand on Trixie's shoulder. "She's worrying about her little guys. The dogs are just fine, Trixie. I called to check right before dinner."

"But they're at Liam and Bev's house," Trixie said.

"I know. That's why they could tell me how they were doing." Hugo offered a lopsided smile. "That granddaughter of yours might need a puppy of her own someday soon. She got out of her crib to sleep with all three of them on the floor this afternoon. The nanny found them napping together in a big pile."

Trixie's face lit up. "Merry would *love* a puppy of her own." She looked around the table with a smile. "She's walking now. Of course she must have a puppy. I'm going to find her one as soon as we get home."

"You might want to check with her parents on that one," Sly said.

Hugo kicked him in the shin under the table. Flinching, Sly gestured at the dance floor, where a waltz was just coming to an end and the costumed duchess was clapping her gloved hands together with detached, chilly poise.

"Why don't you two show us your moves on the dance floor?" Sly asked. "You might not know this, Trixie, but Hugo is a great dancer."

Hugo kicked him again, this time harder. "Sly's joking."

"I am not. I saw you dancing at Camila's wedding." Camila was a cousin on Sly's mother's side. "You're certainly better than I am."

"I'm sure you're a lovely dancer, Sly," Trixie said. "And even if you're not, any woman would love to be in your arms. Isn't that right, Cleo?"

Cleo visibly recoiled. Annoyed, Sly stood up and held out his hand. "Looks like they'll need company, Cleo. Let's make it easier for them."

She put her hand over her purse. "One of us should stay here so our things don't get stolen."

"I'm happy to stay." Trixie stood up and tugged at Cleo's chair. She must've pulled hard, because Cleo fell forward and clutched the table.

"Only if you promise to try the next dance," Cleo said, finally getting to her feet. She set her napkin down and walked over to the dance floor without waiting for Sly.

"Just try not to step on her feet too hard," Trixie said. "Make lots of eye contact, tell her how beautiful she is. Not just her eyes. Tell her she's got nice lips."

"I'm not going to tell her she's got nice lips," Sly muttered, even though he'd just been thinking the same thing. Talking about her body parts was the last thing that would put her at ease. He caught up to her near the musicians, where she'd stopped to listen.

She glanced at him and held out her arms like a robot. "Let's get this over with."

Bracing himself for the pleasure of full-body contact, he pulled her close. "Is it the dancing or the company that you object to?"

Her hand was unyielding in his. "I don't really like everybody staring. We're part of the show now."

"You perform all the time."

"At something I'm good at," she said.

"I'm sure you're just fine." He slid his hand around her waist and led her between the other pairs of dancers. "Try to relax and let me lead."

Her body was as rigid as before. It reminded him of the month he'd tried judo with Mark. As if any second now she was going to hook an ankle around his leg and push him onto the floor.

"I'm kind of jealous of Trixie's dress," she said after a few steps. "I wonder if she'd make me one."

"Really? You hate dresses."

"I don't. Why would you think that?"

"Because you only wear them for work."

"I need a special occasion, that's all."

"Yet you didn't wear one tonight," he said.

Her annoyance must've helped loosen her up, because she stopped fighting and began dancing. "That's because I didn't have one as cool as Trixie's. I went to the store, and everything was ugly or didn't fit or was too expensive. But you wouldn't understand. You're a guy. You wear a suit and that's it, problem solved."

"I didn't wear a suit tonight."

She scowled at his chest. He'd changed into a fitted blue shirt, open at the throat, and dark pants. "I see that. And you didn't shave, either. I thought you were going to shave."

Not if you like a little stubble. "Sorry," he said. "Forgot."

She cleared her throat. "You're wearing the chain I gave you for your birthday."

His next footwork brought her body closer to his. Holding his breath, he splayed his fingers over her back and tried not to imagine unfastening her bra, how her breasts would tumble forward into his waiting palms. "I always wear it." His voice was a little rough.

After a long pause, she said, "I never noticed."

The music swelled and so did he. With as much grace as he could muster, he moved her hips a few inches away from his and concentrated on his feet. He'd screwed up the rhythm a few times now and saw that this musical ineptitude made her flinch.

"Listen for the beat." She tightened her grip and held him closer. "*One* two three, *one* two three."

He liked the closeness and wanted more of it. "Would you like to lead?"

"You could never follow. You're not the type."

"You don't know everything about me," he said.

"I know enough."

"Try me."

She released him, a daring gleam in her eye. "All right, I will." She reached out, taking his other hand in hers and wrapping her arm around his waist. Her knee bumped his. "Remember, *one* two three, *one* two three."

"Yes, mistress." He lowered his eyes and considered telling her she had nice lips.

She lurched forward, then twisted, moving him across the floor with wide, smooth steps. She was surprisingly strong, but he couldn't stop trying to move in the opposite direction.

And the way she handled him so confidently was turning him on.

After another minute, she gave up and threw up her hands. "I give up. Let's give Trixie and Hugo a turn. You're hopeless."

He nodded, following her back to the table, itching to grab her again.

I am. I really am.

14

IT TURNED OUT that Hugo was an excellent dancer. As in, TV-competition quality. Even the professional dancers, who were probably just unemployed Hollywood wannabes who looked good in Downton Abbey costumes, stepped aside to let Hugo twirl Trixie around the parquet dance floor.

Cleo was relieved to be sitting down again where she could admire Sly's uncle's moves. "Where'd he learn to do that?"

Sly emptied the wine bottle into his glass. "Uncle Hugo's full of surprises."

"He's incredible."

Looking sour, Sly slumped in his chair and brought the glass to his lips.

"Are you jealous?" she asked.

"I never pretended to be a good dancer."

"But you like to be good at everything." She patted his knee. "Sorry I wasn't a good partner for you."

His expression softened. "You were great. It was my fault. Would you like me to ask Hugo for a dance?"

"If you think he'd enjoy your company, go ahead. Maybe he could give you a few lessons."

"Aren't you funny?" He leaned into her, brushing her cheek

with the back of his hand. "I'll ask Hugo to take you out on the next one. Tell him it'll give Trixie a chance to watch him."

His touch unbalanced her for a moment. "No, thanks. I'm fine." Twisting her napkin in her lap, she turned to the dance floor.

Waltzing in Hugo's arms around the dance floor, Trixie was glowing, her cheeks pink against her silver hair, her eyes bright. She looked about sixteen. At the edge of the floor, Hugo suddenly brought her into a dip, then another spin, and when the song came to an end, she threw her arms around his neck and stared at him as if she didn't recognize who he was. He held her gaze and said nothing, but a faint smile teased his lips.

"On the other hand," she said, "maybe we should go. I think they're having a moment."

Sly turned to look. His eyebrows rose. "I think you're right."

"If we leave now, they won't have to make small talk with us."

Sly signaled the waiter. "I'll get the check."

Another song began, slower than the previous one. Trixie began to walk back to the table, but Hugo caught her hand and pulled her back into his arms like a yo-yo on a string. She laughed, shaking her head, but he insisted. By the time Sly was signing the check, Trixie and Hugo were swaying in small circles near the musicians, no longer making an impression on those around them but, Cleo thought, making a bigger one on each other.

She grabbed her purse and stood up. "Should I leave a note?"

"I'll text Hugo. Not that he'll care."

They walked out of the restaurant past the crowd waiting to get in, some of them in costumes more elaborate than the staff, and found the elevators. She decided to call it a night. The goal was to get Trixie and Hugo together, after all. That situation was looking very promising.

"Feel free to go to the casino." She pressed the up button. "I'm going to bed."

"Already?"

"I think it would be better if I stayed away from the slots from now on."

He braced a hand against the wall and stared at her, rubbing his jaw. With his hair mussed, his shirt gaping open at the throat, and another two hours' worth of stubble, he was quite a sight.

Of course he was good-looking. That wasn't news to her. Responding to it, however, was a choice.

Choosing no, she hit the button again. And then again. "You'd think all the money people lose here would pay for faster elevators."

"I have an idea," he said, stabbing the down button. "We'll walk to the Bellagio and look at the fountains. It has music. You like music. Perfect."

"I was going to do that in the morning."

"They don't do the show in the morning. You want to see it at night to get the full effect." The doors opened with a chime, a red light indicating it was going down.

From dozens of floors above, her book called to her. Her safe, cozy book.

But he'd be there in the bed next to her, and he wasn't as safe and cozy as he used to be. They'd always been physical with one another, but since Carmel, she worried that every little touch was a sign he was getting confused again. He'd admitted he was just lonely, bored, and searching for meaning, shooting arrows into the dark.

She stepped into the elevator. "Will I need a jacket?"

"You'll be fine."

The elevator was crammed with the Friday night crowd on their way to fun and fortune. Or despair and disaster. Nobody knew which. She peeked at the young and old faces of all colors and creeds and tried to guess which way it would go for each of them.

The African-American couple in their sixties looked calm and determined while they talked hurriedly together about their plan for the night. She heard them decide how much of their afternoon winnings they were going to risk tonight (two hundred-fifty each), how many free cocktails they would drink (three for him, two for her), and when to meet back at the fountain under the dancing-elf statue (never; they decided to stay together).

The women next to them, part of a bachelorette party, were heading to the casino for a few comped drinks before going out to a club for dancing. Based on the signs that they were already drunk, Cleo feared the worst for them.

The doors opened, and everyone shifted to make room for more people. One of the giggling and swearing women lost her balance, windmilled her thin, bare arms, and smacked Cleo on the shoulder.

"Oh! Sorry!" She and her friends burst out laughing.

Cleo, tempted to return the favor, moved away from them, maneuvering into the far corner. She could smell the perfume of a tall woman next to her, which was better than the beer, vomit, and hairspray she'd detected on the bridal party, but was still a bit strong for such close quarters.

Then the woman turned, exposing her profile.

No. It couldn't be.

"I'm going to kill you guys if anything bad happens to my sister tonight," the woman said. Her words were harsh, but her tone was playful.

Yes. It could be. And it was.

Ashley.

"If you really cared," a voice called out, one vaguely familiar to Cleo, "you'd come with us. Some sister you are. Missing my bachelorette party."

"I'll text you after the show and come find you."

Cleo had begun to shake. Ashley was here, right next to her, and the man on the other side of her—

The elevator stopped, the doors opened, and the herd began to move.

"Cleo?" Sly was looking into her face.

Blindly, she reached for his hand, laced her fingers through his, and squeezed, trying not to stare at Ashley or—

Dylan. Now she saw him. In a suit, he looked just like he did in their old wedding pictures.

"My ex," she said under her breath.

Without a word, Sly followed the direction of her gaze, and in the next second was leading her off the elevator with the others. He dropped her hand, moved his arm around her shoulders, and gave her some much-needed support as they walked into the lobby. She felt as if she'd been run over by a bus. One minute, she'd been cheerfully crossing the street, the next—BAM. Airborne. Then landing with a soft, agonizing thud, bloody and bruised.

They must not have noticed her. Thank God. She could hurry out the door with her head buried in Sly's shoulder and they'd never see her.

She plowed Sly across the gleaming marble floor for several long strides, then stopped. Sly didn't protest, just watched her carefully.

Maybe he hadn't let her lead the waltz, but he could follow when it was important. At that moment, she loved him more than she'd ever loved Dylan, that cheating, lying bastard.

"I don't have anything to be afraid of," she said. "Why am I running away?"

Sly nodded. "He's skinny. I think I can take him. Can you handle the chick?"

"I wish. Ashley used to do kickboxing aerobics." Cleo took a deep breath, furious with herself for reacting so emotionally after all these years. "I'd better say hello."

"Why?"

"For my pride."

Sly shrugged. "If you're sure."

"I'm sure." Pushing her shoulders back, she turned to greet her ex-husband and his current wife, Ashley, who had once asked her, at age twelve, if they could be best friends forever.

Turned out the answer had been no.

15

SLY SIZED UP the ex, concluding he was good-looking, arrogant, and charming, but afraid of Cleo.

If Sly didn't hate him for hurting her, he might've felt a kinship with the guy.

"Cleo," the woman said, her mouth falling open.

They stood on the marble floor next to the two-story waterfall gushing into a pool filled with flashing lights. Crowds jostled around them on their way to the casino escalators, the shops in the mezzanine, the Strip.

"I saw you and your sister in the elevator," Cleo said. For the first time, she turned to her ex-husband. "And Dylan."

Sly was impressed by her cool tone. It managed to convey both indifference and disgust. "I'm Sylvester Minguez," he said, holding out a hand. He'd pretend he'd never heard of Cleo's ex. No reason for the prick to think he was special.

Dylan's eyes widened. Slowly, he took his hand. "The tech guy?"

"That's me."

Dylan and Ashley had stepped away from each other, as if they were afraid of getting caught fooling around. Sly thought it was kind of late for that.

"Dylan Baker," the ex said, his gaze flickering between him and Cleo. "Yorentech. Redwood City."

Sly had heard of it but shrugged and shook his head apologetically.

He dropped Sly's hand, then belatedly claimed his wife's. "It's a new start-up. Just got our first VC."

"You're in marketing?" Sly asked.

An eager smile warmed his face. "Cleo told you?"

"No, I just guessed." Sly didn't have a high opinion of marketing guys, even if he did plenty of it himself.

"Well, I just thought I'd say hi," Cleo said. "We should be going. Give Lizzy my congratulations."

"I will," Ashley said. "Thanks."

Sly and Cleo walked away, and nobody said another word. They made their way outside, moving from one throng to another. After the controlled air inside the hotel and casino complex, the fresh air tasted good, even mixed with car exhaust, cigarettes, spilled booze, and fast food. It tasted real.

Cleo seemed to enjoy it too. She let out a long sigh and took his arm. "That was fun," she said flatly.

"You did great."

"I haven't seen either one of them in two years. They've aged, don't you think?"

"I don't know. I've never met them. But I'm sure they look much worse than they used to."

She poked him in the ribs. "OK, you're right. I hope they're miserable together. I'm petty and small." But she was smiling. "Am I walking the right way to get to the fountains?"

"Yes, but it's about ten minutes from here. Do you mind the walk?"

"Not at all. I'm dying for it."

The Strip was crowded with tourists. Most of them were casually dressed families moving in groups past the chain stores and casinos.

"I've never seen so much neon in my life," Cleo said. "Holy moly."

Sly watched her for signs of emotional upset. When they'd met, she'd just finalized her divorce. She told him her ex had cheated on her with a friend, then joked that she'd chosen Sly as a pal this time around because, she hoped, *he* wouldn't be tempted to sleep with her next husband. If she ever married again, which she doubted.

He'd accepted her explanation, but now he wondered.

"Your ex-husband reminds me of somebody," he said.

"Don't say Ben Affleck. Please. He thinks he looks like Ben Affleck."

"I wasn't thinking of a movie star."

"Good," she said. "I admit he's good-looking, but he's no Ben Affleck."

"I didn't realize you had such a crush on Mr. Affleck."

"Not the whole package, just the chin," she said. "Cleft chins get me every—"

He grinned, rubbing his chin. "Every what?"

"Yours isn't a real cleft. It's a scar." She waved her hand. "Doesn't count."

"You're blushing."

"That's the neon lights. You're blushing too. Purple and green."

He tried to remember the ex-husband's chin. He'd been too busy noticing the dark hair, dark eyes, medium height, and strong build. Not too unlike his own. "I thought he looked a little like me," he said.

She laughed—not quite naturally. "That's crazy. He's nothing like you."

"About the same size—"

"He's so pale, he burns in the shade," she said.

"I obviously have a darker complexion, but otherwise—"

"His eyes are a medium brown. Yours are dark choc—forget it. Just forget it."

"Dark chocolate?" He liked the sound of that. She'd once likened dark chocolate to her favorite sonata. Both made her moan.

She accelerated, weaving around two men who were each looking at their phones, walking erratically.

"Which side of the street are the fountains?" she asked over her shoulder.

He jogged to catch up to her. "This side. Not too much farther." He was still thinking about dark chocolate and moaning. "You do look a little younger than him. About how old is he?"

"A little older."

"How much, exactly?"

"Why do you care?"

He suppressed a smile. "I think it might help you enjoy the show if you talk about him now, get it off your chest. It must've been hard to see him with your old friend."

"She did look old."

"Almost as old as him," he said. "Which is…?"

"Thirty-five."

"Same as me. What a coincidence."

"You want to remind me of my ex-husband?"

"I just think it's interesting I might be your type," he said. "Physically, I mean."

"Gorgeous men are every woman's type."

He couldn't help but grin at that one. "You think I'm gorgeous?"

"Don't pretend you don't know. I tell you that all the time."

"But usually you're kidding. This is serious."

"It's not serious, it's just a statement of fact. Are you really so vain you need me to reassure you about how good-looking you are? When you've gone through life having women throw themselves at you?"

"It's not whether or not it's true," he said. "It's that *you* think so."

"It's an objective truth. I've got nothing to do with it."

The crowds became too thick to talk about it anymore. He wanted to lead her to a spot where they could get a decent view, which was going to be difficult on a Friday night, but eventually they found an opening as the previous viewers cleared out.

Cleo began chatting with a woman and her two small children, all of them in lawn chairs, bundled in fleece blankets and holding Starbucks cups. The woman told her about the fountain, which they'd been watching now for two hours on and off, and Cleo kept up the friendly small talk for several minutes. Sly tuned it out until Cleo grabbed his arm and dragged him closer.

"Well?" Cleo asked—not him, but the woman.

"He *is* gorgeous," she said brightly, licking her lips. "Don't you think he's cute, Katie?"

The four-year-old looked around in confusion, not associating the big, scary stranger man with "cute," which obviously applied to creatures like bunnies and herself.

He waved at her. "Sorry."

"Good with kids, too," the mother said. "You two married?"

Cleo laughed. "No, we're—"

"Waiting." Sly put an arm around her waist and pulled her

close. "Cleo's not quite ready for me yet."

"He's just kidding," Cleo said. In the press of the crowd, she couldn't pull away.

"Oh, I know," the woman said. "It's always the man who thinks he isn't ready. Don't worry. He'll come around."

Cleo shook her head. "No, I don't—"

A sudden shift in the lights indicated the show was starting, cutting off the woman's interest. Cleo made a face at Sly, then seemed to forget everything but the hundreds of jets of shooting water dancing in time to Frank Sinatra. Sly had seen it before, but the music was different. Rather than watch the fountains, he watched Cleo, amused by how she scrunched up her nose when she was concentrating.

Only fifteen minutes later, the show was over. By then she was leaning into him, letting him hold her against his side, and he regretted their cuddle was coming to an end.

She broke away from him, waved good-bye to the woman and her children, and started walking back the way they'd come.

"How about a drink?" he asked her.

"Just one, all right? I'm kind of tired."

"Are you sure you want to walk? We could get a taxi or a tram —"

"I'd rather walk. Thanks." She stuffed her hands in her pockets and stared straight ahead, ignoring the men wearing T-shirts declaring STRIPPERS DIRECT TO YOU who were handing out cards with women's photos on them.

He'd expected her to talk more about the fountains. "Didn't you like the show?"

"It was great. I thought about staying for the next one. Maybe tomorrow." She sounded distracted.

It was possible she was just tired—it had been a long day—but he doubted it. Although he'd like to think she was dwelling over the possibility of sex with him, he suspected the couple in the elevator back at the hotel was to blame. The shock of seeing them had finally hit her.

"Want to talk about it?" he asked, absently accepting one of the cards thrust at him.

She saw him take it and raised an eyebrow. "Feeling lonely?"

"Aren't we all?" He handed it to her, relieved to see a spark of humor.

"It really is Sin City, isn't it?" She looked around, then put it into her pocket with a shrug. "I'll hold onto it so I can recycle it."

"So says the Bay Area girl."

"I should get cards of my own," she said. "'Tree huggers direct to you.'"

"I'd take one of those."

Their eyes met for a split second. He grinned.

"I wish you'd cut that out," she said.

"What?"

"Please. You know. The flirting." She yawned.

His ego shriveled. She'd *yawned.*

He couldn't think of what to say. His efforts at seduction were putting her to sleep.

"Sorry," she said. "I know you're going through a thing. I shouldn't be insensitive."

"Thing?"

"Just repeating what you said. You've been a little confused lately about your life, about the future, who you are, and I'm here, it's dark, and I smell good."

Would she remember his words verbatim if she didn't care a little too much?

"You do smell good," he said.

"Thanks, but I'm tired. Let's get that drink and call it a night."

16

THE NEXT MORNING, Cleo rolled over and peered through the darkness at Sly on the other side of the bed. They'd had their drink, returned to the room, and quietly prepared for bed. After a polite good-night, they'd climbed in and turned out the light. Seeing Dylan and Ashley had been worse than she'd feared, and she'd been caught in a loop of bad memories, reliving the night Dylan had told her—tearfully, because he was such the tragic hero—about his passion for somebody else. This love for Ashley, he'd said, was undeniable.

Unlike, obviously, the one for her. He'd denied that one quickly and thoroughly.

But then, although she'd fallen asleep thinking about Dylan, her dreams had been about someone else.

Sly didn't look anything like Dylan. She couldn't say so last night, but Sly was much, much better looking. Mistaking *him* for a movie star wasn't ridiculous. The blackout curtains made it impossible to see his high cheekbones, generous mouth, strong jaw, or his dimpled—or scarred—chin, so she settled for listening to his breathing for a few long moments before getting up and taking a shower.

When her marriage had ended, she'd lost her two best friends.

She'd never been a social butterfly, but since her divorce, she'd withdrawn, devoted more time to her work and solitary amusements.

And Sly. At first she'd seen him as a safe substitute for a real friend and a real partner. A surrogate.

At first. Then she'd decided he was a real friend. And she'd been grateful to have that.

She got dressed and did extra primping, putting on makeup and styling her hair—not because she wanted to look beautiful for Dylan and Ashley, Sly, or anyone, but because she was afraid to leave the safety of the bathroom.

The way he'd reacted to the mother at the Bellagio was nagging at her. Cleo had been holding it together until then. She'd seen Dylan and Ashley, faced them directly, held her head high. She'd accepted Sly's support and joked with him about his good looks.

And then that woman had asked if they were getting married, and he'd said Cleo wasn't ready for him yet.

She knew it had been a joke, but the feelings that had bloomed in her chest weren't funny at all. Even this moment, the thought of living with Sly as true partners had a sweet, natural appeal.

"Stop it," she snapped, scowling at herself in the mirror. She was hurting and wanted comfort, that's all.

She'd put too much mascara on her left eye. Now she had to put more on the right to even it out. And another swipe of eyeliner. My God, by the time she was done in here, she'd look like a showgirl. She could have cards made up.

A knock sounded on the door. "Hugo and Trixie have invited us to breakfast," Sly called out. "Do you think I could get in there for a minute?"

"Sure, I'm done." She opened the door. "Don't say anything. I got carried away."

"With what?" His dark hair was tousled, and the five-o'clock shadow was now a sexy almost-beard. She imagined how it would feel against her chin if they kissed again.

If her dream last night was accurate, it would feel pretty good.

Stop it.

Averting her gaze, she moved past him into the room. "Oh, nothing. Got creative with the makeup." She wasn't sure if she was gratified or annoyed he couldn't tell the difference. "Sorry to take so long in there."

"I can't wait to get my contacts in so I can get a good look," he said.

"Is your vision really that bad?"

"Yup."

"I had no idea," she said.

He turned and leaned against the doorframe. "There's lots you don't know about me, remember?"

The room suddenly felt very small. "I'm surprised Trixie and Hugo want to have breakfast with us. Instead of room service or something just the two of them," she said.

He rolled his eyes. "I think Hugo struck out. He wants me to meet him alone before breakfast." As the door closed between them, Cleo heard him mutter, "As if I'm an expert."

Cleo slipped out for a solitary walk, then met Trixie an hour later near a pet boutique behind the escalators on the third floor. The four of them were planning to eat at the buffet around the corner in ten minutes.

Trixie gestured for her to follow her into the boutique. "I promised Hugo I'd find Zeus something manly to wear. He doesn't approve of boy dogs wearing pink." Frowning, she picked up a leather collar with spikes. "This one might kill the other dogs if he got too friendly."

"I think that's the idea," Cleo said.

Trixie lowered her voice. "Maybe I should get one for myself."

Not wanting to pry, Cleo picked up a fluorescent tennis ball and waited for her to say more.

"I didn't expect him to be such a good dancer," Trixie said.

"He was amazing."

"I should've found that out before agreeing to dance with him."

"You looked great together," Cleo said. "Didn't you have a nice time?"

Trixie bit her lip. The next collar she picked up was green with flashing LEDs. "This would be good for road safety. I should get them all one."

"How's"—Cleo couldn't remember the name—"the other pooch? The one that got run over?"

"Luna's fine. No permanent damage." She ran her hand through her hair, tugging at the short strands. "I wish I were so lucky."

She seemed genuinely distressed. "Would you like to talk about it?"

With a shake of her head, Trixie picked up three collars without looking closely at any of them, went over to the counter, and bought them without making small talk with the cashier. She didn't even say hello.

What had happened? Maybe Hugo had told Sly and he could tell her all about it later. They might be able to help.

They walked over and met Hugo and Sly outside the restaurant. The casual banter of the night before was missing. Now each was lost in thought, tight-lipped, eyes downcast. Only

Hugo seemed quietly content.

The buffet was appropriately excessive and loaded with every edible product she'd ever seen in vast quantities. They walked over, plates in hand, and gazed upon the fifty yards of culinary delights.

Trixie suddenly set her plate down on an empty table. "I'm not hungry." She turned and left the restaurant.

Hugo watched her go, a soft look in his eyes.

"What happened?" she whispered to Sly.

He shook his head, shrugging.

Cleo started to put her own plate down, then asked Sly, "Should I go after her?"

"I don't think so," Sly said.

Hugo scooped up a mound of scrambled eggs. "Let her be. She's not used to having a male invade her territory. If I time it right, she'll come back on her own."

"She's not a dog, Uncle Hugo," Sly said.

"We're all dogs at heart," Hugo replied. "The best of us, anyway."

That comment led Cleo to chase after her. If Trixie really didn't want to talk, she'd say so.

The mall outside was busy with shoppers and tourists but no Trixie. How could she have disappeared so quickly?

Then she saw a flash of white hair in the pet boutique and rushed over. Inside, Trixie was holding a dog collar big enough to for a woman to wear as a belt.

"Hi," Cleo said. "You looked upset. I thought I'd check on you."

"I forgot to get something for Mouse." Her voice was calm, but she had a tear trickling down her cheek. Wiping it away, she looked up at Cleo and offered a small smile. "Wasn't that stupid of me?"

"Want to sneak off and have breakfast, just the two of us?"

Trixie dug a tissue out of her purse and wiped her nose. "How are things going with Sly?"

"What do you mean?"

"Dancing isn't really his strong suit."

Cleo smiled. "No. Can't be good at everything, I told him."

"That's nice. Did you sleep together?"

Cleo choked out a laugh. Apparently Trixie wasn't that upset. "No, I told you. We're friends."

Trixie gaped. "I'm so sorry. It's my fault. We had all that room we didn't need and you two were camping out on the floor like eleven-year-olds at a sleepover."

"Nobody slept on the floor."

"So you did sleep together," Trixie said.

"In the same bed, but not—"

"Of course not! Is that what you thought? Of course you wouldn't have sex together. Such old friends? If he was interested in you, he would've shown *some* sign by *now*." Trixie held up the dog collar, studying it as she twirled it like a Hula-Hoop around her index finger.

Cleo was learning to be suspicious of Trixie's rambling declarations. "You knew I was going to think you meant"—the boutique had hardwood floors and handfuls of other tourists in earshot fondling the pet luxuries, so she lowered her voice—"sex."

"Not all of us have sex on the brain."

"Excuse me?"

"One of the biggest perks of growing older is not having to think about sex all the time. Sex, sex, sex." Trixie's voice was rising with each word. "What's so great about sex?"

Cleo decided that if people were going to be shocked about an earthy conversation, they should shop for pet supplies somewhere other than the Las Vegas Strip. "Sex is great and you know it. That's why you're here with Hugo, right?"

"That is not—" Clutching the dog collar in her fist, Trixie marched to the register.

Trixie was too upset to play along. What had happened?

Watching Trixie slap her credit card on the counter, Cleo stifled a grin. Poor Trixie had played with fire and ended up having a little more heat than she'd schemed for.

Trixie shoved her package into her purse and strode to the entrance of the boutique, pausing to look both ways before marching out of sight.

Her uncharacteristic rudeness had to be proof of just how much heat she'd had the night before. Perhaps even a third-degree burn.

Once again, Cleo chased after her. She'd ducked into a designer purse emporium with two security guards at the door.

"I think you should talk about it," Cleo told her. "Let me buy you a coffee."

"The last thing I need is a stimulant," Trixie said sourly. She held up a small yellow leather purse with a daisy appliqué and a wrist strap. "Look at the price tag. The entire cow cost less than that and they only used a tiny piece of her."

"We could go down to the casino and get a drink."

"It's ten in the morning."

"It's Vegas."

"It is, isn't it?" Trixie set the purse down, giving it a little pat, the same way she handled her dogs. "All right. For your sake. You seem like you need to talk."

Cleo and Trixie found two empty seats in a lounge in the center of the casino floor, which wasn't as easy as it might've been, given the morning hour. Each ordered a Bloody Mary.

"For the vitamins," Cleo said, sinking back into her plush armchair.

Trixie slapped her hand on her knee. "Absolutely." She wore a Berkeley sweatshirt and lime-green Crocs with mismatched argyle socks. The dowager duchess wouldn't have approved, but Cleo felt a kinship.

The circular lounge was lit by blue lights, giving everything an underwater feeling. Behind them in all directions were table games and slot machines, not quite as busy as they'd been the night before, the only indication of the time of day.

"So," Cleo said.

Trixie shook her head. "Let's wait until the drinks get here."

They sat in silence, watching the flashing buzz of the casino around them. When the drinks arrived, Cleo repeated, "So."

"It's kind of boring in here, don't you think?" Trixie asked. "Let's go over to the slots." Holding her drink like a baton, she stood and strode out of the lounge to a row of slot machines fifty feet away.

After taking a bite out of a carrot stick jutting out of her glass, Cleo followed her, skeptical now that any meaningful conversation was going to take place. Her stomach growled, longing for the feast it had missed upstairs.

Trixie sat on a padded stool in front of a slot machine, gulping tomato juice from the side of her glass as she stared at the flickering lights. "This is awkward. I don't know where to begin."

"You could start with the easy stuff," Cleo said. "How long have you known Hugo?"

"A long time. Six, seven years? Maybe more. Since I needed a vet for the dogs."

"And this new thing..."

Trixie stuffed her mouth with celery and carrot sticks. "If I tell you, you'll be annoyed with me."

"I think I've figured a lot of it out already. You didn't intend to get involved with Hugo, did you?"

Her eyes dropped. "We're close. Good friends."

"But that's it," Cleo said. "No third base. You wanted me to think there was more so I would come with Sly. Right?"

"Go ahead, I deserve it. Call me a liar." Trixie took another bite of celery.

"That's not the word I would use."

"What word would you use?"

Cleo laughed softly. "Hopeless romantic?"

"That's two words."

"Which would you prefer—hopeless or romantic?"

"Romantic, definitely," Trixie said.

"Then that's what I'll call you."

With a sigh, Trixie patted her knee. A cocktail waitress came by and asked if they wanted another drink. Already buzzed, Cleo refused, but Trixie asked for a refill.

"More vitamins," she said, reaching for the handle on the machine. "I had quite a workout last night."

If it weren't for the morose way Trixie had said it, Cleo would've smiled. But she looked so miserable. "Was it that bad?"

The reels spun. They stopped and Trixie set them moving again. "It was that good."

"I'm sorry," Cleo said. "I don't understand."

"I think you'd be the only one who would."

Cleo looked down into her glass. The celery stick she'd ignored sagged against the ice. "That's different."

"Not the way you think. I was married once already. Now I have my children, my first grandchild, my fur babies. I don't need anything more."

They weren't close enough for Cleo to argue with her, but she asked, "Aside from all that, how do you feel about Hugo?"

"Last night I was feeling all kinds of his things."

Choking down a laugh, Cleo said, "Maybe you're getting ahead of yourself. Just enjoy the moment, don't worry about what happens later."

Turning, Trixie stared at her with raised eyebrows. "Interesting advice."

Cleo felt her cheeks get warm. "Drink your damn drink."

"I'm more than twice your age, you know. I'm full of wisdom."

"Says the woman wearing mismatched socks."

"You love my style," Trixie said. "You just haven't matured enough to dare it yourself."

"I dare it all the time," Cleo said.

When her second drink arrived, Cleo gave in, ordered another for herself, and settled in the seat next to Trixie's for a few therapeutic pulls at the machine. After a few minutes, she asked, "Are you feeling better yet?"

"I told you. I'm feeling too much better for my own good." Trixie lowered her voice. "It's so easy to get hurt."

Murmuring her sympathy, Cleo pulled the lever. "You can handle it."

"He's smart and kind, dark and handsome," Trixie continued. "What's not to like?"

"Exactly."

"If he's willing to go for it, why not give it a shot? Even if it ends badly, it could be worth it anyway. Life's short."

"I totally agree," Cleo said. After a few long moments, she noticed Trixie was grinning at her. "What?"

"You didn't realize I was talking about you and Sly," Trixie said.

Turning away, Cleo looked at the reels. She'd won. An evil impulse struck her to give Trixie a taste of her own medicine. With a straight face, she asked, "How do you know I didn't?"

Trixie squealed as if she'd won the million-dollar jackpot at the giant machine near the restroom. She flung her arms around Cleo and kissed her cheek. "I'm so glad. You've really lifted my spirits. I don't feel depressed at all anymore."

Now Cleo felt guilty. "Trixie, I'm sorry. I was just kidding."

With a wink, Trixie stood and plucked the celery stick out of her drink. "Sure you were."

"Seriously, I was. I really was."

But Trixie was already walking away, chomping on her celery. "Enjoy your evening."

17

MIDAFTERNOON, FEARING THE worst, Sly found Cleo at the blackjack table. Her face was scrunched up the way it did when she was listening to a complicated musical composition. And she was exchanging her empty drink for a full one with the cocktail waitress.

Sly hadn't wanted to let her get away, but Hugo had convinced him to stay for breakfast.

"She's so beautiful," Hugo had said at the table, gazing at his orange juice.

"So, you two..." Sly hadn't wanted the details, just the basics.

Sipping his juice, Hugo had smiled but said nothing. Sly had given up trying to help and resumed brooding about his own troubles. His confidence, although unlimited thus far in a professional setting, was under strain when it came to Cleo. She liked him, she'd kissed him, but was that as far as it was ever going to go? Was she really not interested? He thought they had chemistry, but maybe he was lying to himself.

"She'll come around," Hugo had said after the meal as they hugged good-bye near the hostess station. "Cleo, I mean. I know Trixie will."

But Cleo hadn't answered her phone since then, and he'd

been searching for her for an hour when he found her at the blackjack table.

"Hey," he said, touching her shoulder. She'd just finished a round and was preparing for another.

To his surprise, when she saw him, she gathered her chips and got up from the table. "Hey," she said. "What time is it? My phone is dead."

"Are you OK?"

"I'm great." She grinned. "I have a knack."

"You're rich."

"Almost."

The makeup she was wearing made her eyes look enormous. Some of the mascara had smudged, leaving a shadow on her cheekbone. He gave up fighting the impulse to touch her and brushed it off with his thumb.

Her smile fell. "I need to cash in my chips."

He shoved his hands in his pockets as she walked away. He wasn't getting any closer to winning her over. He needed a knack. Or at least a new plan. The going-slow thing wasn't working. It just gave her the space to ignore him.

He chased after her and waited with her at the cashier. When she was done, they walked together toward the elevators. Silently, he counted the hours before they flew back to San Francisco tomorrow. Thirty. A lot could happen in thirty hours. There were shows, restaurants, clubs.

"I'm going upstairs to take a nap," she said.

Or nothing at all.

"Will you be all right on your own?" she continued.

"I'll come up with you and you can tell me about Trixie," he said. A Hail Mary pass.

"Right! What did Hugo say?"

"Nothing. He's very old-school. Being a gentleman."

"I think they... you know. Slept together."

Lucky them. "Why was she so upset?"

"I hate to laugh, but her plan backfired on her. Get this—she admitted that she'd been pretending all along."

"We could tell her we slept together to make her feel better," he said.

"We can't encourage her, Sly. She doesn't realize this is some crisis of yours that has nothing to do with me. She senses your weakness. Single men set off all her alarms. You shouldn't have encouraged her."

"I came for Hugo," he said. "He's not faking anything. I'm here to help." That was true enough. He checked his phone. "Set your alarm before you fall asleep. I'm taking you to dinner and a club. Reservations are at seven for the first, none needed for the second."

"We should invite—"

"We're not inviting anyone," he said.

She stared at him. "Well, I don't know..."

"What are you afraid of?"

"I'm not afraid of you, I'm afraid of your... crisis."

"I think maybe it's not my crisis you're worried about," he said. "It's your own."

"I am fully crisis-free, my friend."

"Good. Then you'll have no problem spending a few hours having a good time." Waving his phone, he pivoted on his heel and began to walk away. "Be ready at six thirty."

He was ten steps away when she called for him to stop. If she insisted on not coming, he didn't know what he would do. Strip, maybe. Get her a T-shirt that said TECH MOGUL DIRECT TO YOU.

"Where should we meet?" she asked.

Cleo didn't go back to the room for a nap.

How could she sleep? Her conversation with Trixie had been nagging at her all day. And she was nine hundred and fifty-three dollars richer than she'd been a few hours ago. Ironically, she'd only gambled the thousand she'd won from Sly in Carmel, and instead of losing it as she'd expected, she'd doubled her money.

No wonder people got addicted to gambling.

Risks could pay off.

Even if it ends badly, it could be worth it anyway.

She pushed that thought aside. In fact, she pushed all thoughts aside. Her natural caution had been eroding since she set foot in Sin City. By the time she got home, she'd be a pile of sand.

Therefore, right now, she'd go shopping. She'd brought an old dress she wore on gigs, and although it was black and stylish, it could use a little something more.

Within the hour, she found the *more* she needed. The shoes were more expensive than they should've been, but they had bows, buckles and silver glitter that made them sparkle like radioactive angels in a disco. They were perfect. She wouldn't have spent so much at home, but she wasn't at home, was she?

Life's short.

Because the killer shoes exposed her toes, she headed over to get a pedicure in the nail salon she'd seen near the pet boutique. It was busy and they made her wait. After forty minutes, when it was pushing five thirty, she was considering giving up and going upstairs to get dressed without the pretty toes when they finally led her to a seat.

She melted into her massage chair throne, kicked off her boots, and glanced at the pair of empty seats next to her, wondering why she'd had to wait so long.

"Those are reserved," the cosmetician said, clasping her bare foot. "But they're late."

Videos of relaxing forest settings played while her hands and feet soaked in a tub of flower-petal-dappled hot water. She closed her eyes, let the electronic fingers in the chair vibrate out the tension in her back and legs, and saw Sly's face. His grin. Felt his lips slid across hers, warm and hungry.

With a sharp inhalation, she opened her eyes and glared at the relaxing forest. So very relaxing, a forest. And empty. She'd never seen Sly in a forest.

The young woman on a stool at her feet confirmed her choice of polish and began massaging her feet and calves with jasmine-scented oil. "Eye wrap?"

"For me?" Cleo asked, then realized how stupid her question was. As if she'd want the woman scraping her toes with metal implements to wear one. "Yes," she said quickly. "Please. Thanks."

The woman waved and an older man rushed over and placed a chilled, padded, sea-green mask over eyes. "Good?" he asked.

"Fine." She exhaled, enjoying the coolness. "Thank you."

Just as she was deciding she needed to do this more often (although it was hardly in her budget, even with a knack for blackjack), she heard a couple of noisy women arrive and sit in the empty recliners to her right.

"I can't believe how late it is," one of them said. She had the silly, high voice of a helium-breathing eight-year-old.

"I know. We got up just in time for dinner." The second woman was hoarse, as if she were ill or had been screaming all night. Given the city they were in, it could've been either one. Or both.

"Will your sister be mad about Monique and Kelsey skipping

her dinner?" asked Helium.

"She couldn't care less about my friends," Hoarse said. "Especially now. I'll be impressed if she shows up herself."

"I don't think she should've told you about it," Helium said. "Given you're getting married next week. It's bad luck."

Unwillingly drawn to their conversation, Cleo wished she could close her ears as easily as she closed her eyes. She was grateful when her neighbors were interrupted by the salon staff for a few minutes as they confirmed their procedures from the menu.

"I told her Dylan was bad news," Hoarse continued when the Platinum Deluxe Mani-Pedi was settled. "Cheaters always cheat. And she had it coming, anyway. Karma, you know? Not that I can tell her that."

The woman holding Cleo's hand tapped her wrist lightly. "Relax, please."

Cleo had been digging her nails into the vibrating armrest. With effort, she uncurled her fingers and tried to keep them limp for the delicate beauty operation underway.

Of all the nail salons in the world, Ashley's little sister had to walk into hers. Liz. And hadn't that helium-voiced woman been in the elevator the night before?

Cleo's head was spinning with the comments about Dylan and karma.

Had he cheated on Ashley? How could that be? He'd destroyed everything because of how much he loved Ashley. How much he wanted and needed her.

So much more than Cleo.

"I still think she should've waited to tell you," Helium said. "I think it's really annoying she might spoil everything for you. This is totally your time, you know?"

"Yeah, it sucks. She confronted him last night. At least he's gone now though. Flew home this afternoon to pack up and move out." Liz sighed, and the noises coming from her massage recliner changed from a slow throb to a staccato hum. "My mom's going to have to pretend she's not happy about it. She never liked him. His first wife, the one they cheated on, used to play at our house when I was little."

Cleo rolled her head away, hoping Liz didn't have a photographic memory for human profiles.

Helium's voice rose to glass-shattering heights. "What?"

"They were friends in high school," Liz said. "I don't remember her. I was little. But my mom told me."

"That's sick," Helium said. "I'll never look at Ashley the same way ever again."

Cleo's wished she knew Helium's name so she could call her something more complimentary in her mind.

"Like I said. Karma." Liz let out a long sigh. "Let's not talk about it. It pisses me off and I've already got a headache."

"Good thing the wedding isn't until next week," Helium said with a laugh. "We've got another night to party."

Liz mumbled something in agreement, and their conversation turned to the details of a honeymoon in Kauai.

Cleo gazed blindly into her eye mask. How was she going to get out of here without Liz seeing her?

How was she going to get out of here without throwing up?

Dylan had cheated on Ashley. She couldn't wrap her head around it. How could he ruin two marriages doing the exact same, horrible, stupid thing?

Gentle fingers removed the eye mask. "You're all done," the young woman said. "Want the dryers?"

Turning away from her neighbors, Cleo looked down at her

neon-cranberry toenails and shook her head. She noticed a small purple clipboard holding her bill sitting near her left hand. Rather than deal with a credit card, which would take too long, she plucked several twenties out of her purse and handed them over. "I don't need any change." She reached down for her boots.

The woman nodded politely at the huge tip, then hurried to help her with her shoes. "Careful. No sandals?"

Memories were washing over Cleo. The night Dylan told her that he'd never felt that spark with her that he had for Ashley. That she was his best friend and he loved her, but that he was *in* love with Ashley, that Ashley aroused a passion in him that Cleo never had.

Belatedly realizing the woman didn't want to ruin her pedicure, Cleo lifted the box of new shoes, and the woman, smiling, took them out and carefully slipped them on Cleo's freshly presentable feet.

Did Dylan's new woman arouse a passion that Ashley never had? Is that what he told her last night, here in Las Vegas as they celebrated Liz's wedding?

It was almost enough to make Cleo feel sorry for her.

She got out of the salon without glancing at Liz or Helium, then went directly upstairs to the room.

When she got to the door and pulled out her key, she noticed she was humming a cheerful pop song to herself. And had just sashayed down the hallway in her sparkly new shoes and cranberry neon toes like a happy prom queen whose daddy had just replaced her totaled Bimmer.

Chagrined by her *schadenfreude*, she bit her lip and went inside to get ready.

Her good mood only got better after she'd put on her dress and touched up her face.

He was a bad guy, a horrible husband, and she was sorry other women had the misfortune of falling in love with him and believing his lies, but...

It hadn't been her fault. The divorce, the humiliation, the pain —it hadn't been her fault. Somehow, deep down, she'd been carrying this boulder in her heart that hinted at a difficult truth: she hadn't been desirable enough to satisfy him. The way Ashley was.

Except Ashley wasn't either, and Ashley was classically gorgeous, sexually adventurous, and rich too.

Shoving her cash, ID, and a credit card in her purse, Cleo flew out of the hotel room, eager to find Sly and tell him everything. He brought flowers every year on the anniversary of her divorce, and a bottle of vodka for the date of the wedding. He would understand what this meant to her.

She found him standing next to the waterfall fountain with his back to her. Although he wore a charcoal suit and blended in with many of the other men, she recognized him instantly—the way he stood with one hand in his pocket, weight balanced more on his right hip, his dark hair curling at his collar. When he turned and saw her, he smiled, eyes shining, but otherwise didn't move.

Thoughts of Dylan Baker fell away.

With each step that drew her closer, Sly's gaze burned brighter. She became aware of her own bare shoulders, her exposed cleavage, the slit up her skirt. It wasn't a special dress— she'd worn it a dozen times before—or maybe it was, she just hadn't known it before. Maybe she was the most beautiful woman in the world.

If Sly was the one looking at her.

When she was several feet away, she stopped to catch her

breath. They stared at each other, neither saying a word.

18

SOMETHING HAD CHANGED. It was written all over her. Sly wanted to get closer and read every word.

"What happened?" he asked, forcing himself to stay a few feet away. "You look... excited."

"I do?" Her voice was throaty. It made him want to get her talking and listen to it for hours.

"Yes," he said softly.

"I'll tell you at dinner," she said. "Where are we going?"

"A little place."

She wore a sleeveless black dress with a loose skirt, but not too long for him to miss her girly shoes and even-more-girly toes. Had she dressed up for him?

A hint of perfume drifted over to him. He'd warned her before what happened when she smelled too good. Yet she'd done it again.

Heart rate quickening, he turned and began walking the convoluted route to the exit. "It doesn't have any dancing."

The sound of her laughter was like a kiss. He smiled, ridiculously pleased.

"Does it have music?" she asked.

"Don't spoil it. Just be patient."

"Then it does," she said.

He was trying to seduce a musician. Of course it had music. "Maybe."

"What kind?"

"Will you be patient?"

"Seriously. I just want to make sure we'll be able to talk."

He stopped walking and looked at her. Her fair hair was loose, framing her face with a platinum curtain he imagined sliding between his fingers. Now that he'd given himself permission to think about her in his bed, it was all he could think about. She was the same person, but she was a stranger. A familiar, delicious mystery.

"We'll be able to talk," he said.

She stared back at him. Her pupils were dark pools in the center of a blue sky.

"Is it far?" she asked.

"We could get room service."

Smiling as if he were joking, she walked through the doors to the hotel's circular drive entrance where several uniformed valets waited at a podium. "Are we driving?"

He paused, taking a deep breath before he followed. "No."

"I don't mind walking." She unfurled a wrap and slung it around her shoulders. "I bought this today for fifteen bucks. Can you tell?"

"That you just bought it?"

"That it was only fifteen bucks," she said. "Duh."

"Well, yes, but only because you left the price tag on it."

In alarm, she craned her neck around, picking at the fabric as she searched for the tag.

"Just kidding," he said.

She smacked him on the shoulder and, to his happy surprise,

slipped her arm through his. "Funny guy."

He was feeling funny, but not the way she meant. "Oh, good. Right on time." Ahead of them sat a black stretch limousine. "Our ride."

Her pace didn't slow down.

"Seriously," he said, flagging the driver. "The restaurant sent it for us."

She frowned. "Oh, come on."

The elderly chauffeur jumped out and opened the back door for them.

"Thank you," Cleo said to him, giving Sly a skeptical smile as she climbed in, and in minutes they were seated in the vast backseat, creeping through the Saturday-evening traffic.

"Do you like it?" Sly asked.

Her hands stroked over the leather. "What's not to like?" But she didn't say anything else until they'd reached the restaurant and were climbing out again.

She thanked the driver and reached for her purse, but Sly was already handing him a few bills. "Cut that out," he told her.

"I was going to give him some of my blackjack winnings," she said.

"Save it. This is my treat."

The restaurant was old-school Italian, with dim lighting, black-and-white Sinatra photos on the brick walls, and a drum set and keyboard on a small stage near the bar. Most of the tables, small and close together, were already filled. Their waiter led them to the dark corner booth Sly had negotiated over the phone. He watched Cleo's face as she took it in, not happy with the unease he saw there.

The waiter took their drink order, mentioned the specials, and left them with the menus.

"What's the matter?" Sly asked her.

Shaking her head, she opened the menu. "Do you like calamari? Let's get that as a starter. And maybe the baked clams. Too much seafood?"

"Not too much." He inched closer on the smooth, padded seat. "Whatever you want."

Without moving her head, she looked at him out of the corner of her eye. Then back at the menu.

Their drinks arrived. He didn't want to seem too eager to pour it down her throat, but she was too tense. He sipped his own and smiled at her like a mother encouraging her baby to eat the mashed peas.

A moment later, she did pick it up, her frown melting away, but not because of him. Two guys had started playing jazz on the small stage, one on drums, the other the keyboard. Warm, crusty bread and a plate of olive oil appeared, and soon she was actually smiling and wiggling in her seat to the music.

"This is great," she said, staring across the room at the band.

"You're great," he replied, staring at her.

She froze with her head turned away from him toward the stage.

"Cleo," he said.

Slow, sensual jazz drifted around them. A bassist had joined them. *Boom-da-boom-boom-boom...*

She turned. "Sly..."

He had to fight down the impulse to compliment her lips. They were pink and rosy, round and soft-looking morsels. Instead, he broke away and sipped his martini. "Sorry. What happened to you earlier?"

After a pause, she tore a piece of bread apart and dipped it in the oil. "I'm not sure I want to spoil the... meal... talking about it here."

Spoil the date, she meant. He moved another infinitesimal sliver closer. "It looked like good news. You seemed happy."

"That's because I'm a bad person."

"Something bad happened to the ex?"

Her mouth dropped open. Then she smiled. "I'm that predictable, aren't I? But no, it wasn't Dylan. I wouldn't feel guilty if it was Dylan. It was Ashley. Which I do feel bad about, sort of. Almost. If I try really hard." She shoved the bread in her mouth. "In time."

"She lost the Prius at craps?"

"She and Dylan are getting divorced," she said. "He's cheating on her."

"Who told you that?"

"I heard it from her sister during my pedicure." She cleared her throat. "She was talking to a friend of hers, didn't see me."

"Wow."

She tapped her glass against his. "I know. I couldn't believe it. I still can't. He did it *again*."

"The wow was for the coincidence of overhearing. I'm not surprised he cheated again."

"Oh, come on. If you'd seen him back then, you would be."

"Why?"

"He was obsessed with her," she said, rolling her eyes. "When he told me about what they'd been doing, he was weeping, begging me to understand. He said he'd never—whatever."

"Never what?"

"Nothing."

It was dangerous to push her now, inviting the ghost of her failed marriage to join them, but it haunted her, berating her to stay safe. Time to kill it for good. "He'd never what?"

"All right, listen. This is the thing. He'd said he'd never felt that way about me. And I believed him." She popped an olive into her mouth and licked her lips. The sight of her tongue distracted him for a moment. "Because I was an idiot."

"Don't beat yourself up. You trusted him. That makes him a dick, not you."

"Yes, yes, he's a dick. But... this is different. Do you know what this means?"

"His next wife should get a prenup?"

"It means it wasn't my fault."

"Of course it wasn't your fault."

"Not anything I did, of course," she said. "But even the things I couldn't help. You saw Ashley. If he could do it to *her*, well then. What chance did *I* have? You see?"

If Dylan had been there at that moment, Sly would've stuffed his fist down his throat. He looked at Cleo, saw the remnants of shame in her blue eyes, the hurt pinching the corners of her mouth, and almost got up and left her there so that he could go find the asshole, wherever he was, and kill him.

"So that's why I'm happy," she continued. The calamari had arrived, and she picked up a long, crispy tentacle between her fingers and wiggled it at him. "I'm not repulsive after all."

He wrapped his fingers around her wrist and gently guided the fried cephalopod onto her plate. Then, with his other hand, he caught her by the back of the neck and kissed her.

Cleo's first thought was that the music was all wrong. Soft instrumental jazz was a terrible soundtrack for pounding, burning lust. Fingers stroking her nape, Sly licked the seam of her lips and teased them apart. She sank against him, aware only of the feel of his tongue sliding into her mouth and how good he tasted. His strong hand behind her head held her in place, but she wasn't going anywhere. Ever since Carmel, all she'd really wanted was to kiss him again. And do everything. Everything.

But he broke the kiss and rested his forehead against hers, gazing into her eyes. His breath was warm and coming fast, mixing with her own. "I have really, really bad timing. I planned to do that a little later," he said in a low voice. Tangled in her hair, his fingers brushed the skin of her neck, arousing a shiver.

Every cell in her body screamed for him. She leaned in for more, not caring where they were.

"See? Not repulsive." With a grin, he pinched the tip of her nose.

His comment struck like ice water down her back. He was just proving a point. He was playing around, teasing, not really serious.

She shouldn't do this. They were too mismatched. She wouldn't call him a womanizer, but she knew he'd had plenty of one-night stands in his life, relationships that lasted three dates or a weekend. As his friend, she could hold her own. A good listener, fun at a party, quick to order a pizza or remember a birthday—she was confident in her friend skills.

But this... she didn't know how to be this woman who necked in Italian restaurants while Sinatra looked on in chilly, sexy cool. Her speed was to date, fall in love, have sex, and get married. Except for the order of sex and marriage, she was embarrassingly traditional.

"Gee, thanks," she said, pulling away. Hand shaking, she picked up her fork and impaled a tangle of calamari.

He leaned in again and nuzzled her cheek. "Cleo," he said softly. His hot breath tickled her neck, standing the hairs all over her body at attention, a sensual electrocution. Molten pleasure pooled between her legs, ready for the next step.

The other diners at the restaurant, however, certainly weren't ready for any more steps than they'd already taken. A girl, not quite a teenager, was watching them from the next table while her parents were feeding each other cannoli.

"Eat," she said. "Please." They'd enjoy their meal and the show and figure out the finer details of their friendship later. Or never. Never would be smarter.

Slowly, he moved away. "That's probably for the best."

"I'm glad you think so."

"I'm going to need my strength." He took a bite, eyeing her while he chewed.

"Earlier you said you were just having a crisis."

"If I am, I'm really enjoying it." He signaled the waiter and ordered a bottle of wine to go with their meal.

"I shouldn't drink any more."

"Whatever you want, Cleo."

"You're not listening to me."

He propped an elbow on the table and gazed at her. His heavily lashed eyes were dark and inviting. If she leaned forward a few inches, she could kiss him again.

With the hint of a smile, he turned away and put a clam on her plate. "I'm listening to the music," he said. "Just like you."

"Fine. We'll argue later."

"If that's what you want to call it," he said. "I'm looking forward to it."

They sat in silence until the rest of the dishes were served. She wiggled a foot away from him on the seat and picked at the meal. It was probably delicious. It could've been leftovers from a junior high cafeteria's Dumpster and she wouldn't have noticed. Focusing on moving the utensils around the plates and bowls used up all her limited executive functioning. Lift, cut, lift, chew, swallow. Mostly she just moved the food around the plate.

"Good drummer," she said.

"They stopped playing five minutes ago."

She looked up from her eggplant, now a brown hill on the side of her plate, and stared at the empty stage. "I knew that."

"Ah," he said. A moment later, she felt his hand stroke her thigh. Just a feather touch but enough to leave a trail of fire along her skin.

It took her a moment to suck enough air into her lungs to say, "That's my leg."

"Is it? I was so engrossed in the music, I didn't notice." With his free hand, he lifted his wineglass to his mouth. The other stayed where it was. Just resting there like a kitten.

Ten long, dizzying seconds passed before she said, "Leggo my Eggo, buddy."

He laughed and, after a tantalizing squeeze, moved his hand away. The mirth continued for several minutes as he ate, drank, and shot her admiring glances. "I'm crazy about you, Cleo. Did you know that?"

"You're crazier than you used to be. That's for sure."

He lifted his glass in a toast. "I'll drink to that. No, I'll drink to you."

"Drink all you want, just leave my limbs alone."

"I've always been creative within the parameters I've been given," he said, dropping his gaze to her chest. "Define 'limbs.'"

"Is this biological, do you think? Have you had your hormones tested? Some men go through a mini menopause. A *man*opause. I think you should see a doctor."

He only laughed and kept eating. "Are you going to want dessert? Their cannoli is supposed to be good."

Her stomach was already suffering enough. Nerves, liquor, olive oil, tomato sauce, garlic, cheese. Churning, unrequited, impractical lust. "No. I couldn't."

"Fine with me. Let's pay up and get out of here."

The service was quick and efficient, perhaps because of the demand for the table, and in several minutes he was holding out his hand to help her out of the booth. Reluctantly, although not reluctantly enough to refuse, she put her hand in his and felt his warm fingers slip around hers and tighten. He didn't release her as they walked to the front. She hadn't thought he would. She'd also known she wouldn't insist.

Was it so bad to hold hands with an old friend? It felt so right. She stifled a moan as his thumb stroked her knuckle.

They stepped out into the parking lot, a small square of concrete set between a strip mall and the palm-lined entrance to a gated housing development. The temperature had dropped into the low fifties, and she used her free hand to tug her wrap over her upper arms. Sly reached over to help, bringing his dimpled chin into view.

He hadn't shaved again. The feel of those whiskers on her cheek was burned into her sensory memory. Unlike a bite of whatever she'd eaten inside.

Just past the stubble-shadowed dimple, a full harvest moon that would've looked huge over a rural field was just a small bright orb hovering over the power-plant-draining city, like a firefly in the Milky Way.

The parking lot felt more intimate than the cozy restaurant. Without Frank or the candles, the night was theirs alone. A wave of longing struck her for this man and his confident grin, quick mind, and good taste in serial television. What was life for but to connect with other people? She'd been so alone. It wasn't her fault. It hadn't been—but it would be if she ran away now.

Too much alcohol made her sway on her feet, holding on to him for balance. If they couldn't go back, they'd have to go forward. It was past time she lived like other adults, enjoying physical pleasures, and who better to experiment with than an old friend she liked and trusted?

Wasn't she always telling her students how important it was to practice?

She said none of this aloud and got into the limo for their return to the Strip without hinting at any of her thoughts.

He looked good sitting in a limo. At ease. Confident. Gorgeous. Delicious. In a suit. Although a birthday suit would be better.

She rested her head on the back of her seat, feeling the world spin.

"What's so funny?" he asked.

"I was imagining you naked." A laugh bubbled out of her. Not a cute feminine giggle, either, but a throaty guffaw.

He didn't answer right away. "Hilarious."

She hauled his hand to her lips and kissed it. His skin smelled like men's cologne, which seemed terribly unfair. Hers probably smelled like parmesan.

She rotated their hands and sniffed her own fingers. Yup. Cheese. She laughed again.

"I wish I'd cut you off after the second martini," he said.

"No you don't." She dragged her lips to the underside of his wrist, trying to tell if his pulse was racing as fast as hers was. "Then I might not have decided to sleep with you tonight."

When he didn't say anything, she glanced over at him. He was staring at her, unblinking, the muscle in his jaw twitching.

She turned his wrist again and opened her mouth over the

skin that smelled so good, mouthing the little hairs.

His voice came out strained. "You can't make any big decisions when you've had so much to drink."

"You have too many scruples."

"We'll go dancing. You can metabolize just enough of the alcohol to let me take you up on your offer."

"I don't feel like dancing. That didn't work out so well last time."

"Not that kind of dancing," he said. "We'll go to a club."

She brushed her lips across the swell of his thumb pad.

"Cleo," he choked out.

In response, to draw the pointless dancing conversation to a close, she licked his palm.

In one sudden move, he wrenched his hand free and captured her face in both hands.

19

FINALLY, CLEO THOUGHT, arching into him. She didn't care how irrational this was, considering she'd been pushing him away so long. They could never go back to the way they were before, so why try? The ship had left the barn. The cow had left the station. The metaphor was as mixed as the drinks she'd poured down her throat and the emotions churning inside her.

She tunneled her fingers through his hair, fisted the thick locks, and kissed him deeper. Their tongues tangled. A low moan escaped him, filling her with a sense of her own power. He wanted her, he wanted to kiss her, he wanted to make love to her. Before now, she'd been shoving it aside as humorous and unlikely, a comic accident of biology and bad timing. She couldn't remember why she'd thought any of this was funny. She couldn't remember anything.

His hand roved across her body, snaked around her waist, and was hauling her on top of him when the driver's voice drifted back to them.

"We're here, folks," he said cheerfully. "Sorry to rush you, but I've got another party waiting."

Not registering what he was saying, Cleo slid her hand around Sly's neck and played with the wavy hair behind his ears.

Sometimes, when they watched TV and he sat on the floor and she sprawled above him on the couch, she'd stared at this spot, wondering what it felt like.

Now she knew. It felt excellent.

"Cleo." He gave her a quick, hard kiss on the mouth before pushing her away. "We have to get out."

The door opened, sending in cool air. With effort, she moved away from Sly, tugging her dress over her thighs, and clambered out of the low seat, grateful the driver averted his eyes.

"Thanks," she said, stifling a giggle. A giggle? Her? Lord. "Great driving." She watched Sly to make sure he tipped the old guy before walking unsteadily toward the huge ornamental doorway into their hotel. The valets greeted her, and she waved at them, hoping she looked like a fun-loving party girl, because that's what she needed to feel like to keep going. Not a woman who was fighting the instinct to run and hide. No. Just a party girl without a care in the world.

"Careful," Sly said, capturing her hand. "You're weaving."

"Don't be ridiculous," she said. "I've never weaved in my life. A little crochet, that's it."

He pulled her against his side as they walked, his hand stroking the side of her waist. She knew she wasn't herself when she didn't adjust her underwear to smooth out the soft rolls that formed where the elastic dug into her. He was feeling her, rolls and all. Cinnabon had nothing on her.

Oh God. She wanted him so bad. She wanted him to touch her everywhere and she didn't care what he thought, what he saw, what he felt, just that he would do it and keep doing it all night. All night. Right now. Right here. Sly. Her strong, sexy friend with the bedroom eyes and dimpled chin and talented fingers.

Sly tightened his hold around her waist. "Are you OK,

sweetheart?" he whispered in her ear. "Let's sit down for a minute."

Tucked off to their left was a seating area with red velvet sofas and leather club chairs. He guided her over to it and pushed her down in one of the chairs while remaining standing himself. He bent over to kiss her on the forehead, lingering there a moment with his lips brushing her skin, then turned as if to go.

She gripped his wrist. "Where are you going?"

"Wait right here." He caressed her cheek, dragging her hand with him. "I need to do something."

"Do what? Check your email? What?"

"No. Nothing like that. It's a surprise. Will you wait for me?"

"You're just going to leave me here?"

"Only a few minutes," he said.

"Will I like this surprise?"

"Stop asking me questions. It's a surprise."

She looked up at the chandelier over their heads. It didn't look familiar. "Are you sure this is our hotel?"

"I wish you'd had more to eat tonight. You'd be handling the liquor a little better."

"So much better I wouldn't be doing this," she said, staring at him as she licked her lips, slow and seductive. Or she hoped it was.

"Don't say that." He closed his eyes for a moment. "I'll be right back. Don't move."

The lights in the chandelier were blue, she realized. Not all of them, just some of them. She wondered where you could find blue chandelier lights or if it was a custom-made kind of thing.

Sly said, "I don't think you're going anywhere," and strode out of sight. Head spinning, she pondered the lights some more. When she got home, she'd go shopping for lights. They were so sparkly. These little ones twinkled like the high notes of a harpsichord.

"Here you go."

She lifted her head to see a paper cup with a plastic lid and a familiar green logo hovering in front of her. No, not hovering. Sly had returned. The cup was connected to his arm.

"You need to sober up a little," he said. "Before we go on."

"You have the totally wrong idea about that."

"That's what I'm afraid of."

Crossing her arms over her chest, she looked at her raspberry-neon toes. Lights in a pink color like that would be pretty too. "I don't drink caffeine after six."

"Because it keeps you up all night," he said in a low, gravelly voice.

She met his gaze. His left eyebrow was arched in a way that, several months ago, she would've called obnoxious. But now it was hopelessly, frantically sexy. She wanted to kiss it.

"Good point." She took the cup with both hands and brought it to her lips.

"While you drink that, I've got one more thing to do."

"This is very anticlimactic."

"Just drink that, will you?"

"You're so bossy. Are you always this bossy with your women?"

Not smiling, he leaned down and kissed her. Hot and hard. Just as she was feeling a trickle of hot coffee burn through the polyester of her dress, scalding her thigh, he drew back, righting the cup, and said, "You're my only woman, Cleo. Only you."

Holy mother of Beethoven. Was this really happening? She felt as hot as the coffee.

His hand brushed her cheek. "Drink it," he said, then disappeared again.

She craned her neck around to see where he was going. God, that arrogance. That stride. That ass. He was headed toward reception. When the fountain blocked her line of sight, she turned back to her coffee with a long, lusty sigh.

This city needed a warning label. She'd already become a gambling addict, an alcoholic, and a sex fiend. What vices had she missed? Cigarettes had killed her grandparents, which was unforgivable, and she was too conscientious to become a criminal. She was trying to remember the Ten Commandments, a little hung up on the coveting your neighbor's wife part, which reminded her of her failed marriage, when her date returned.

He took the cup away from her and shook it a little. "You didn't drink it."

"It was as hot as your ass," she said, then smiled at him.

"God."

"I forgot that one! But I already do that." She hauled herself out of her seat and wrapped her arms around his waist. Because she could.

"Lots of people forget God here."

"Taking the Lord's name in vain," she said. "I was trying to think of new sins I could commit."

He moved both hands down her spine and cupped her bottom, right there in the lobby. "Let's go upstairs," he said into her hair, "and I'll help you with that."

This wasn't how he imagined their first night together. The smart, capable Cleo he knew didn't act like a drunken teenager who groped his crotch in the elevator and then broke down giggling. He wanted her to lose control, but not like this. If they had sex when she was in this condition, he'd be taking advantage of her.

The elevator passed the floor for the room Hugo and Trixie

had given them and kept going. She was too busy trying to cop another feel and collapsing with laughter to notice they were going somewhere else. Unrequited lust was making him tense, and her behavior annoyed him. He blamed himself, of course. She hadn't kept the drinks coming, he had. Now he had her lush, inviting body in his arms and he was going to have to push her away until she'd sobered up. Which could be hours. By then she might change her mind.

He couldn't bear to get this close to having her and then lose her. But if she woke up feeling ill-used, she'd never forgive him.

She stopped groping him and stared, eyes wide. Unfocused, but wide. "What's the matter?"

Her sweet face knocked the breath out of him. He bent his head and kissed her lightly, then stood there, inhaling her scent, heart pounding with wanting her, until the doors opened at the top floor. He gathered his wits and led her off the elevator to a door at the end of the hallway.

She didn't notice they were in a new suite until they were inside. "This isn't our room."

"It is now."

The suite cost him more than he'd ever spent on a hotel room before in his life, and he'd traveled around the world with an expense account for over a decade. Of course, as an entrepreneur, he'd never enjoyed draining the company's coffers and had been known to be thrifty on occasion. In fact, Mark had always accused him of being cheap.

Well, he wasn't being cheap now. "Chocolate?" Holding her hand, he walked over to the plate of truffles waiting for them under a vase of red roses.

"You got us another room?"

He picked up a cocoa-dusted pyramid, pulled her against

him, and pushed it between her lips. While she chewed, moaning, he pressed his hips into her soft curves and told himself he could resist tearing her clothes off as long as he got to hold her.

"There's champagne too." Her hands found his ass again and squeezed, inspiring another round of giggles.

"None for you," he said.

She pulled away, eyebrow arching. "Excuse me?"

"I'm waiting for you to sober up."

"I'm waiting for you to pull that stick out of your ass." She lunged, as if going for the stick, and he twisted out of reach. Her humor faded. "Come on, you've got to be kidding me. I'm finally ready to go, and you're saying no?"

"I'm saying let's take it slow."

She closed her eyes, dropping mascara-darkened lashes over her cheeks. Nostrils flaring, she took a deep breath, then spun away from him and strode into the room. As she walked past the wet bar with the chocolates and champagne, her arm swung out and caught the bottle. She took it with her through the sunken living room to the sliding balcony doors, where she stood with her back to him, hand on the window, looking out on the view. The flashing city lights put her hourglass figure into stunning silhouette.

"We can't wait," she said, setting the champagne bottle on the floor. "We have to do it now." She turned, leaning against the glass, and reached up to the neckline of her dress. With a tug, one side fell down her arm, exposing a red bra strap and a pale, creamy shoulder.

He hurried over. "It's not a chore to get over with." Breathing hard, he grabbed the dress and yanked it back up, trying to tune out the feel of her velvety skin under his fingers and the seductive way she leaned into him. The scent of her perfume. The memory of her taste, sweet and forbidden.

Tilting her head, she touched the hollow of his throat, then trailed a featherlight finger up to his chin, across his jaw, his lips. He froze, struggling to hold himself back, trying not to show how her touch undid him, but his heart was pounding and he was aching hard for her. If she didn't stop, he'd have to leave. He'd have to. He'd have to. He closed his eyes.

"So beautiful you are," she said, mockingly, a hint of Yoda in her voice.

He felt her chest press against his as she drew closer. "So drunk you are," he managed to say, his voice unsteady. "Sober up you must."

He opened his eyes just as she kissed him, light and teasing, on his chin. "But then I won't be happy fun girl. I might remember we can't do this."

"We can."

She began pulling his shirttails out from his pants. "Yes we can, yes we can," she chanted between giggles, hooking her fingers around his belt. Powerless for a moment to stop her, he froze, indulging in the fantasy of her fumbling to unfasten the leather, unfasten his pants, and touch him.

She withdrew her hands suddenly and reached down for the champagne. "You're wrong about me, you know."

He swallowed over his dry throat. "Am I?"

"I'm not nearly drunk enough to do this." She tore off the foil and began untwisting the wire over the cork.

Not nearly drunk enough. Not nearly.

He ducked his head. "Neither am I." Hardly believing he had the willpower to move, he pivoted and headed for the door.

20

"WHERE ARE YOU going?"

Hearing the vulnerability in her voice, Sly paused at the door, not able to make himself open it. "I'll leave the extra key next to the roses. There are spare toothbrushes in the bathroom." He'd arranged for all the amenities, wanting it to be special.

She came up behind him. "That's it? You're just going to walk away?"

"I can't do this." Slowly, he turned to face her. "Not if the thought of having sex with me is so repulsive to you that you need to be semiconscious to do it."

Her mouth fell open. "No, wait. Please. I thought you wanted…" She looked down at herself. "To do this."

"I do want this. I do." He shoved his hands in his pockets to stop himself from reaching for her. "You have no idea. But I can't be the only one."

Her voice fell to a whisper. "You don't understand."

"Sure I do. We've known each other a long time." He thought of the long, happy years of platonic camaraderie. "Maybe it's just too late."

She made a sound that might've been a laugh.

"I can't be here with you and not want you, Cleo. I can't do it.

I could before, but now that we..." He turned and reached for the door handle.

She lunged past him, arms out like an airplane, and flung herself in front of him. "You can't leave now," she gasped, bracing her back on the door. Her chest heaved with exertion, and he forced himself not to look at the way her breasts were spilling out of her dress. "Just trust me on that. It's OK, OK? Totally OK. Better than OK. Great."

"If you still feel that way tomorrow, and I really, really hope you do—"

"No!" Her eyes widened with panic. "I mean, I will. Yes. If you still, I mean after we... oh, God. I should've told you before. Now I can't. But I have to."

"Told me what?"

She pushed part of her dress off her shoulder again and reached behind her back to undo the zipper. "First I'll strip. Then we'll do it. After that, I'll tell you everything."

He strode forward and caught her hands in his wrists, pinning her to the door. "Nobody's stripping."

With a choked giggle, she went limp and dropped her head, hiding her face behind a curtain of shimmering blond hair. After a tense silence, during which he tried to release her wrists but couldn't make himself, she said, "But I want to."

He looked away, drawing her scent into his lungs. "I have to go."

"Please," she said, and then her voice dropped, suddenly cool and sober. "This isn't alcohol doing this to me. I wish it were."

What game was she playing now? He didn't release her, afraid of what she might do. "I'm listening."

She didn't lift her head. "I'm nervous."

Hope began pounding in his chest. Some parts of him

softened; other parts, quite the opposite. "Don't be," he said softly.

"I haven't... it's been a long time."

He knew she hadn't dated anyone more than a few times since the divorce. "I understand." He stepped closer so their bodies were touching. But he couldn't let go of her hands.

"A really long time," she whispered.

After a deep breath, he kissed the top of her head. "Nobody since Dylan?"

She shook her head.

Moving closer, he breathed in a lungful of her perfume. "We'll go slow."

She nodded.

He caressed the pulse in her wrist with his thumb, glad she couldn't see him smile. The silence between them became tighter, more pleasurable. "I understand," he said.

"You... don't quite. God. This is embarrassing." Finally, she lifted her head, bumping it against the door, and looked into his eyes. "I've never been very good at this."

He brushed his lips across the soft hairs at her temple. "I'll be the judge of—"

"Not before Dylan and not after." She leaned away from him and caught his gaze. "Listen to what I'm saying. Please."

The tone of her voice broke through his renewed lust. Belatedly, the implications sank in. "You've never slept with anyone else?"

She closed her eyes with a long exhale and nodded.

"Never?" He couldn't believe it. "What about in college? I dropped out, but you were there for, what, six years—"

"Tease me and I'll kill you."

The arguing, the giggling, the inconsistent behavior all made sense now. "I wish you'd told me."

"You wouldn't understand."

"Sure I would."

"With all those girlfriends, so many years, a grown man like you?" She leaned into him, pressing her breasts against his chest. Her voice dropped to a throaty whisper. "How could you possibly?"

"I would try." He pushed her against the door, pinning her soft, sexy body under his. "Really, really hard."

Their rapid breathing filled the silence.

"That's what I was hoping," she said quietly.

Oh, baby. He released one of her wrists to caress her arm, her cheek, the silky skin where the fabric of her dress arched over her shoulder. "Kiss me, Cleo. I'm dying here."

"I'm not stopping you."

"Show me you want it." He released her other hand, lowered both of his arms to his sides. "Show me you want me."

Nibbling her lip, where the hint of a smile threatened, she put her hands on his chest, splayed her fingers, and went still. "I don't know what I'm doing. I don't have any moves."

"I'm very patient."

She licked her lips. The smile was gone. "Thank God." She went up on tiptoe and kissed him like a grandmother at church. Closed lips, no tongue, tipping forward at the waist.

"Come on," he said.

"Hey, I warned you."

"Kiss me like you did in the limo."

"I was kidding." She cleared her throat. "And, yes, a little drunk."

"Do it or I'm out of here."

She stepped closer. "You couldn't bear to leave me. You want me too much."

"That was good. Now say it without laughing."

"I can't."

In spite of himself, he thought about opening the champagne. "How about if I close my eyes? One little kiss, like you mean it, and then I'll give you what you want."

"A pony?"

He made a growling sound in the back of his throat.

"Sorry, sorry," she said, throwing her head back and inhaling like a woman about to sing the national anthem at opening day of the World Series without a mic. "OK. Ready. Close 'em."

He closed his eyes.

Cleo waited a moment before stepping close and lifting her hand to Sly's cheek. His jaw felt warm and firm, very real. Alive. It wasn't a fantasy or a dream. She was awake. She dragged her thumb across his lower lip, enchanted with the way he sucked in a breath but didn't move to take over. With growing confidence, she leaned in and dropped kisses along his neck, breathing heavily along his skin, licking the shadow of his jawline while her hands splayed out on his stomach and began to explore.

Being a virgin would've been worse, she told herself. Much worse. Until the miserable discovery of Dylan's cheating, she would've said they'd had a good sex life. If she could just forget how painfully she'd learned otherwise, she could enjoy this night with Sly. If she could just forget how Dylan had faked his satisfaction, his pleasure, his desire...

She moved her hand down over the bulge in Sly's pants. He shuddered.

"You want this?" she asked, hating herself for needing to hear it again but unable to resist.

Before she took her next breath, he captured her face in his hands. His nose brushed hers, but he didn't kiss her. Hot current snapped between them.

Then he released her. "Last chance," he said in a low voice, staring at her.

She flung her arms around his neck and pressed her mouth against his, sloppy but heartfelt, just wanting to feel and taste him. Her heart was beating too fast, and the lack of oxygen going to her brain made her dizzy, but she gave the kiss everything she had, fondness and desire, love and lust, and knocked him off-balance so badly he fell against the wall.

Not stopping then, even though he had to throw his arms out to either side to keep himself from hitting the floor, she gripped his face in her hands and kissed him deeper. Openmouthed, with tongue, breasts pressing against his chest. Everything she had.

He staggered a little and then put his arms around her, encouraging her, taking it all and demanding more. She felt his hands at her waist, stroking her curves, exploring her belly and her hips and the small of her back. And then he spun her around and pushed her back against the wall. His knee forced her legs apart. Now she was the one off-balance, reaching for support, trying not to fall.

"Cleo," he said in her ear, his voice giving her shivers. "Cleo."

"Don't say my name."

"What? Why?"

"Pretend I'm someone else," she said. "Then I can too."

He reached around and pulled the zipper down her back. Fabric slid down her torso, exposing her upper body. She felt chilly air-conditioned air, then his warm hands. "And who am I?"

Her thoughts were too splintered to understand. "Hmm?"

"Are you imagining I'm somebody else, too?"

Shaking her head, she unbuttoned his shirt from top to

bottom, exposing his chest so she could bury her face in him, inhale his scent, and kiss his skin. There was nobody else she wanted to think about.

"Are you sure?"

She wrapped her arms around his waist and gazed up at him. "Very."

"What about"—he shoved her dress to the floor—"the pizza guy? With the tattoo?"

His own clothes were harder to remove, but she was a piano player and had agile fingers. In three seconds, his pants were around his ankles and his shirt rested on the floor. She admired his erection pushing through his boxers. "Take off your shoes."

With a grin, he kicked them off. "I like your bossy side."

"Same here."

"Really?"

She traced a circle around his nipple, loving the way it hardened under her touch. "Ah. Yeah."

His fingers came around her wrist in an iron grip. He brought her hand to his mouth, isolated a finger, and sucked it between his lips. The sensation of teeth and suction and tongue made her knees weak.

"Good," he said. Still holding her wrist, he pulled her with him into the suite, past the doorway to the bedroom, down the steps into the living room, and then over to the floor-to-ceiling glass overlooking Las Vegas. There he stopped to kiss her hard on the mouth before opening the sliding doors and pushing her onto the balcony.

She turned back to the interior, suddenly aware of what he was doing. At the moment she was still wearing a bra and panties, but that wasn't going to last long.

He moved quickly, blocking the doorway. "Nobody will be

able to see you. We're on the top floor."

"They can see me right now." She flung out her arms. It was hard to care if anyone could see her in a bra that was more modest than most bikinis, but soon she'd be completely exposed... doing things with this unbelievably gorgeous guy...

Oh, God. The thought was making her hot.

"I've got a plan." He kissed her shoulder before jogging back inside, grabbing the back cushions on the sofa, hauling them out onto the balcony, and flinging them down.

"But—"

He knelt at her feet, stroked her through the panties, then hooked his fingers over the waistband and jerked them down her hips. With a cry, she looked wildly around for spectators, seeing millions of potential eyes in the windows of other hotels, the open streets below, the balconies to either side.

And then she pushed aside the rest of the world.

There was only him.

She leaned back against the solid balcony railing, about hip-height, and concentrated on keeping her legs from buckling beneath her as he buried his face between her legs.

He was good. Maybe he hadn't spent any effort on practicing the piano, but he'd clearly put a few hours into this lovely skill. She didn't want to think about how many hours, or with whom.

"Oh, God," she said, her throat tightening.

His strong fingers spread her wider. She tried not to think of all the times she'd seen those same fingers holding his phone, pushing the buttons on the TV remote, driving a car. Because now they were touching her, in her, claiming her in a way she'd never let herself imagine. Every one of her nerves sang with erotic, forbidden excitement.

Sly, her old friend, was licking her between her legs. And she wanted him to do it.

She'd die if he stopped.

His tongue slid deeper. Breathing heavily, with her elbows braced on the railing, she looked wildly over her shoulder at the city. Its energy poured into her, pushing her higher.

His hair tickled the skin of her inner thighs. When she put her hand on the top of his head to encourage him—to make sure he didn't stop—he grabbed her ass with both hands and rewarded her with another long, hard stroke of his tongue.

Was it wrong to compare his technique to her ex-husband's? Was there some ethical or psychological reason she shouldn't acknowledge how much more she was enjoying this than she'd ever enjoyed it before?

His head lifted. Cool air brushed her wet flesh.

"Let go," Sly said in a low voice as his hands continued to stroke her ass, her thighs. "Cleo. I've got you. Let go."

"I'm really," she gasped, "enjoying this. You're very talented."

"You're delicious. And so beautiful. Stop thinking." He trailed kisses along her inner thighs, blowing air across the moist flesh—which had excited her a moment earlier but now was painfully inadequate.

She arched her hips to show him where she wanted him to be. "Stop talking."

With a low rumble of laughter, he lowered his face again into the aching spot between her legs and got back to work.

Now she let herself think about all their mundane, ordinary moments together. It excited her to imagine him wanting her all this time, to think about how this handsome, high-profile friend of hers was now on his knees before her, worshipping her body, both of them primal and exposed.

One of his fingers drove between her folds and touched her

somewhere deep and unexpected. With a strangled cry, she shattered and rocketed up into the stars. The dark night and bright lights pushed and pulled at her, spinning her senseless out of herself. She hadn't expected to come so quickly but here she was, broken and soaring.

Just as she hit the sky, she had a moment of perfect clarity. She saw herself, she saw Sly, she saw the universe and their place in it. They were nobody important, but they were in the heart of the world.

21

CLEO HAD NEVER been alive like this before.

And then he was there, holding her shoulders and guiding her down onto the cushions. Legs trembling, she let him help her. They faced each other on their knees, gazing into each other's eyes. Still dazed from her climax, she clung to him and waited for her pulse to return to a manageable rate.

"Christ, Cleo," he said roughly. "Or whoever you are. You're beautiful when you come."

Not wasting time on words, she caught the waistband of his shorts and pulled them down his hips.

Oh, my. Her pulse never had a chance.

As a general principle, she always tried to avoid judging another person's body, especially their most intimate parts, but...

Lord, he was beautiful. All over. And there was a lot of all over.

"Hello," she said, reaching out to feel him. Never looking away from his face, she wrapped her fingers around him. His nostrils flared. High on power, she slowly tightened her grip. With a groan, he tilted his head back, exposing the muscles of his neck. It reminded her of when he'd fall asleep on her couch in front of the TV, except now he was throbbing in her hand.

She had to kiss him. "Sly," she whispered, burying her face in his chest and inhaling as she stroked. His hair was springy under her tongue, thick the way she liked it, damp with sweat. She nibbled a strand between her teeth and heard him suck in a sudden, pained breath.

"Did I hurt you?" she asked, drawing back.

"You're killing me." He pushed her away and onto the cushions. "I can't wait any longer. God knows I've been patient." He slid an arm under her legs and tipped her onto her back. The padded fabric was soft under her bottom and shoulders, reminding her she was naked. He climbed on top of her, ducking his head to kiss her hard on the mouth. "God knows," he growled against her lips.

Fresh desire exploded inside her. All at once, she felt the years of deprivation, the nights alone. All at once, she recognized the longing she'd had for him when she'd sat at his side, laughed with him, enjoyed his company. Now she let the lust engulf her. She spread her legs and hooked her ankles around his hips, drinking in the feel of his bare skin sliding along hers. She explored the contours of his lean, muscled body with both hands. Licking his nipple until it hardened under her mouth, she knew she was losing control and didn't care. "I want you inside me," she said. "Sly. I want you."

"I'm working on it, beautiful," he said, pushing away from her. A foil packet appeared in his hands. He fumbled with it, breathing heavily. "Stupid thing won't open."

"I'll do it."

"Got it." He tossed the foil aside. "My hands were shaking. Good thing I'm not a surgeon."

"You can play doctor on me anytime."

Anytime.

He looked at her in surprise, a slow grin spreading across his face. "I'm glad to hear that."

She wouldn't think about the implied lack of an expiration date on her offer. *From now on*, she was saying, *I'm yours.*

City lights shimmered across his dark, muscled torso as he put on the condom. She reached up and caressed the trail of hair dusting his abdomen. How could somebody so perfect ever…?

She wouldn't think about it. *I don't care about what happens after tonight*, she told herself, *so long as I can have him right now.*

Dropping her hand, she leaned back and watched him stroke himself as his gaze slid up and down her body. Heat blasted through her. What did he see? Heart pounding, she let her legs fall open and waited, letting go of the last of her fear.

His eyes were hungry but gentle. Loving. They'd cared about each other for a long time, but this…

He climbed on top of her and pressed his mouth against hers in a hard, openmouthed kiss. Their tongues came together, rushed and tangled, as his hands explored her body. One hand claimed her breast, the other dove between her legs. Kissing his way down her neck to nuzzle and lick her other breast, he forced her legs wider apart and settled between them.

Her back arched, inviting him, wanting him, demanding him. "Now, Sly, do it."

His hand stroked her wetness. "You want me?" His voice was low and ragged.

She nodded her head, unable to breathe.

"I want you," he said. "I want you really bad."

"Take me. For God's sake, take me."

Bracing himself on one elbow, he positioned himself and looked into her eyes. "Say my name."

She slid her hands up and down his muscled back, frantic for him to enter her. "Sly," she whispered. "Please."

Closing his eyes, he thrust into her with a loud exhale. She cried out, not expecting so much pressure all at once, but the pain quickly turned into intense, sweet heaven.

"Cleo, God, Cleo," he moaned, pulling out, thrusting again harder. She rose up to meet him and take him deeper, and they fell into a frenzied rhythm, perfectly in sync, their cheeks pressed against each other, then their lips, their tongues, matching the pace of their hips.

He came with a shout. She held his face in her hands and watched him wonderingly for a second before she felt her own body join him.

22

SHE WAS GONE.

The curtains were open, and the dawn light shining into the suite left Sly no doubt that he was alone.

He fell back on the bed, a wave of unease washing over him.

Last night, after the first spike of triumph he'd felt after finally having her, another feeling had crept up on him and taken hold in the front of his thoughts. Well, after he'd had his fill of her and he'd had any thoughts worthy of the name.

Fear. Where was this going to go? Were they dating, like he and Teresa had—a few months or a year of shared meals, social events, and a bed and then, finally, a breakup?

Or were they just friends with benefits, just great pals who got naked and had great sex while the rest of their life happened elsewhere, later?

Were they even friends at all?

He'd pursued her because that's what he always did after setting his sights on something. He was a goal-oriented guy. Because of his persistence, he'd made a fortune and a name for himself by his early thirties. He'd never been the type to give up just because it was hard or even question the decision to go for something in the first place. During the pursuit, you couldn't question yourself or you'd make excuses and succumb to failure. He'd decided he was going to prove to Cleo that this attraction lurked between them and he had.

Now what?

Now he couldn't breathe. He felt like Frank Sinatra himself was standing on his chest, using him as a stage, grinding him into the empty bed with his well-shined shoes. He should be relieved that she'd probably run away to the other room, maybe even to the airport, and saved them both from an agonizingly awkward morning after.

But he wasn't relieved. He was having a panic attack. She couldn't leave him again. He had to—

"Look what I found." Cleo stood in the bedroom doorway with a wheeled cart laden with covered plates, a white vase with a single red rose, coffeepot and cups, various cutlery, and the paper. "They left it at our front door. I could get used to this." She lifted a strawberry as big as a plum and admired it for a moment before sliding it between her lips.

The air rushed back into his lungs. He sat up to drink in the sight of her in a hotel robe, barefoot, with her blond hair cascading down her shoulders and her cheeks flushed.

Thank God. His relief made him dizzy.

And then another emotion struck him: lust.

He jumped out of bed and strode over to her, catching her in a kiss before she'd swallowed the strawberry. With a choked laugh, then a gulp, she returned the kiss, a little more cautiously than he'd hoped.

She tasted better than a ripe berry. "Morning," he said, then kissed her again while he unfastened the belt of her robe and pulled her against him, reuniting their bodies, skin against skin.

"Did you order this?" she asked.

He made a show of looking down at her body. Cupping her breast in his palm, he smiled and nodded. "I did, but I wasn't sure it would come."

"Oh, she came all right." Smiling, she flushed and tried to pull away.

He held her. Her bottom was soft and yielding under his roving hands. When she sighed, high-pitched and erotic, he moved his hands up to her shoulders and pushed the robe down, making her as naked as he was but far more beautiful.

His breath caught. "Look at you," he whispered.

"I'd rather look at you," she said, sighing again. "I'm tempted to take pictures for later."

"I'm game." He grinned.

"God, just what my career needs. When people search online for piano teachers, they'll get me. Butt naked."

"Not that I'd upload the pictures," he said, raising his voice when she squawked in protest, "but if I did, you'd see a surge in business."

"The kind that uses little cards to hand out on the Strip."

"No, no. You'd be teaching piano, just... in the buff. I'd find it quite inspiring. I might even practice." Slipping his hand between her legs, he lowered his voice. "I'd practice all the time. Every hour. Every day. Over and over and over, as hard as I could. Thinking about how to make my teacher happy."

"With one hand, you mean."

"There's a lot you can do with one hand." Gently, he explored with his fingers, wiggling as if on the keys.

"Mmm," she said, melting into him. "Practice makes perfect."

He lowered his head and kissed the side of her neck, nibbling softly and blowing against the damp skin while his hand stroked and circled between her legs.

When her knees buckled, he guided her onto the bed, pushed her onto her back, swallowing her sighs with his mouth, and climbed on top of her, suddenly desperate to make love to her again as soon as possible.

His phone buzzed. He ignored it, kissing his way down her throat to her breast and pulling a nipple into his mouth. Her body arched beneath him, responsive and welcoming, and he didn't hear anything other than the little moans in her throat after that.

Until a few moments later, when he was feeling her other nipple pebble under his tongue, the phone began ringing again.

"Answer it or turn it off," she said, running her hands through his hair. "Please."

He let out a frustrated sigh, rose, and staggered over to his pants. "Sorry," he said to her, slapping at the fabric for the offending device. Why the hell hadn't he turned it off last night? Or thrown it out a window?

Hugo's face was on the screen.

"What?" Sly barked.

But it was Trixie who answered. "We need your help. You and Cleo."

"We're busy." Sly cleared his throat. "Sorry, but we are."

"What kind of busy?" Trixie asked. But she didn't sound like her playful, impish self. More serious.

"Just sitting down to breakfast," he said.

"So you're up," she said. "We need you to meet us here."

Cleo was watching him with a questioning expression.

"I'm very sorry, but it'll have to wait," he said. "We're about to eat." He flashed Cleo a wolfish grin.

"We'll eat together," Trixie said. "Please."

"We could do that, but it'll have to be later." His gaze took in Cleo, deliciously ready on the bed from her beautiful head to her lovely toes. "Two hours." He tilted his head to get a better angle. "Maybe three."

"We need you now. It's about to start." Trixie began talking away from the phone.

Suddenly it was Hugo talking. "We're getting married, and she wants you as witnesses," he said. Then he cleared his throat. "I'd rather like it if you came as well. I've texted you the name of the place. Get here as soon as you can."

Sly helped Cleo out of the taxi, not believing they were standing in front of a bubblegum-pink building with a drive-through window, flashing neon lights, and architecture painfully reminiscent of a Taco Bell. They should be back in bed at the hotel.

"It's not too late," he said. "We can talk them out of it."

"Why?"

He frowned at her, surprised. Given her messy divorce, she was the last person he would've thought would approve of a rushed marriage. "Because, until yesterday, Trixie was only pretending to like Hugo for our sakes?"

"She's not pretending. I think she really likes him. She must. Look where we are."

He raised an eyebrow. "*This* convinces you? The Taco Chapel?"

"Why are you so upset? Hugo's been in love with her for years." She looked around for the entrance, then saw something in the front window and clapped her hands together. "He's here!"

"Alone, hopefully. It's going to break his heart when Trixie wants an annulment next week."

"Not Hugo," she said, patting his arm. "Elvis."

"I hate Elvis."

She gaped at him. "What's the matter with you?"

"The same thing that should be the matter with you," he grumbled.

Grabbing his hand, she led him to the front door, which was painted gold and covered with faded plastic flowers. "You just didn't get enough sleep last night."

"I got the same as you."

"You did more of the work," she said, shooting him a naughty smile that made him resent his uncle even more. They could be in bed at that very minute, not walking into a converted fast-food joint to greet a white-suited Elvis impersonator holding a ukulele.

Sly groaned inwardly. Cleo would never criticize any event that featured a ukulele. They'd probably end up getting married themselves.

He tripped over something on the carpet. Looking down, he saw his own feet and nothing else. But he paused a moment to calm himself, recognizing he was upset.

Of course he and Cleo weren't going to get married, ukulele or no. He glanced at Cleo. She wouldn't want to. Not today, not for a long, long time.

The queasiness that had come over him when he'd woken in an empty bed settled over him again.

Cleo might not be able to imagine settling down again, but *he* didn't mind the idea of living together for an extended, indefinite period...

Which only made his stomach clench more tightly. The idea *should* be unthinkable. Minguez men made terrible husbands. He cared too much about her to inflict his innate workaholic nature on someone as sensitive and affectionate as she was. She deserved a guy who cared more about her than his career, a guy who woke her every morning with a kiss and went to bed with her in his arms. Every woman he'd ever dated had complained about how often he'd been in a different time zone. You couldn't Skype your marriage.

He wouldn't do that to her. But he could help her get over her first husband so that she'd be ready for the right guy when he came along. They'd already crossed the line. There was no going back. Might as well get as much out of it, within reason, as they could.

Trixie rushed over from a side door. She wore an ivory peasant dress and had flowers—real ones, not plastic—pinned in her hair. "You made it. Thank you. We want to get it over with before I change my mind."

"If you think you might—" Sly began.

Hugo smacked him on the shoulder. "Did you bring the ring?"

"What ring?" Sly asked, startled to think that he'd screwed up somehow. Then sanity reasserted itself. "Of course I didn't bring a ring. I didn't know you were getting married."

"I told you an hour ago." Hugo reached down and captured Sly's right hand. "Don't worry, you've got it. I'll get you a new one later." He began unscrewing the heavy gold band that Sly wore on his third finger. It had come to him after his grandfather's death several years earlier.

"Dad's not going to be happy," Sly said. "He'd wanted me to have that."

Hugo's voice dropped low enough that only the two of them could hear it. "I need it more than you. Your grandparents were married for over sixty years. I'm going to need all the luck I can get."

"And I don't?"

"You're not the marrying kind," Hugo said.

Although his uncle's words echoed his own thoughts, Sly was annoyed. "I don't know that."

"Trixie will be glad to hear it." With a low chuckle, Hugo turned Sly's hand over and pressed his grandfather's ring, as well as a smaller one, into his palm. "Hold onto these until the big moment."

"You're seriously doing this?"

"I sure as hell hope so." His craggy face split into a smile. "But not seriously. We've got Elvis."

Trixie was talking to Cleo. "I'm so glad we'll have music for the ceremony. He usually plays guitar, but I asked for the uke. As a thank-you to my maid of honor." Trixie smiled, but it was strained.

They couldn't let them go through with this. Sly tried to catch Cleo's eye, but she was staring at Elvis, who was strumming the ukulele and singing "Let's Get This Party Started."

"That one's so seldom attributed to the King," Cleo said.

"Well, none of this will be quite the way I might've done it if I weren't in such a hurry," Trixie said, pushing back her shoulders. "We'll have to make the best of it."

Sly raised his voice. "But why do it now? If you love Hu—"

Hugo hit him again. When Sly spun on him, his uncle replied, "There was a scorpion on your shoulder. It's dangerous here in the desert."

"Right," Sly said, rubbing the point of impact. Years of handling unruly pets had given Hugo quick impulses.

"Let's get this party started," Hugo said. "Right, sugar?"

"We're not getting any younger." Trixie marched forward a few steps, then looked over her shoulder at Hugo, who'd frozen in place. "Change your mind already? I've got a flask in my purse if you need a little more courage. I just had a hit myself."

Hugo met Sly's pained glance, shrugged, and jogged over to Trixie. "I'll save mine for the honeymoon." He held out his arm. "Shall we?"

A fortysomething showgirl with stunning legs, a feather boa, and a clipboard appeared behind the altar and picked up a microphone. "Dearly beloved, are you ready?"

"You all go up there," Trixie told them. "Elvis is going to walk me down the aisle. It's part of the package."

Elvis, giving her a playful, characteristic sneer, joined Trixie, and before Sly could stop them, Hugo and Cleo walked to the altar and turned, waiting for the arrival of the bride.

"Come on," Cleo mouthed to him.

What else could he do? With a shrug, he trotted down the narrow aisle past the flimsy fiberboard pews and stood next to Hugo. "You aren't really going to do this, are you?" he muttered.

"Wait until you hear him. He's really good." Hugo spoke as if the event's musical accompaniment had been Sly's primary objection.

"Mark's going to kill me," Sly said. "Letting his mom marry you without even a phone call."

"You can call. Just wait a few minutes." Hugo's smile stretched from ear to ear.

"What if she regrets this and hates you?"

"She won't," Hugo said calmly. "It was all her idea."

Sly was going to continue to argue with him, but Elvis began to sing "Can't Help Falling in Love," and somehow, impossibly, the campy atmosphere turned serious.

The guy was actually good. His voice was rich and powerful, and even his playing on the ukulele seemed flawless. Sly saw Cleo's eyebrows rise in admiration.

Fools rush in, he thought. Hugo had waited almost twenty

years to marry again. Was it really a rush?

Sly decided to let it go. If they wanted to do this, it was their own business. To show Cleo he wasn't going to cause any more trouble, he turned to her with a smile, and then was shocked to see her biting her lip, a tear streaming down her cheek. She didn't see him, only Elvis and Trixie, who were walking at a snail's pace up the aisle during the song.

Her sweetness touched him. She really was a softhearted person for all the sarcastic attitude she flung around.

Elvis handed Trixie over to Hugo, who was also overcome with emotion. His deep-set dark eyes were shining with unshed tears as he took Trixie's hand in his and turned to the altar. Elvis finished his song, greeting everyone in the traditional manner, and asked if anyone had any objections to the marriage.

Sly felt Cleo's gaze turn to him. He glanced at Hugo, saw him wipe away a tear, and kept silent.

The speedy vows centered on loving each other tenderly, not being cruel, and promising to avoid Heartbreak Hotel.

He couldn't believe this was really happening.

Then they exchanged rings, Elvis proclaimed they were married and couldn't be returned to sender, and they kissed.

"I'm all shook up," Elvis declared, lifting the ukulele. "Join me in welcoming the married hunk and hunkette of burning love, Hugo and Trixie."

The speakers began blaring "Viva Las Vegas." Elvis and the showgirl belted out the lyrics while Hugo took Trixie in his arms and danced her down the aisle.

Cleo and Sly, clapping along but not dancing, stared at each other.

"They really did it," Cleo said, her blue eyes like saucers.

Sly took her hand and pulled her into his arms. A light show had begun, flashing in time to the music. "Yeah." He wondered if his parents were going to be annoyed he'd let it happen. In their family, weddings usually involved several hundred people, international flights, and five days of celebration. Hugo's decision to elope wasn't entirely because of his fear Trixie would change her mind. He probably wanted to avoid all the fuss.

The singing and dancing led to signing legal documents, giggles and hugs, generous tips, a few package-approved photographs, and a hurried exit to the parking lot. Another group, all in Hawaiian shirts and bikinis, were waiting for their turn, and they traded smiles and high fives as they passed.

Tucked under Hugo's arm, Trixie was back to her old self again, relaxed and cheerful, her eyes twinkling with amusement. "That was perfect." She turned to Cleo and Hugo. "Don't you think? No wonder he was the best-selling solo artist in the history of recorded music. I read that on Wikipedia."

"We're lucky he's nice enough to marry people now," Hugo said.

"I really felt his spirit in there," Cleo said. "Gave me chills."

"I had chills, but that was just nerves." Trixie gave Hugo a bear hug. "I'm better now. Sometimes you just have to hold on and jump."

Over Trixie's flower-clad head, Hugo beamed at the world and said nothing.

Trixie went up on tiptoe for another long kiss that went on and on. Cleo snapped a few pictures and even turned to take a selfie with them in the background.

Breaking the kiss, Trixie turned to them. "Now we have to ask for that favor."

23

CLEO SCROLLED THROUGH the pictures she'd just taken, deleting the bad ones, only vaguely aware of what Trixie had just said. Standing in the parking lot was a bit of a letdown after the Elvis revue, and she put a hand over her mouth to cover a yawn.

"Favor?" she heard Sly ask sharply.

"This wasn't it," Hugo said. "Although we do appreciate you coming."

"Thanks for inviting us," Cleo said. She was sincere, although the busy night before was catching up to her. Gravity was pulling at her eyelids, inviting her to rest.

"This is about the dogs," Trixie said. "We'd like to travel a few days before we go home."

"A full week, darling," Hugo said. "You deserve a real honeymoon."

"Would you be able to watch our fur babies? It would be best if you stayed in the house. My house, I mean our house, since Hugo has agreed to live there, even though he's never been upstairs."

Sly's voice was wary. "Are you asking me or Cleo?"

"Both of you, of course," Trixie said. "You spent the night together, right? But everything happened so fast, you don't know how it's going to be when you get back home. Staying at my house will give you a little time to figure it out."

"Please," Hugo said. "If she thinks she's playing matchmaker, she won't feel so guilty about leaving the dogs for another few days."

Trixie turned to Hugo with a flushed, melting smile. "Am I that obvious?"

In response, Hugo cupped her cheek and kissed her on the lips. Sly glanced at Cleo and smiled.

He's a nice guy, she thought, going all squishy inside. *For an alpha mogul, he's quite the sweetheart.*

Trixie broke the kiss and said somewhat breathlessly, "Mark's room has the best bed since it wasn't that long ago that he was living there, but maybe that would be a little awkward."

Cleo couldn't think of what to say. She was too busy wondering what excuse Sly was going to come up with.

"Liam's old room is set up for guests," Trixie continued. "The mattress is only a double, but since you've just gotten together, you'll probably like being on top of each other."

Elvis's melodious warbling reached them from inside the chapel. Another wedding had begun. The sun was still low in the sky but shimmered brightly over the tile roof. At that moment, reality as she'd known it felt very far away.

"I'd be happy to stay at the house with the dogs," Cleo blurted. The entire weekend had been one crazy impulse after another. "My wedding gift to you."

"Wonderful! Of course you can use the piano as much as you'd like." Trixie handed her a set of keys on a Chihuahua-shaped fob. "Liam and Bev have been watching my babies this weekend, but they have to go to work tomorrow. And they've got a human baby. I didn't want to impose. Not with Mouse too."

"Isn't he at the vet clinic?" Sly asked.

"Bella wouldn't mind keeping him another—" Hugo began, but Trixie patted him on the chest.

"No," she said. "He can't spend another day there. He's going to be living at the house and should get to know it as soon as possible."

"Even if you're not there?" Sly asked.

"Why not? It might be better if the changes happen in stages. Stage one, the house and other dogs. Stage two, all of us together." Trixie cast an appealing look at Sly, then at Cleo. "Are you willing to do that? He's a doll. A gentle giant."

"Why not?" Cleo wasn't in any hurry to go back to her old life just yet, since she didn't know how Sly was going to fit into it, if at all. "The more the merrier."

"I'll give you Bella's number," Hugo said. "Let her know whenever you're settled, and she'll bring him by."

Trixie threw her arms around Cleo. "Thank you. I was going to invite you both to breakfast, but I think you'd rather get back into bed. To sleep this time." She released Cleo, pinched Sly's cheek, and returned to Hugo's side.

Dragging Trixie with him, Hugo shook their hands and thanked them a few more times. "Viva Las Vegas," he said finally, offering a lopsided grin, and soon they were climbing into the rental car, then smiling out the window as they drove away.

"Congratulations!" Cleo shouted, waving at the taillights. Too bad they hadn't had time to put on any streamers. She waved again. What a crazy weekend.

Sly put an arm around her shoulders and turned her around. "Our ride's here too."

They climbed into a taxi, and Cleo removed a piece of stiff paper from her pocket that was digging into her thigh. Reminded of what it was, she smiled and started to put it into her purse.

"What's that?" Sly asked.

Cleo waved the postcard. "It's Elvis's card. He was really good. Much better than I expected."

"You took his card? For the wedding chapel?"

"I didn't want to forget his name."

"Just in case you needed an Elvis impersonator to marry you?"

"You never know," she said with a laugh. When he didn't join in, her humor drained out of her. "What's the matter?"

He looked away and traced the door handle with a long, lean index finger. Reminded of last night, sexual awareness shivered through her.

"They're really married," he said. "Now we're the ones who have to face the music while they avoid reality for a week."

"No problem. I'm a musician," she said, smiling again. "I love facing music."

"It might be OK for you—you're not close to any of them. I've got my parents and sisters and cousins to answer to, not to mention Mark and her other kids."

"Then I'll stay there by myself. I'm the one who volunteered."

He held her gaze for a moment, then put a hand on her thigh. Another shiver rippled over her. "You aren't getting rid of me that easily," he said, drawing a circle on her flesh with his thumb. Finally a smile curved the corners of his mouth, but he didn't say anything more.

"I didn't expect you to give up a week of your life for Trixie's dogs," she said.

"I'm not." He nuzzled her neck. "I'm giving it up for you."

Closing her eyes, she leaned into his touch, trying not to think about anything but how wonderful the tip of his nose felt against her pulse point. Nothing was the same and the future was unknown, but they couldn't figure everything out now.

When they got to the hotel, Sly began taking off her clothes as soon as the door closed behind them. But when they fell onto the bed, the feel of the expensive sheets against her bare skin reminded her of how tired she was, of how little sleep she'd had the night before, and she yawned like a cat. "I'm so sorry, but I'm not up for anything right now. I need to sleep for a little bit."

Kissing her neck, he ran a hand down her belly and stroked her inner thighs. "Your skin is so soft. I had no idea skin could be so soft."

His matter-of-fact tone sent shivers down her spine. "Really, Sly, I'm warning you. I'm too tired to do anything but just lie here."

She felt his hand capture her breast. Intense pleasure-pain struck her as he sucked her nipple into his mouth. After a long moment, he lifted his head and murmured, "I don't have a problem with that."

Her body melted under him, tingling and limp, apparently more than happy to passively accept his attentions.

"Guess there are *some* advantages to sleeping with a workaholic," she said sleepily.

"Glad you're finally catching on." He grabbed her hips and abruptly rolled her over.

Jolted by his strength—she wasn't easily flipped—she lifted her head. "What are you—?"

Climbing on top of her, he brushed her hair aside and nibbled on her ear. "I noticed you like to sleep on your stomach," he said in a low voice. His erection brushed her back, then her exposed bottom.

"I'm not sure I'm up for—"

"I'm up so you don't have to be." He reached between her legs and stroked her wet heat. "But this might feel better. Lift your hips."

"What? Why?"

"Pillow." His teeth gently bit down on her earlobe. Then he spanked her ass. "Up."

"Sly—"

Somehow he hooked an arm under her and lifted her hips off the bed a few inches. Warming to the idea—burning up, actually —she braced her weight on her forearms and arched her back, high enough for him to shove a pillow beneath her pelvis. "Up," she said.

He stroked her bottom with large, strong hands. "God, Cleo," he said, his voice strained. "Your ass is unbelievable."

She'd thought the same thing for years, but not quite with the same admiration. "Shopping for jeans is a bitch."

He slid his erection between the cleft of her bottom, each of his hands caressing the flesh to either side. Then he moved one hand around her hips and lifted her again while the other slipped between her legs and spread her apart. He entered her with a single thrust.

She let out a strangled groan. The sensation of him filling her was more intense than the night before, so intense she wasn't sure she could take all of him. He drew back slowly, then thrust again. Deep inside, her body began to sing, ache, and beg for more.

She was wide-awake now.

His weight came down on her, pressing what little air she had left out of her lungs. In spite of being pinned beneath his body, she was able to tilt her hips up to meet him in a position that gave her the most pleasure. Almost too much pleasure. It was almost too much. She felt tears forming in the corners of her eyes.

"You're so sexy," he said, his lips against her temple. "I want you, Cleo. I've wanted you for so long."

She arched her back, inviting him deeper. "Take me, take me," she gasped.

"Oh, I will." He pushed into her. "You're mine, Cleo. Mine."

"God," she gasped. "Don't stop. Whatever you're doing, don't stop."

"You're going to come for me, aren't you?" He slipped his hand beneath her and found the small, hard center of her desire. His voice fell. "Aren't you?"

Words failed her. Openmouthed, she clung to the mattress and let go of her mind.

"Aren't you?" he asked.

"Yes, yes," she said, barely able to make a sound.

He pressed into her from below and behind, and the tightness exploded. She closed her eyes and cried out as the current rippled through her.

He pounded into her, going deep, hard, fast. Then, with a shout, he shuddered into her, his fingers never letting her go.

They slept until they had to pack, check out of both rooms, and go to the airport. There, waiting at the gate for their flight, she lost all her winnings from the day before in the slots. She didn't care. The shimmering sexual afterglow prevented her from minding anything. And a budding hope for a future she'd never let herself think about. Her and Sly. Not just one night, not just one weekend, but from now on.

Unwillingly, she wondered what a child of theirs might look like. Fair or dark, round or lean—it would be fun to find out.

Fun. Sure. Just fun. Not heartbreakingly wonderful.

They landed in San Francisco around seven thirty that night. Sly drove her to her apartment, then parked and escorted her upstairs to her door. For a moment, Cleo felt uncomfortable. They'd kissed on the plane and indulged in a little groping on the Bay Bridge, but they were entering familiar territory now. Her apartment, where they watched TV and teased each other about bad taste in beer.

She unlocked her door and pushed it open.

"I can't wait to make out on that couch with you," Sly said. "We've got a lot of catching up to do."

"Too bad we don't have time tonight."

"Too bad." He brushed his lips across her cheekbone. "Do you have Trixie's keys?"

She took them out of her purse.

"You don't have to stay there." He grabbed the keys and held them against his chest. "Really, if you go back far enough, I'm the one who got you into this. I'll do it."

"We'll stay there together." She tried to liberate the keys, but his grip was too strong.

"You don't have to."

"I said I would. I like dogs. It'll be fun."

He nibbled on her earlobe, inhaling deeply. "The nights will be, anyway."

"Only the nights?"

In response, he traced her lips with his fingertip. "Every minute."

"Mmm," she said, sighing.

He shoved the keys into his pant pocket. "But I'll get there first. It should be me who talks to Liam. Mark's brother, next door. He can be difficult. He's not going to be happy about his mother eloping with a moody veterinarian he's never met."

"No, I should tell him. I'm a stranger. He can't blame me."

With a quick kiss, he broke away and opened the front door.

"By the time you get there, it'll all be settled." He grinned. "I'll be waiting with bells on."

"But—"

The door slammed shut. She opened it and saw the back of his dark, handsome head as he ran down the stairs.

She smiled. The man was too accustomed to getting his own way.

As she was emptying her suitcase and refreshing its contents for another journey, she reflected that she *was* grateful she wasn't going to be the one to tell Trixie's son about the quickie Vegas nuptials. Nice of Sly to insist.

Dangerous feelings enveloped her like a warm blanket. She savored the sensation for a moment before digging out a scarlet-red silk nightgown from the depths of her dresser. She shoved it into the suitcase. Whatever their relationship was in the future, right now it was a sexual adventure. She should focus on that.

It took her more time than she'd expected to load up her car. She had to bring her keyboard—pianos were nice, but they wouldn't hook up to her laptop—and pack up the perishable items in the fridge. By the time she was parking next to Sly's car in Trixie's driveway in Oakland, it was almost eleven.

She hated to leave her most valuable belongings in the car, but it was the hills, not the flats where she lived, and there probably weren't robbers crouching in the rosemary.

The porch light was on, and she heard yappy barking inside. Without ringing the bell, she opened the door and stuck her head in. "Honey, I'm home!"

24

SLY WAS FILLING the dogs' water bowls in the kitchen when he heard Cleo arrive. The ugly dog, Zeus, who was only slightly larger than a football, kept trying to climb him like a tree. He lifted and carried him to the front door, surprised by the dog's enthusiasm.

"Welcome," he said to Cleo. He bent over to kiss her but found Zeus's tongue slipping into his mouth instead.

She laughed as he sputtered. "Friendly little guy."

"A little too friendly." He pushed Zeus into her arms and walked past her through the doorway. "Need help carrying stuff in?"

"That would be great. How'd it go with Liam?"

He smiled at her over his shoulder. "We dodged a bullet tonight. He wasn't home. The dogs were with the nanny."

When the woman next door had told him Liam and Bev were out at the movies, Sly had almost kissed her. He was too tired to argue with Liam tonight.

"I'm surprised they weren't lying in wait for us," Cleo said, joining him at the car. "To hear about how it all happened." They carried the bags and keyboard into the house. The three little dogs began yapping again.

"Maybe they don't know," he said.

"But she must've told them."

"Why do you think that?"

Her blue eyes, no longer adorned with makeup, widened with alarm. "She must have. If just to explain why we're moving into the house. Was the nanny surprised to see you?"

"She seemed glad to get rid of the dogs. They kept eating the baby's toys, she said."

Cleo looked down at the three animals. "They're cute. I wonder where they sleep."

"Not with us." He caught her hand and pulled her against him.

"So, we're really doing this then?"

"You'd rather go home?"

"No, I mean us." She leaned away from him. "This."

He slid his hands down over her round bottom and stroked. His voice lowered to a growl. "I sure hope so."

That night, the dogs expressed some anxiety with the new living arrangements. During the frenzied lovemaking Sly and Cleo began the moment they got upstairs, they were able to ignore the dogs' pitiful cries, far too engaged in their own feelings. But afterward, when the two tired humans curled up together in the guest room's bed, the whimpering became unbearable. And so when they woke up the next morning, three little animals stretched out between them on the quilt, lined up tail to tail like a furry chastity belt.

Sly reached across them and stroked the soft curve of Cleo's exposed breast. Her skin felt chilled. "Are you cold?"

"Mmm," she mumbled, wriggling under the sheet. The dog's weight pinned the quilt down at her waist.

As much as he enjoyed the view, he dislodged Zeus, who was nestled under her breasts, lucky dog, and pulled the quilt up to her chin. She smiled, not opening her eyes, and burrowed into her pillow.

Something softened inside him. They'd been nice to each other in the past—they were good friends—but now he was compelled to be a different kind of nice. Macho protector nice. He couldn't fight off any wild boar, but he could deal with the family before the shit hit the fan. It was Monday morning, just past eight. Liam had never come by the night before; Mark hadn't called. This had to mean Trixie hadn't told them about the wedding.

Quietly, watching Cleo, he climbed out of bed. Her lips were parted, slack with sleep. He fought the urge to kiss her. She needed her rest. And he had that morning-after feeling that maybe they'd gone too far, too fast. As she'd said, he was only the second man she'd ever slept with. Had he considered how much power that gave him to hurt her?

While he was pouring kibble into the dogs' bowls in the kitchen, he decided to call Mark. As soon as that unpleasant task was accomplished, he'd call his father. Or not. Maybe he'd lie low on that one, at least for a few days. He never knew how his father, a chronically logical, serious man, was going to react to things. Family could bring out the hidden passions in him.

Cursing under his breath at the spot he was in, Sly made coffee, relieved to find some fresh beans and a grinder. As cheap as he could be, he didn't skimp on his java.

Mark could also be a mystery. The famous introvert wouldn't express his unhappiness verbally but would probably withdraw into himself, avoiding social conflict until he'd calmed down or it had blown over.

Deciding he could deal with that, Sly picked up the phone and called him. Mark didn't answer the phone right away, and when he did, he sounded short of breath.

"If this isn't an emergency," Mark said, "call me later."

Sly heard Rose's voice in the background. "I have to go to work anyway."

"No, don't go. It's only Sylly," Mark said, his voice muffled.

Sly heard her shout hello from a greater distance than she had been a moment earlier.

"Damn it," Mark said into the phone. "This better be good."

"Sorry to interrupt the married bliss."

"She has this crazy idea she has to go to work and leave me here alone all day." Mark had not only written software for WellyNelly, the health website they'd started up together, but also other software, some of it far more profitable than WellyNelly. Mark was sitting on millions.

"Your wife doesn't want a sugar daddy?" Sly asked.

"I understand she wants a career. But can't it start after noon? So she can stay in bed with me a little longer?"

"Maybe she doesn't want to," Sly said. "Your personal hygiene used to be a bit sloppy. Have you fallen into old habits?"

"The only old habit I've fallen into is answering your calls. You're not my boss anymore." Mark had worked briefly recently as an engineer at WellyNelly before marrying Rose, who still worked at the company. "Why are you bothering me so early?"

Here it came. Sly walked over to the back door and let the dogs out to do their business. "Guess where I am?"

"You were in Las Vegas this weekend, weren't you? That's what my mom said."

Suddenly, telling his old friend about witnessing his widowed mother's wedding to his lovesick uncle at the Taco Chapel wasn't so easy. Standing in the man's childhood home, Sly couldn't make himself say it over the phone.

"Are you busy this morning? We need to talk," he said.

"Don't tell me you lost all your money and you need your job back," Mark said, "because I already hired Poppy. Thanks to you."

"No, no. Nothing like that."

"Then what?"

"Look, I'll explain when you get here. I'm at your mother's."

Mark's voice sharpened. "What happened? Is she all right?"

"She's fine," Sly said quickly. "You haven't heard from her?"

"Why would I hear from her? Let me talk to her."

"She's not here. She extended her trip." This wasn't going the way he'd intended. "I agreed to housesit. Watch the dogs. Since I'm a bum these days. But you should come by and I'll tell you the rest of it."

"You're sure she's all right?"

"She's very happy." That was true enough. "Come over, all right? Oh, by the way, Cleo is here with me. You've met her a few times. The musician."

"The cute piano teacher?"

Unexpected jealousy stabbed into Sly's gut. Mark was hardly a ladies' man, and he was passionately in love with his wife, but Sly didn't like him expressing the slightest hint of attraction to Cleo. "Yes."

"She's there with you? Like, overnight?"

Sly cleared his throat. "Yes," he said again.

Mark whistled. "I was wondering when that would happen. Mom strikes again." He chuckled.

"It's no big deal. Just having a good time." He didn't want Mark to embarrass Cleo when he came over. "See you soon." He hung up and let the dogs back in. They rushed in as if they'd been gone a month, sniffing and jumping on him.

Cleo spoke behind him. "Who was that?"

Startled, he spun around. She wore a men's red plaid flannel robe that hugged her hips and plunged low between her breasts. "Mark." He caught her by the waist and reached under the robe, already hungry for the feel of her.

"He's coming here?"

He nodded. "I called to tell him about the wedding, but I couldn't bring myself to tell him over the phone."

With an odd expression on her face, she leaned away from him. "I'd better take a shower."

"Sorry," he said. "I didn't realize this was how it was going to go."

"What?"

"Mark. Coming over. It was just going to be a phone call."

"Oh. Right. It's no big deal." She patted him on the shoulder and broke free. "Just having a good time, right?"

She'd disappeared into the kitchen before he realized what she'd said. The same words he'd used with Mark.

Not good.

He jogged after her. "I said that to Mark because I didn't want you to be uncomfortable."

"It's fine. Good times are good." With a wave over her shoulder, she went upstairs.

Cursing under his breath, he picked up Zeus, who continued to shadow him, and succumbed to a face licking. Affectionate little guy.

Did she really mean it? She wasn't upset?

From another woman, he would've thought no. He'd screwed up, and she was hiding her true feelings. But with Cleo, he wasn't sure. They had a long history of being brutally honest with each other.

Of course, they also had a long history of keeping their clothes on.

He set Zeus on the floor and wiped the dog spit off his cheek.

Had they gone too far, too fast?

◇ ♡ ♤

To calm the waters, Sly made pancake batter. Cleo loved pancakes. Trixie's kitchen was well stocked, and Cleo had brought butter from her place. Butter could make so many things better. It was a reliable happiness lubricant.

Before he'd heated the pan, the doorbell rang. He set aside the batter and went to the door.

"You could've come right in," Sly told Mark, surprised he'd rang the bell. "Your house, not mine."

Mark, in a sweatshirt and old jeans, stepped inside and looked around. "I didn't want to interrupt anything."

Cleo appeared on the stairs. "Was that the doorbell?"

"It's Mark," Sly said. If she and Mark had ever met, it had been a couple of years ago, and Mark had changed since then. His wife Rose had burned the rags he used to wear, and sexual triumph had given him a taller stature. "Mark, Cleo."

"Hi, Mark," she said. "Nice to see you."

"Hi." Mark managed to smile at Cleo before turning his gaze to the floor, cheeks flushed. Marriage hadn't cured him completely from his natural shyness around women.

Sly patted Mark's shoulder, stalling for time. How was he going to tell him about Trixie and Hugo? He caught Cleo's eye and gestured for her to go back upstairs. No reason for her to get caught in the crossfire.

She hesitated, then said, "I have to dry my hair. Then I'm going to take your mom's dogs out for a walk like I promised. Did you feed them, Sly?"

"I fed them," he said, gesturing again for her to go. Finally, she turned and walked upstairs.

When she was gone, Mark said, "You're like an old married couple." Something in Sly's face must've amused him, because then he laughed. "Let's go into the kitchen. My mom hides chocolate in the back of the junk drawer. She thinks I don't know."

"Good idea. You can eat a pancake when they're done."

"Who's making pancakes?"

"I am."

Mark strode into the kitchen and opened a drawer by the fridge. "I didn't know you could cook."

"I'm thirty-five. I would've starved by now if I couldn't."

"You can afford to eat out," Mark said, untangling a chocolate bar from a wad of string, screwdrivers, white earbud cords, tape. "But I suppose that's why you're cooking breakfast foods. Not so easy to get delivery."

Sly turned on the heat under a nonstick griddle. As much as he'd love to continue talking about himself, it was time to get to the point. "Listen, about your mom," he began.

The chocolate bar froze halfway to Mark's mouth. "I thought you said she was fine."

"There's no easy way to say this. I tried to stop it. But nobody would listen to me."

"For God's sake, what?" Mark asked.

Sly took a deep breath. "She and my uncle Hugo got married."

"Excuse me?"

"They called us first thing in the morning from one of those all-night wedding chapels off the Strip, asking us to be their witnesses," Sly said. "They really went through with it. I'm sorry, I really am, but there wasn't anything I could do."

To his surprise, Mark barely reacted at all. His brow furrowed the way it did when he was absorbed in an engineering problem. "This was yesterday?"

"They didn't seem intoxicated, but they'd probably been up all night having a good time." Sly cleared his throat. "My uncle has, ah, liked her for a long time."

"Interesting." Mark took a bite of the chocolate, his gaze fixed on Sly's face. "So, they called you and Cleo, you came, they got married."

"You're taking this really well."

"Just trying to get the whole picture," Mark said. "The ceremony, it was just the four of you?"

Sly paused. "And Elvis."

"Wow," Mark said flatly. "No wonder you were upset. You hate Elvis."

Sly felt that Mark wasn't taking this at all the way he should've been taking it. "They really did it. They're married. My Uncle Hugo is now your stepfather."

"Having a vet in the family could come in handy. Rose and I are thinking about getting a cat."

Smelling the butter burning, Sly turned off the heat and shoved the pan to a back burner. "I should've told you over the phone and saved us both the trouble. I assumed you'd want to know."

Mark took another bite of chocolate. "I do want to know. Now tell me exactly," he said, "how it is you and Cleo ended up living here in my mother's house."

"Your mom wanted a honeymoon. She asked Cleo to watch the dogs."

Mark laughed softly, shaking his head. "Of course. And you're here because...?"

"My uncle has a new dog, a really big one, and he's sensitive..." Sly realized how absurd that must sound. "Look, I couldn't let her face you and your family by herself. Liam's right next door. I know how he can be."

"That's true. He'd jump to conclusions, lose his temper. He's a little like our father sometimes. My mom's said so herself." Finishing off the chocolate, Mark looked around. "Coffee?"

"What conclusions would he be wrong to jump to?"

"Come on, Sly, think about it."

"You think it was all just a joke."

"She's up to her usual games," Mark said. "Playing Cupid."

"You weren't there. Yes, at first she was bluffing about the thing with Hugo. But then she really fell for him. It was funny and then it wasn't. They were dancing and she looked up at him and there was this—" Sly made a face. "Trust me. She lost control of the situation."

"I sympathize, buddy. I've been in your shoes myself. You think she's crazy and harmless, and then..." Mark found the coffee Sly had made and poured himself a cup. "Then you realize she's pulling all the strings."

"If you'd seen her face..."

"I know. She's very convincing." Mark sat down and kicked out chair for Sly. "You look like you need to sit down."

25

NOT SURE WHAT to believe, Sly refilled his cup. In spite of the Elvis impersonator, the wedding had felt genuine. Hugo, he knew, hadn't been faking his love or intentions.

Sly sank into the chair. "Whatever she's doing, Hugo better be in on it."

"I'm sure he is. She'd never hurt anyone on purpose."

"Tell Liam, will you?" Sly asked. "And the rest of your clan? I don't want Cleo dealing with it."

"Why tell them anything? Liam might not believe it's fake. Better just to say Cleo's house-sitting while our mom enjoys another week in Las Vegas." Mark sipped his coffee. "Question is, what are *you* doing to do?"

"What do you mean?"

"Are you going to stay here?" Mark asked.

"Of course. There really are dogs to take care of. I promised Cleo I'd help."

"Lots and lots of helping," Mark said.

If the wedding was phony, nobody would be upset with him and Cleo for not interfering. The situation was better than he'd feared. "I'm a helpful guy," he said, grinning.

"You must know this was her plan all along. The two of you...

you know."

Sly lowered his voice. "Cleo didn't have a plan. It was almost impossible to get her into bed."

Mark choked on another bite of chocolate. "I meant my mother. Having you and Cleo living together."

"Oh." Cleo had always claimed that people thought she must be in love with him but was too afraid—or sensible—to admit it. Those people were going to have a lot of ammunition now that they were sleeping together. It was going to annoy her.

He took a deep breath. Had he ever seriously considered the price of finally having sex with her?

"I bet she'd been hoping for more," Mark continued, "when she got you to a quickie wedding chapel yesterday. But you didn't bite, so she had to initiate plan B."

Sly rubbed the back of his neck. The muscles were starting to spasm. "Bite what?"

"Eloping yourself. You and Cleo."

"It wasn't like that at all." But Sly remembered how Cleo had taken Elvis's card and put it in her purse.

"I've been to one of those before," Mark continued. "Friends of mine renewing their vows. Everyone wore costumes. It was really fun. Touching, even."

"It was Sunday morning. We were cold sober. If your mom had wanted us to get carried away, she would've called us the night before." Sly lowered his voice. "Cleo and I had just—for the first... never mind."

"She probably knew that. I don't know how she does, but she does. Trust me. She's scary." Mark leaned back in his chair. "She set up me and Rose, April, the neighbors, and God knows how many others. Maybe even Liam. She's a force of nature."

"I don't like it. People might get hurt."

Mark glanced at him, a sympathetic smile on his lips. "Cleo's tough. I'm sure she knows what she's doing."

In a very low voice, Sly said, "I hope so." She'd been burned before. She couldn't want to go through that again, not so soon.

"It's not so bad, you know," Mark said. "Settling down."

Sly held up a warning hand.

"Married men live longer," Mark continued, grinning.

"You're as bad as your mother."

He shot out of his chair. "God forbid. If that's what you think, I'm getting out of here." He put his coffee cup in the sink and strode directly to the front door. There he turned and said in a more serious tone, "Seriously, Sly. Marrying Rose is the best thing that's ever happened to me."

"You wanted a wife when you were sixteen. You're like that. I'm not."

Mark frowned. "Really? You don't ever see yourself getting married?"

"It's been two days."

"Come on, it's been years."

Sly opened the door and escorted him out onto the landing. "Nice seeing you, Mark. Give my best to Rose."

Frown deepening, Mark shook his head. "My mother wouldn't be doing this if she didn't see something serious happening."

"I need to go make some pancakes." Sly shut the door with more force than was appropriate, afraid that he himself had lost his appetite.

$$\diamond \ \heartsuit \ \spadesuit$$

From the upstairs bathroom window, Cleo watched Mark get into a black Tesla and drive away. As far as she could tell from her aerial view, he didn't look upset, and she hadn't heard any yelling, physical assault, or tears. She pulled her hair into a ponytail and went to find Sly.

It was surreal, she thought as she walked downstairs, to think how much had changed so quickly. She was living in an unfamiliar house, where she'd shared a bed and her body with Sly, and when she walked into the kitchen, he took her in his arms and kissed her.

Sly had said they were having a good time, but it wasn't feeling quite as good as it had the day before.

"Well?" she asked. "How'd it go?"

"He doesn't believe it."

"Did you show him the pictures?" Even Sly had taken a few shots with his phone.

"He believes there was a ceremony, but he thinks it was all a ruse."

She wriggled out of his arms. "No, it was real. You saw the way they were looking at each other."

"That's what I told him. But he's still not buying it. He knows her a lot better than we do."

"No," she said. "Nobody would get married just to set somebody else up. And how would that work, anyway?"

"Either we got inspired to get hitched ourselves, or we ended up here at her house living together."

Uneasiness crept over her. "I don't believe it. Hugo wouldn't do that."

Eyebrows raised, Sly shrugged.

"He wouldn't," she said.

"Not for me," he said, "but if he thought it would get him closer to Trixie..."

"Yeah, like, married is pretty close."

"Exactly."

She tore the ponytail elastic out of her hair and dragged her fingers over her scalp. "I hate this. Have we been had?"

"I don't know."

Eating would help her think. A bowl of a promising yellowish batter sat on the counter. She pointed. "What's that?"

"Oh yeah, I forgot. Sit your sexy ass down and prepare to be amazed." He grabbed a paper towel and wiped out a pan. "Or at least fed. I'll have to make more coffee. Mark drank yours."

"I didn't know you could cook."

"Why does everyone think that? Thirtysomething guy who's never been married—of course I can cook."

"I assumed you lived on pizza and bad beer. Like all confirmed bachelors."

"Don't call me that. It makes me sound like a closeted Victorian. Do you want pancakes or not?"

When they were friends, she could tease him about being perpetually single and it didn't mean anything. But now it made her sound like she was fishing. Which stung her pride. "Of course I want pancakes. Have you learned nothing about me all these years?"

He smiled at her over his shoulder. His jaw, she just noticed, was clean-shaven. No wonder their kiss had been so silky.

Her body tingled. The man had more sensual appeal than a dozen tech moguls bundled together and dipped in chocolate.

"I thought you might worry about my ability to make anything edible," he said.

"I figured you could feed yourself on occasion."

"Or my…" He turned back to the stove. "My friends."

"Your girlfriends," she said.

The word killed all conversation for a long, tense minute. Worries that earlier she'd been able to smother with mindless lust began to surface. Were they going to date for months or a year or break up next week?

Memories of her divorce played like an unwanted pop-up ad in her mind. Ashley's emails apologizing for giving in to love, curling up in a ball on the floor while her mother rubbed her back, signing the final papers...

She'd refused to go through that kind of pain ever again. Yet here she was, rushing in like a fool...

"When does Hugo's dog get here?" she asked.

"Don't know. I'll call after breakfast."

A few minutes later, he set two plates of pancakes on the table, a bottle of syrup, the butter dish, and a cup of coffee. "We'll eat healthy later."

"No pressure." She found silverware in a drawer and gave them each a set. "This looks great. Thanks."

"My pleasure. Hope you like it."

They ate in silence, staring past each other at the unfamiliar kitchen, the window overlooking the San Francisco Bay, the family photos on the walls. "Nice house," she said.

"I think Mark might be right."

"He wasn't there. He didn't see—"

"But he knows her and says this would be like her. You've got to admit, it didn't feel right. It was rushed."

"Of course it was rushed."

"Look, I was wondering. When you came by for that piano lesson. Maybe she got the idea then. Did you give her any reason to think you might want—I'm not saying you *meant* to suggest it, but given who she is, maybe she misconstrued it."

Her stomach twisted. "What are you talking about?"

"Me. Us." He looked down at his plate. "I'm sure you didn't say you were hoping we'd fall into bed together or anything, but maybe you said something complimentary and—"

"Complimentary about you? Like, by the way, Sly's so sexy and I dream about his hot body every night?"

He raised an eyebrow. "OK, so you didn't say anything like that."

"I can't remember. I may have. I probably did. I mean, look at you. How could I not?"

"All right, all right. Forget it."

"Everyone knows I've been in love with you for years," she said. "Just ask my mother."

He sighed. "I'd rather not." The first and last time they'd met, Cleo's mom had asked him if his opinion of his parents' marriage was the source of his lifetime of emotional avoidance.

"She's going to be pretty annoying."

"You're going to tell her?"

A mouthful of pancakes got caught in her throat. So he *had* assumed it would be short-lived. Why bother telling anyone?

It's no big deal... just having a little fun...

She gulped down a mouthful of coffee. "Were you thinking we'd keep it a secret?"

"She lives in Oregon," he said, "there's no hurry. If it's going to bother you to talk to her about it."

"Before the farm, she was a clinical psychologist for twenty years. She can smell a lie from hundreds of miles away."

"I'm not saying you should lie. Just don't bring it up."

Although she'd considered waiting a week before calling her mother, she knew she wouldn't be able to wait that long. She was dying to talk to her about Sly, about what she was feeling, even if Mom couldn't help saying *I told you so.* "She can read minds. Even if I don't say anything, she'll bring it up on her own within the first two minutes."

"You're exaggerating."

"Fifty bucks, buddy." She held out her hand. "Shake on it."

He took her hand and brought it to his lips. "I was just trying to save you from getting mad at her. I know you hate it when you lose your temper."

"She's going to think she was right all along."

Lips brushing her knuckles, he glanced up at her. He didn't say anything, just held her gaze.

She pulled her hand away. "She wasn't."

He laughed. "I know, sweetheart. I was just kidding."

Looking away, she stood up and began clearing the table. "Why don't you call about the other dog? I've got to teach this afternoon, so we should deal with it now."

He came up behind her at the sink and took the dishes from her hands. "You don't have to do anything. I'll call and go get him after I clean up. Then Hugo's employee doesn't have to drive all the way up here. Isn't this your work time? When you compose?"

"Well, yes, but..."

"Then get going. I'm here to serve."

"Nice. Very sexy," she said.

"You're procrastinating. Go on."

"Say it again," she said, turning and grabbing his shoulders, eager to banish the feeling that she was his infatuated sidekick. "The serving thing. It makes me hot."

He pushed her against the sink, captured her face in his hands, and gazed into her eyes, his nose barely touching hers. His fingers, warm and strong, stroked her cheeks.

Raging desire flared through her body. She licked her lips, expecting his kiss.

But he released her and stepped away. "I'd better deal with that dog before I get into bed with you again and never want to get out."

She watched him leave, wondering if he was really in any danger of that.

26

SLY DROVE OFF an hour later to get Hugo's dog, leaving Cleo alone in the house with the Chihuahuas and a lot on her mind. The urge to seek confidential counsel from her professionally trained mother struck her at once. When the best friend you usually talked to was the guy you were sleeping with, your options for other qualified listeners were limited.

Her mom had been eager for her to start dating again. She could give Cleo the encouragement she needed to be brave. Loving Sly was potentially wonderful, but she was too scarred from the past to let herself. Her mother would seize the chance to tell her so.

Sitting at the piano for confidence, she played silent chords with her left hand while she selected her mom's cell number on her phone. Neither of her parents bothered to answer the landline anymore, and they were probably out in the garden anyway, harvesting the last fall vegetables for next weekend's farmer's market at the town square. They called themselves farmers, but their operation wasn't much larger than what Cleo had seen in Trixie's backyard. Everything they grew, they grew by hand, by themselves. They didn't make much money, and their house was so small they used the garage as a living room, but they were happier than she'd ever seen them. She knew what a successful family was. Although her own first try was a disaster, how could she not still want it, someday, for herself?

"Please tell me you're coming up here this weekend to help us with the last of the winter squash," her mother said, not bothering to say hello.

"Relationship drama," Cleo said.

"Oh?" There was a long pause. "Someone new?"

"No." Cleo said it forcefully, knowing that would be enough.

"Not Dylan, I hope."

Cleo nearly dry-heaved. "God, no. But it is somebody you know."

Her mother let out a long whistle. "Give me a minute. I'm out in the back forty." Which referred to feet, not acres. There was the sound of a thud, footsteps, then her mother swallowing. When she was working, she always wore a water-reservoir-containing backpack with a straw on her shoulder. "Is he there?"

"No."

"We are talking about Sly, correct?"

Cleo made an affirmative grunt.

"When?" her mother asked. "Saturday, I'm guessing? That would give you a day of afterglow and then another night to see if it was still as good as the first. Which it was, so you're starting to worry."

Cleo sighed. It really was hopeless. "You never should've given up clinical practice. You're robbing the world of a truly scary gift."

"My happiness will do more good. It can be catching, you know, like a virus."

Having heard this philosophy before, Cleo got to the point. "I need you to tell me it's OK. I'm feeling the urge to sabotage."

"It's not my place to tell you anything is OK. You have to

come up with that decision on your own."

"Drop the shrink act, Mom. You're not an impartial observer here. You've wanted me to do this for years."

"Are you sure about that?"

"Oh, come on. You've never believed I was happy just being friends with him."

"And you think that means you'll be happy being his lover?"

Flinching, Cleo closed the lid on the piano. In her mind, *lover* was a pretentious word you couldn't say without a fake French accent. "I don't think that's all we'll be."

"Has he talked about the future?"

"As you guessed, it's only been two days."

"So you haven't."

Cleo's hands balled into fists. "We were flying back from Las Vegas in a crowded airplane, and then we got to the house where we're—you don't know the whole story, but you think—" She jumped up and groaned in frustration, startling the three dogs sleeping on the sofa. "No. We haven't."

"Does Sly have any interest in having children?"

"Mom, come on."

"You haven't discussed it? In all these years?"

"No," Cleo said, realizing only then that that was odd. That she'd always assumed he'd be a great father—not for her kids, but in the abstract—but she couldn't remember him expressing any interest.

"Do you think that's something you might want to discuss now?"

Cleo dug her fingers into her ponytail and twisted it around her fingers. "You can't just be a normal mother for once, can you?"

"How do you think he'd react?"

"I think he'd freak out. It's too soon."

"And what would he do? When he freaked out?" her mother continued.

Crap. Mom was going for the jugular. There was no escaping the drilling down into the deepest secrets of her mind. Her mom wasn't a headshrinker, she was a power tool. "He might decide this isn't something he wants to do after all."

"Decide *what* isn't what he wants to do?"

Cleo sat on the couch near the dogs, stroking them for comfort. "You know."

"You need to say it."

Cleo couldn't. "It's not normal for women to demand that sort of thing anymore. Or a man. If that guy I went out with a couple of times last year had asked me if I wanted to have his children, I would've run screaming in the opposite direction."

"You did just that, as I remember."

"I could tell he wanted more than I did," Cleo said.

"And is that what you think about Sly?"

Oh, her mother was evil. "Possibly."

"And you think it's better that you found that out later rather than sooner?"

"Are you capable of saying anything without making it a question?" Cleo asked. But it was the issue she'd been wondering about herself. She stroked Zeus's back, watching him close one eye and smile, his tongue lolling. His ecstasy brought her comfort. Giving pleasure could feel as delicious as receiving it. It made her feel powerful and good, godlike.

Is that what had happened with Sly in Vegas? He was getting off on making *her* feel good?

"I'd like to know as soon as possible," Cleo admitted.

"Then maybe you should ask him."

Cleo made a face. "It's embarrassing."

"Why? Of course you'd like to have a happy, rewarding union with someone. You were hurt before, but you'd still like a family. Why not say so up front? Don't be ashamed of what you want."

"I don't want him to think I'm in a hurry."

"You called me because something was bothering you," her mother said. "Putting it off isn't going to make it easier."

Cleo slumped over on the couch, completely horizontal now, and let the three dogs climb all over her. "I'm not even sure if"—she bit her lip and rushed on—"marrying him is what I want. We just... it's only been..."

"You know my suspicions about that," her mother said.

Unbidden, tears burned in Cleo's eyes. Love? All along?

She touched her lips, remembering the feel of his kiss, and her insides melted like plastic wrap on a flatiron.

Cleo's voice dropped to a whisper. "I don't think it's mutual."

"What's the worst thing that could happen?"

"Don't make me say it."

"Then write it down," her mother said.

"That would be worse." The last thing she wanted was a paper trail.

"I think it's important to get it out."

Cleo hugged Zeus to her neck. "He won't want to see me again."

"But if he doesn't love you by now, Cleo, would you still want him in your life?"

Sly sat in late-morning traffic in Berkeley with a giant dog slobbering on his shoulder from his spot in the backseat.

"Sorry about the change of plans, Mouse," he said, hitting the gas to turn before the light changed.

Not expecting the change in gravity, Mouse teetered off the

seat with a muffled thump. A moment later, his head reappeared in the rearview mirror, his droopy eyes reproachful.

"Sorry about that," Sly said. "It's impossible to turn left in this town. Ironic, don't you think?"

With a sigh, Mouse replaced his chin on Sly's shoulder, which was already soggy from their first mile on the road.

Sly reached up and stroked his massive head. Except for the parts that were sticky with drool, Mouse's fur was silky and thick, a tactile pleasure. "I hope you like your new house. Whichever one that is. Not quite sure yet if this is a forever thing for Hugo."

His words echoed in his ears. A forever thing. Not quite sure yet.

He hadn't anticipated how accelerated his relationship with Cleo would be. They'd had their first real date less than forty-eight hours earlier, but already he felt as if everyone expected them to get married tomorrow. According to Mark, Trixie had hoped they'd elope yesterday.

"I care about her a lot, but come on," he told Mouse.

Mouse sighed.

"She doesn't even know what she wants herself. Maybe I'm the first of a hundred men she's going to sleep with to make up for lost time." The idea didn't bring him any comfort.

He was approaching the turn for his condo in Rockridge. Trixie's house was another ten minutes of twisty turns up into the hills.

If he had a job, he'd be at work right now. Maybe that was his problem. All this free time made him neurotic. He'd founded a multimillion-dollar corporation and started a few smaller ones, never wasting time doubting himself the way he was now.

And his personal life hadn't ever bothered him this much, either. Even Teresa, who had meant more to him than any of the other women he'd dated, had never given him insomnia. But since his first night with Cleo, he hadn't slept more than two hours in a row. Even when she'd been asleep, he'd stared at the ceiling, or at her.

Mouse began kissing his ear with long, wet strokes of a tongue as big as a man's hand. His loose jowls leaked drool down the collar of Sly's shirt. The creepy feel gave him gooseflesh.

"You're a handsome guy," Sly said, patting Mouse's head away, "but I prefer a certain blonde these days."

All he needed was a decent night's sleep. No sense trying to think about anything right now.

The closer he got to Trixie's house—and Cleo—the better he felt. He wondered when her first lesson was, if they'd have a little time together. As he got out of the car and opened the back door for Mouse, he vowed to make time.

The dog, however, stared at him from the backseat, not budging.

"Come on, Mouse." Sly spoke in the voice he'd used for team-building retreats. "You can do this."

Mouse lay down, rested his chin on his paws, and closed his eyes.

Sly clipped the leash on his collar and tugged. It was like trying to move a redwood with a jump rope.

"You can do this!" Sly repeated, but his confidence was fading.

The advantages of having a dog from Chihuahua, Mexico, instead of Newfoundland, Canada, struck him with full force. Newfies had been used to haul lumber over the tundra. And to rescue drowning fisherman in icy Atlantic waters.

Mouse wasn't going anywhere unless he wanted to.

Sly looked up at the house, imagining Cleo naked, and sighed.

Inside the car, Mouse also sighed.

While Sly stood there pondering the volume of a Newfoundland's bladder, Cleo came out of the house and walked down the steps to the driveway.

"Hi," she said. Something about her seemed strange, but he was too preoccupied with the dog to pursue why.

"He won't get out of the car," he said, turning back to Mouse.

Her gaze moved to the backseat. "Holy moly. He's huge."

"Yup."

Moving past Sly, she reached into the car and stroked Mouse's blocky head. "What a handsome fella."

"Too heavy to lift. I can't convince him to move."

"Maybe he's scared."

He glanced at her, hearing the empathy in her voice. "I'm not scary."

She buried her fingers deeper into the black fur. "Maybe it's not you, it's me." The dog watched her with sad eyes. Drool puddled on the leather under his paws. "I'll go get a treat, see if that'll move him."

But nothing she got appealed to him. They tried ham, cheese, peanut butter, crackers, kibble, and even the dried bull penis Bella had given him at the clinic with his other gear.

"That's just wrong," Cleo said, wrinkling her nose at the two-foot-long brown stick. It was like a magic wand. Except without the magic.

"I'll bring him back to the clinic." He let the unwanted bull penis sag in his hand at his side.

"Maybe you should try bringing him to your place."

"And what, stay there with him all week?"

"If he's happy there."

He turned, about to make a joke about making her happy,

then saw the tightness in her lips. "Would you rather I did that?" he asked.

"I was just talking to my mother."

"Oh, no wonder," he said.

"She thinks I should ask you if you want children."

His bark of laughter made her flinch. He sobered instantly, feeling the hairs rise on the back of his neck. "And this is how you're doing it," he said.

"Apparently." Her restless hands twisted the fur around Mouse's neck.

"What else did she say?"

"Don't blame her. I'm the one taking her advice."

"I'm just curious," he said. "You're obviously upset."

"You haven't answered the question."

"You didn't really ask me," he said, knowing he was being a jerk but unable to help himself.

"Do you want to have children someday?"

The world around them faded away, leaving them in a silent bubble, frozen in time. "You're serious."

"That's another thing my mother pointed out." She raised her chin. "I am serious. I'm serious about us. Are you?"

He heard the blood rushing in his ears and felt his legs twitch as if the starting gun had just blasted.

They were friends. Everything had always been so easy. He'd thought he understood her, that she understood him. "Is this really the time or place to discuss this? I've got this huge animal stuck in my car, we're standing in some random driveway…"

Her cheeks were as pale as the haze hanging over the bay. "I need to know before we take this any further."

"That's unfortunate," he said. "Because I'm not prepared to answer that question right now."

"I see."

Their eyes met for a moment, then both turned to stare at the dog. A car drove by but didn't stop. The sun hadn't come out yet and didn't look like it was going to.

"I have to get to my first lesson," she said. "The dogs are on the porch off the kitchen. I can check in on them between lessons. You don't have to be here."

"It sounds like maybe you'd rather I weren't."

"Maybe I would."

Hands shaking, he pushed Mouse's furry head deeper into the backseat and slammed the car door. "Just as well. I have to deal with this guy anyway. Who knows how long it'll take?"

"Right," she said. "Who knows." It wasn't a question.

Angrier than he had any right to be, he got into the driver's seat and started the engine, dismissing a thought about his overnight bag still in the house. He didn't want to drag this out.

"I'll see you later," he said.

Her eyes were downcast, so he couldn't read her expression, but he saw her hands clench into fists.

Yeah, he was angry too. Not waiting for her to say good-bye, he backed out of the driveway.

27

CLEO RETURNED TO the house just after nine that night. Monday was her busiest evening for lessons, and driving all over the East Bay was making her question her policy of doing house calls. When she had a home of her own with a real piano, she'd set up a proper studio and…

Her thoughts trailed away. She didn't really care about any of that anymore. After letting the dogs out for a while, then playing with them to make up for leaving them alone all evening, she went upstairs to bed. Her heart was heavy and bruised but intact. As much as she craved his presence at the empty side of the bed, she had no regrets, either about sleeping with him or what she'd said that afternoon.

She couldn't repeat the past. She wouldn't. People tended to make the same dumb mistake, loving the wrong type again and again, never learning their lesson, but she wasn't going to. Dylan hadn't loved her enough, and she had refused to see the truth until it was too late. It had taken her years to even consider dating again. If she let Sly hurt her like Dylan had, she'd be in her late nineties by the time she recovered—and as her mother had astutely pointed out, she would like a family someday. It wasn't first on her list, but it wasn't last, either.

Sly called around ten, while she was staring at the ceiling in the darkness with two dogs on her feet and one curled up near her hip. Her phone was still programmed to let his calls go through, no matter the time.

Sucking in a breath, she rolled over and picked up her phone. Her heart shuddered a little when she saw his handsome, grinning face glowing on the screen. How quickly things could change. She'd looked at that same photo a hundred times and never experienced the slightest change in blood pressure. She sat up in bed before she answered. "Hi."

"Hi," he said. Even his voice did things to her it hadn't before. It was like he was licking secret parts of her through her ears.

Although she couldn't breathe, she tried to sound normal. "How's Mouse? Did you bring him back to the clinic?"

"He's with me. At my place."

Since he was the one to call, she made no effort to fill the silence.

"I thought we could talk," he said.

"OK."

"I thought I could come over."

She knew what would happen if he did that. "Maybe we should just talk right now like this."

"I hate the phone."

"It's safer," she said.

"Safe. Well, that's what this is all about, isn't it?" Before she could hang up, he rushed on. "I'm sorry. That was what I called to say. I was rude earlier. Today. You surprised me."

"I should've picked a better time." But she'd known if she hadn't challenged him then, when her mother's words were fresh in her mind, she might never have.

"As to your question," he began.

She bit her lip. She couldn't help him out on this one.

"I care about you, Cleo..."

Here it comes, she thought, closing her eyes.

"But how about we take our time here and see what we have before we rush into anything?" His voice was charmingly apologetic. "I'm sure your mother meant well, but this is a woman who's been convinced you've been in love with me for years, and naturally she—"

"I think she might've been right."

For a moment she was sure the phone had disconnected.

"But you've always—just yesterday you were swearing to me —"

"My capacity for self-delusion is infinite, I guess," she said.

He let out his breath. "Cleo," he said softly. Charmingly apologetic again.

She grasped at his earlier words like a lifeline. "How about you take your time there and see what you have before you rush into anything?" she asked, hearing the edge in her voice. "I'm going to hang up now, get some sleep, and maybe we can talk later. OK? OK." Finger trembling, she hung up and powered down the phone. Even if he called her back, she wouldn't know. But she didn't expect him to.

"Dad, we should talk," Sly said into the phone.

It was Wednesday evening, forty-seven hours after he'd last spoken to Cleo. He and Mouse sat together on the floor in front of the washing machine inside his condo, watching the spin cycle. His place felt emptier than usual in spite of the enormous dog. Cleo had never spent much time there, but her absence was palpable.

"I'm crunching some numbers right now," his dad said from

their house outside of San Diego. Sly could hear the TV playing some game loudly in the background. He never bothered to turn it down just for a phone call. The ultimate multitasker, his father. His parents had owned their own accounting and bookkeeping business for thirty years. There was always work to be done, all of it a priority, even in the off-season. "But go ahead. I'm listening."

"It's about Hugo. He got married this weekend. In Vegas." If Sly had tried to tell him the whole story, his father would've hung up before he got to the climax.

"What?"

"It probably wasn't real. Just a Vegas thing, nothing to take seriously. But I thought you should know."

"Are you sure?"

"I was there," Sly said.

"In Vegas?"

"Yes."

"Why?"

"It was kind of a double-date kind of thing," Sly said.

"Are you married too?"

"No."

His father let out a breath. "Shame. But Hugo is."

Sly frowned in surprise. His dad thought it was a shame he hadn't eloped? Looking into Mouse's droopy eyes for insight but finding only sympathy, Sly said, "Yes. To Trixie Johnson, Mark's mother. You remember Mark?"

"The Bill-Gates-Steve-Jobs-wannabe guy."

"Something like that," Sly said.

"He got married too, didn't he? I seem to remember you writing a toast."

"Mark is married too, yes."

"But not you," his father said.

"Come on, Dad, don't you want to ask more about Hugo?"

"Why?"

"He's your brother."

"I'm sure he'll call me when he's ready," his dad said. "But I'm glad you were there. You two always got along so well. I remember that year you spent every day after school at the clinic."

"I liked seeing the animals. You never let us have any pets."

"Didn't see the point having them around the house."

Sly hooked an arm around Mouse's neck and rubbed his cheek against his fur. When he'd been a boy, having a dog had been his ultimate dream. Before he'd begun to think about starting companies or getting rich and famous, he'd fantasized about having a dog. Any dog. Big, small, old, young. Even a friendly cat would do. But his father, who hadn't taken a day off his entire life, had always insisted they were too much work.

"I thought you might be upset about Hugo," Sly said. "Or that I was there and didn't tell you."

"Upset? Me?"

"You have your moments. I never know how you're going to react."

"You sound like your mother."

Sly's jaw tightened. His parents had never gotten the modern memo about healthy family functioning and often used their children as pawns in their battles.

"Speaking of Mom," Sly said, "maybe I should call her. She'll want to hear about the wedding from me."

His father cleared his throat. "She's here. You want me to give her the phone?"

"She's home?" For a second, Sly thought he'd forgotten it was a major holiday or birthday. Why else would they be in the same house? "Does she know you're there?"

"I believe she noticed me across the dining table," his father said. "Want to ask her yourself?"

They were eating together? Without a major family event to force them to? "Yeah. I do."

Sly heard a grunt, footsteps, a door opening, muffled talking. Then his mother's voice came clear and bright over the phone. "Sly, how nice."

"Hi, Mom. Why are you there?"

"I'm fine, thanks for asking. How are you?"

"Did you know he was going to be there when you flew back from Kona?"

"That's wonderful, honey. I'd glad you're doing well. How's work going?"

"I quit, just like I told you I was going to," Sly said. "Did you and Dad finally sign a treaty or something?"

"I'm glad you're taking a break. It means there's hope for you."

"You're not going to tell me what's going on?"

His mother paused. "Your dad and I have decided to work on a few things."

"Like being in the same continent at the same time?"

"Be good, Sylvester."

The washing machine's spin cycle came to a rumbling stop. Ears perking up, Mouse stood up and peered through the glass at the wet clothes. Sly scratched his shaggy belly from below, trying to absorb the shocking news about his parents apparently not hating each other anymore. "Sorry. I called to tell Dad that Hugo got married last weekend. He can tell you all about it, not that he seemed to care very much."

She sighed, then said in a low voice, "You shouldn't have told him. Hugo asked me not to."

"You talked to Hugo?"

"He didn't want to upset your father."

"Don't worry," Sly said. "He's not upset."

"You never know with Victor. Still waters run deep."

He got to his feet and was suddenly aware of how tired he was. "I'm more worried about Hugo." He didn't want to explain about Trixie and her plots, because that would lead to Cleo, and anything that made him think about Cleo made his guts churn. "I've got to go. Doing my laundry." It took both hands and some leg muscle to push Mouse aside so he could open the door to the washing machine.

"There's going to be a ceremony," his mother said.

He frowned. "For Hugo and Trixie?"

"No, no. For us. Me and your dad. We're renewing our vows."

"Come on, Mom, what happened? Why now?"

"When you receive a save-the-date card in the mail, please do so," she said. "It'll be sometime in the spring."

Too much was going on and nobody was being straight about it. "Fine. Great. Congratulations."

"You kids wanted us to talk, so we did."

He cleared his throat. "Well, good. I'm glad. But we've been wanting that for decades."

A long moment of silence stretched between them. "I had a lump. But it's fine. We weren't sure, but now we are."

"God, Mom—" he said, gripping the phone.

"It was just a false alarm. But it got us thinking. That's all I'm going to say about it."

"You're sure you're—"

"Yes, yes. It was nothing. I'd rather you didn't tell your sisters. They'd worry."

"I worry," he said.

"You know how they are. Emotional. Not like you," she said.

"I have emotions."

"But they aren't a big priority for you. You've got your career. Like your father."

That comment struck him between the eyes so hard that he blinked. "I'm glad you're all right," was all he managed to say.

"Thank you. Me too."

Mouse was blocking his access to the machine again. Before Sly could stop him, he snapped up a wet sock between his jaws and bolted down the hallway with unlikely speed. Sly admired his burst of ambition. "I should go."

"We'll talk more later," she said. "Promise."

"Right." After a small pause, they both hung up.

His parents were spending time together, and not just because it was tax season. A month ago, the news would've compelled him to get on a plane and fly down to see for himself. He would've called his sisters and maybe even a cousin or two.

But today?

Today he couldn't muster the energy to interfere. Who was he to give advice? Demand explanations? Celebrate?

How about you take your time there and see what you have before you rush into anything?

Two days since Cleo had said that, and he'd done nothing. Not a text, not a call, not a visit.

I think she might've been right...

Two days.

He was happy his parents didn't hate each other anymore. But it wasn't enough to distract him from how much he hated himself.

28

ON WEDNESDAY EVENING, when it had been two full days since she'd scared Sly away with talk of love and marriage, Cleo decided she had the courage to turn on her phone again.

She'd just finished her last lesson for the day and was hurrying to her car, which was parked with ambiguous legality in a faded delivery zone, when she reached into her purse and held down the power button.

Before pulling it out to look at the screen, she lifted her head and took a deep breath as she gazed at the fog clinging to the hills. Behind her, the sun was already setting into the Pacific. The days were getting shorter and shorter, gloomier and gloomier.

You did the right thing, she told herself, then looked down at the cold phone in her hand.

The only message was from Trixie.

URGENT. Call me please. 8-0

Not Sly, just Trixie.

Exhaling loudly, she got into the car and slammed the door.

Not even a text. She picked up the phone and stared at Trixie's message.

She was stumped by the numbers at the end, assuming Trixie had forgotten to type all the digits, but then she realized it was an emoticon of alarm.

Reluctantly, she called Trixie's cell.

"Cleo! Hello!" Trixie cried.

"Where are you? Is everything all right?"

"I don't know. That's why I'm calling," Trixie said. "Where are you? I hear traffic."

"I'm in Albany. Just finished a lesson."

"Is Sly with the dogs?"

Living alone in Trixie's house for the past three days with plenty to dwell over had made Cleo more suspicious now of the older lady. The numerous prominent photos of her late husband had convinced her the marriage to Hugo was not only a sham but a shame. Poor Hugo. Even if Trixie had warned him it was all for fun, he was going to get hurt.

Cleo sympathized in a deep and heart-stabby kind of way. Every hour she was tempted to text Sly and suggest they hook up again, no strings attached, friends with benefits, sex in the city, touch me again you animal I can't live without you.

But then she'd make herself think of her marriage.

The next guy she dated would be unambiguously crazy about her. She wasn't going to go into her next relationship as a supplicant. Whoever this dream guy was, he'd beg for her. She might even insist on occasional groveling.

"Sly is at his place with Mouse," Cleo said. "I'm at your house with your dogs."

"Oh, Father Christmas," Trixie said. "Who chucked whom?"

Because the call was already over the speakers, Cleo started the car. "None of your beeswax," she said. "When are you going to tell your family about the wedding?"

"Well, Mark already knows by now, doesn't he?"

"I didn't tell him," Cleo said.

"But Sly would have."

Cleo didn't reply.

"And Mark wouldn't believe it, of course. It's just as well he didn't tell Liam. April, well, I'll have to talk to her myself in person. Our flight comes in Saturday morning."

Not willing to participate in any more of Trixie's games, Cleo pulled out into traffic. "I'll feed the dogs and pack up before my Saturday lessons then. If I don't see you—"

"When's your first lesson?"

"Well, not until one, but it's in El Sobrante, so I have to hit the road early enough—"

"Plenty of time. We'll be there before noon," Trixie said. "By the way, I'm making dinner for you on Saturday night, nothing fancy, just to say thank you—"

"I won't be going to any parties, Trixie."

"It's not a party! It's just food. And drinks."

"And who else did you invite?" Cleo asked.

Trixie hesitated.

"I'm on to you, lady," Cleo said.

"This is all my fault," Trixie said. "You've got to let me make it up to you."

"Then leave me alone." Cleo softened her tone. "Sorry. Please leave me alone. I just want to go back home and get back to real life."

"I don't know what happened, but—"

"I have to go," Cleo said, fumbling on her steering wheel for the hang up button. She couldn't resist adding, "Give my love to Hugo. And I mean that. He deserves it."

Sly woke up on Thursday morning when Mouse rolled over in bed. Already teetering on the edge of the mattress in a fitful sleep,

Sly wasn't prepared for the furry weight coming at him; he fell off the bed face-first. As he threw out an arm to break his fall, he knocked over the nightstand. His phone, previously on the nightstand, slid to the floor, belly flopping onto the hardwoods at the precise angle necessary to shatter its screen.

All in all, Sly thought as he rubbed his elbow and stared at his broken phone, it was a typically shitty way to start yet another day of his shitty, empty life. Maybe Teresa would come by and make his shitty world complete.

Above him, Mouse grunted and took to the air. Sly rolled over just in time to avoid one hundred and sixty pounds of dog landing on his face. After a scramble to regain his footing on the slippery floor, Mouse turned and looked down at Sly with a huge wet smile as if he couldn't believe how lucky he was not only to be alive, but to be living with such a great guy.

Sly reached up and scratched him behind his ears. "You're awesome, Mouse."

Mouse closed his eyes and panted.

"Hope I didn't worry you when I screamed," Sly said. "It's all right. I like falling on the floor."

Mouse suddenly shook his head, sending a ropy strand of drool flying through the air. It landed on the window blinds, then grew long and skinny as gravity pulled it down. Mesmerized, Sly watched it stretch over the slats.

I've got to talk to Hugo about this dog, he thought. *Sooner rather than later.*

Nudging Mouse aside, he got to his feet. He rubbed the broken screen on his phone, hoping to at least unlock it. But it was hopeless. He might as well expect a genie to pop out and grant him three wishes. His favorite and most important piece of technology was now a brick.

Since he hadn't had a landline in ages, he had to use his laptop to call Hugo. The wonders of modern communication technology.

Not so wonderful. He didn't answer. Sly opened a second window to check the Skype settings and phone number. But then, on the seventh ring, the call went through and Hugo's gruff voice rumbled over his earphones.

"I told her I wouldn't call you, but here you are calling me," Hugo said. "I don't know how she does it. She's a sorceress."

His uncle didn't sound as infatuated as he had a few days earlier. Maybe he'd finally struck out for good.

"This is nothing to do with Trixie," Sly said. "It's about Mouse."

Hugo sighed. "Ah. Well. I warned Bella you might bring him back. She's happy to have him until I get home."

Sly noticed he'd said *I* instead of *we*. "I don't want to bring him anywhere."

Hugo snorted. "Having trouble getting him out of the car, are you? He's funny that way. Try putting opera on over the speakers. Works every time. Jumps out of the car like a jackrabbit."

"That's not what I meant."

"I suppose I could ask Bella to drive to—"

"I want to keep him," Sly said. He picked up a drool rag—an item he'd learned was necessary when living with a Newfoundland —and wiped away a puddle at Mouse's feet. "But I don't see how that's going to happen."

"You want to steal my dog?"

"I thought about leaving town and not leaving a forwarding address," Sly said.

"Are you sure that's because of Mouse?"

Sly adjusted the headset mic and said nothing.

"Trixie talked to Cleo, you know," Hugo continued. "Heard things didn't work out."

Sly's throat tightened. "Cleo said that?"

"You've gone to ground with a scheme to kidnap my dog. It doesn't sound promising."

"What exactly did she say?"

"I'd let you ask Trixie herself," Hugo said, "but she's gone to the movies."

"Without you?"

Hugo cleared his throat. "She said I wouldn't like it. She's probably right."

"Sounds like things aren't going so well for you either," Sly said.

"They're going fine. Don't worry about us. Focus on your own problems."

Sly buried his fingers in Mouse's black mane. "My parents are getting back together."

"Your mother is a remarkable woman," Hugo said. "I've been telling your father that for years."

Thinking of lumps and close calls, Sly buried his second hand in Mouse's fur. "She is."

"Some men should never marry," Hugo said. "They don't know how to make time for it. But I don't have to tell you that. You've learned from your father's mistakes."

"Yeah. I'm a fucking genius."

"I'm sorry it didn't work out with Cleo. I really am. How about you and I go fishing in a week or two? Just us. Two men out in a boat."

"It's November."

"Great time for bass. Trout too. I'll set it up. Keep your calendar open."

Sly picked up his dead phone and twirled it between his fingers. "I don't have a calendar anymore."

"Christ, you're in bad shape."

"I'm keeping the dog."

"I think you'd better," Hugo said. "I'll call you when I get back."

Not sure he understood, Sly cleared his throat. "You don't mind if Mouse stays with me?"

"I wouldn't have left him for so long if I planned on keeping him myself."

Sly stood up, pulling the earphone cord with him. "What?"

"You needed a dog. If ever a man did, it was you. Thought so for years, but your job made it impossible."

"Mouse was a setup?"

"When his previous owner asked me to find a home for him, I thought of you right away. He'll get you out of the house and keep you from working too hard. You'll slow down. Smell the roses. Best thing for your health, a dog. Unless you're allergic."

"Why didn't you just ask me if I wanted him?"

"You would've said no."

Sly rubbed the knot growing in the back of his neck. "You and Trixie were made for each other."

"That's what I keep telling her," Hugo said.

29

IT WAS THURSDAY night. One that would've been a TV-and-beer-with-Sly Thursday.

Cleo had been playing the piano for two hours straight. Her frozen curry dinner from Trader Joe's sat uneaten in the microwave. Her wineglass was empty. The bottle of two-dollar Chardonnay next to it, also empty.

The two female Chihuahuas, sensing trouble, huddled in a pile on the sofa. Zeus, sensing an uneaten meal in the kitchen, waited at her feet.

She played "Ode to Joy" because she was masochistic and Joplin because she wasn't. She made her way through the sheet music she used for beginner's lessons. She played her own compositions.

When she was too drunk to play with both hands, she called Ashley.

"Cleo?" Ashley's voice was faint, incredulous.

"Hello, Ash." She ran her finger over the corner of a chipped G key.

"I—hi. How are you?"

"Great, totally great," Cleo said. She burped into her hand. "Wonderful. Awesome. And you?"

A pause. "Have you been drinking?"

"Why, yes, I have. Would you like to join me? I'm in Oakland. Nice view up here."

Ashley paused again. "Actually, I'm at my grandmother's funeral."

Cleo slapped her forehead. Sometimes hitting the right notes wasn't as important as the timing. "Shit. Sorry. Really sorry. I'll let you go."

"No, no. It's all right. We've been here all day. I was just about to go back to the hotel."

"Where are you?" Cleo asked.

"Santa Barbara. She was my mom's mom."

"I remember her. That sucks."

Ashley sighed. "Yeah."

"Give my love to your mom."

"I will. Thanks." Ashley's voice turned weary. "She'll like that. She asks about you, you know."

"She was always really nice to me."

Ashley fell silent. Cleo heard a delicate nose-blowing. "Unlike me," she said finally.

"Yeah." Cleo picked up the empty bottle of Chardonnay and peered through the glass at Zeus, further distorting his already-distorted features. "Well, that's life."

"You're not mad anymore?"

Cleo laughed. As if. She didn't say anything.

"Dumb question," Ashley said. "But I'm glad you called. Why did you?"

"Impulse. Alcohol. Depression. Felt like feeling worse."

"Great. And I'm at a funeral."

"It's kind of a jackpot," Cleo said.

"You looked great in Vegas. Are you serious about that guy?"

"Nope. Just sleeping around. As one does."

"Oh," Ashley said. "Too bad. He looked nice."

"If you liked him, it's a good thing I dumped him," Cleo said. "We've got terrible taste, you and me."

"God, isn't that the truth. Dylan cheated on me. Did you hear that?"

"How would I hear that?"

"I don't know," Ashley said. "Bad news gets around."

Cleo rolled her knuckles over the black keys like a seven-year-old. "What are you going to do?"

"What do you mean? I told him to move out."

When Dylan had cheated on Cleo, she'd asked him to go into counseling with her. "Just like that?"

"He'd already packed a bag," Ashley said. "I was hardly going to beg him to stay."

Cleo had done just that. But she'd been so young and didn't have Dylan's track record to give her perspective. "Good for you." Cleo's head was spinning. Was she really talking to Ashley, or was she passed out next to the piano having a bad dream? "Well, gotta go. Sorry about your grandmother."

"Thanks."

"And your marriage."

"Right. Good-bye, Cleo."

"Bye, Ash."

Tempted by the idea of resting next to the piano, Cleo slid to the floor and rolled onto her back. The underside of a grand piano was a beautiful thing. Too bad this was an upright.

While Zeus licked her face, Cleo thought about how she was a better person than Ashley. She hadn't walked away from *her* marriage without a fight. She'd tried to talk it through, work at it, go to counseling, see what she could do to salvage a relationship that had been so important to her.

Because she was a good person.

But Ashley, who'd ruined her best friend's marriage and started one of her own, *she* throws up her hands and calls it quits at the first sign of trouble.

Nyah-nyah, I'm better than you, Ash.

Well, she used to be. She hadn't been very patient with Sly, and Sly hadn't ever promised to love her forever in front of God and everyone the way Dylan had.

"But he didn't even text," she said to Zeus, rolling on to her hands and knees. "Not even an emoticon."

Excited that she was staggering to her feet, which might propel her into the kitchen, Zeus danced in a circle around her. Swaying, Cleo caressed Sly's face on her phone. He had such a yummy face.

She closed her eyes and tapped the screen, then lifted it to her ear.

It rang and rang.

And rang.

On the eighth ring, Zeus gave up, collapsed on the floor, and fell asleep.

Cleo threw the phone, still ringing, into a wastebasket. Then, following Zeus's wise example, she went to bed.

Maybe it was too late to make a social call. But Sly had been thinking all day, had gone to bed still thinking, gotten out of bed and into his car, still thinking, and driven over to Trixie's house in the misty night—not thinking anymore. Just feeling.

He didn't have a plan. If he'd known what he was doing, he would've arranged for Mouse to go to Bella or the clinic. Since he hadn't known, his new dog was at that moment drooling down his neck from his spot in the backseat of the new, red Volvo V60 wagon he'd purchased that afternoon. The Audi hadn't been big enough for a dog bigger than most fifth graders. And the Volvo had all those safety features.

He turned into Trixie's driveway, parked next to Cleo's little Honda, and stroked Mouse's loose jowls, dislodging a handful of drool onto his shoulder. "Lots of room back there. Next time, go ahead and stretch out."

The house was dark. Well, no surprise there. It was past midnight.

Sucking in a deep breath, Sly got out of the car. "You coming?"

Mouse ducked his head and stared at him, the car dome light gleaming in his round brown eyes.

"No problem. Like I said, make yourself comfortable." Sly opened all the windows before closing up the car and walking to the front door. Once he'd talked to Cleo, they could use opera to compel Mouse to exit the vehicle.

He hit the doorbell and waited. Hit it again. And again. Finally a light went on upstairs. Then he saw glow flicker through the downstairs windows.

Figuring she was looking at him through the peephole, he smiled and held up a hand. "It's me."

The pause that followed was longer than he'd expected, long enough to make him uneasy, but eventually she opened the door.

"Hi," she said.

"Hi." The sight of her, sleepy and tousled-haired, adorably sexy in an old heather-gray T-shirt and polka-dot boxer shorts, made him forget what few words he'd rehearsed during the drive over.

His meager plan had been to tell her he cared about her and

wasn't going to let her sabotage things between them just because she was scared of repeating the past. That she wasn't in a hurry to get married any more than he was, that to bring it up now was a clumsy attempt to drive him away. He'd planned to say that they should take it slow because that was the best way to make it last.

And if that didn't work, he'd try the nuclear option and tell her he loved her.

Of course he did. He'd said so a few times already, like on her birthday, or when she'd made him cookies. But this time he'd say it while he kissed her. While he held her in his arms and heard her sigh in his ear.

"Is that your car?" she asked.

Grabbing onto a neutral subject, he grinned at her. "Just bought it today. Guess why?"

Her face froze. Her eyes widened. He thought she looked like she might throw up.

"Are you all right?" he asked.

She shook her head, stared at him.

To stop himself from grabbing her prematurely, he pointed at the car. "See who's inside?"

Slowly, she looked away from Sly and peered at the car. "Hugo's dog?"

"My dog."

"Your dog?"

"I told Hugo I couldn't live without him. He agreed. It was a setup all along."

Something changed in her face. She wrapped her arms around herself. "You bought the car for the dog."

"I couldn't resist. He seemed to like it, so I traded in the A4 and drove it home this afternoon. He's already drooled over most of the leather." He laughed, trying to get her to smile. "You wouldn't believe how much that animal can drool."

"Lots of drool," she said.

"Yeah. But it's no problem really. I just mop it up with a rag."

"Yeah, no problem."

"They gave him a bath at PetZone this morning. Did wonders for his aroma. They clipped his toenails too. He hated that." He didn't like that she wasn't smiling, didn't look interested at all. "I felt so bad I bought him a new dried bull penis. Still in its shrink-wrap."

She rubbed her temple, looking pained.

"Are you sure you're OK?"

"Had a little bit too much Two Buck Chuck tonight," she said. "And it's cold out here."

He cleared his throat. "How about we go inside?"

"I'm not—you didn't—" She wrapped her arms more tightly around herself. "You didn't even call."

"My phone broke."

"It broke?" She blinked. "When? How?"

"It fell off a table this morning when Mouse knocked me out of bed."

"This morning." She raised an eyebrow. He realized then she'd wanted him to call her any of the days previous to this one, not just before he'd come over tonight.

"I didn't think you wanted to hear from me," he said.

She was looking at her fingernails. "You're sleeping with him?"

"He was so needy. It makes him feel good."

Her mouth tightened. "You couldn't resist that, could you?"

"Please, let me come in. I won't—we won't do anything. We can watch TV." He smiled. "It's Thursday."

"That's what you want to do? Watch TV?"

"I'd be happy just being with you."

"Just like old times," she said.

"Just like." His heart jumped. She was going to let him stay. "I'll try to get Mouse out of the car."

"Wait."

He turned, holding his breath.

"I can't do this," she said.

"It's late," he said. "I know. I should've tried earlier."

"Yeah. Much."

"Let's get together tomorrow. Not TV. Breakfast. Or lunch, so you can sleep in. Royal Café?"

Shaking her head, she took a step back into the house and began to close the door. "I can't do this," she said again.

"It's late. I understand." He put a hand on the doorframe, right where it would get crushed in a moment if the door continued moving. "I'll call you tomorrow morning, late."

"On what? Your broken phone?"

"It's easy to get a new one."

"That's so true. Too bad you didn't think of that earlier." She gave his hand on the doorframe a pointed look. "Good night, Sly."

"You're angry."

"I wish," she said.

"You wish you were angry?"

"It would make it easier to say good-bye."

Good-bye. Feeling the blood draining out of him, he withdrew his hand.

The door closed in his face.

30

SLY KNEW HE'D screwed up. Bad.

He needed help, and had a crazy idea where to get it.

Your average thirtysomething guy might not be at home on a Friday morning, but Mark wasn't average. The reclusive software engineer had always preferred working from home. In the past, Sly would call before dropping by and warn Mark to put on some pants. But today he'd risk seeing Mark's tighty-whities.

He brought Mouse with him. When he had the thought to leave him alone in the apartment, he imagined Mouse's sad face and reached for the leash.

Mark and Rose's driveway was gated but open, and he was able to park near the front door. Making soothing yet slightly operatic noises, he led Mouse out of the back of the Volvo and walked him to the door of the modern house perched in the hills that had once been his own. He'd never lived there; it had been just an investment. Mark had bought it from him as part of his Rose-wooing process a couple of years earlier. Because the wooing had been so successful, Sly decided he was just the guy he needed to talk to.

He banged the knocker and scratched the top of Mouse's skull while he waited. He knew his world had changed forever if he was seeking romantic counsel from Mark Johnson.

To his surprise, it was Rose who answered the door. She looked as beautiful as always. A large, curvy blonde, Rose had a natural sex appeal that bowled over most men who saw her. But not him. He'd thought he'd always been immune to her charms because of Mark's feelings for her, but now he wondered. Would it have been so easy to resist Rose if he hadn't had Cleo in his life already?

In fact, he hadn't been seriously involved with any woman since he'd met Cleo, but he'd attributed that to his break with Teresa.

What if it had been something else?

What if his affection for Cleo had been serious for a lot longer than he thought?

"Sylly! This is a nice surp—" Rose began. Her eyes rounded. "Oh my God, is that a bear?"

"It's a Mouse. Can we come in? I was hoping to talk to Mark."

"Please. He's taken apart my laptop and swears he knows how to put it back together." She looked at her watch. Long blond hair tumbled down around her face. Her hair was a little darker than Cleo's, and longer and wavier. Stunning, really. So model perfect, it was hard to believe it was real.

But it wasn't as beautiful as Cleo's.

"He took it apart last night," Rose continued. "I'm going to have to go to work without it."

Sly stepped into the foyer. Mouse lumbered in and collapsed next to a hall table that held a vase of arching blue and white flowers. Sly's own image reflected back at him from a gilt mirror on the wall over the vase. "You've kept the decorating from the sale."

When he'd put the house on the market, Rose had lived in the house while it was artificially staged to look irresistible to buyers.

"We have fond memories of those days," Rose said, "so we replicated some of the decorating."

"Like the pillows?" The bed in the master suite had been piled high with dozens of them. Mark had admitted to him (or bragged) that repatriating them to their assigned positions after his and Rose's first night together had been a challenge.

Rose's smooth skin flushed pink all over. "Actually..."

Mark popped out from the doorway to the kitchen and put his arms around her waist. "Especially the pillows," he said, burying his face in her neck. "We enjoy knocking them to the floor every night. You know, while we—"

"Hey," Sly said, holding up his hands. "Please. I don't need to know any more." Once, while Mark and Rose were working at WellyNelly, Sly had interrupted them at the very wrong time. On top of Mark's desk in their Berkeley offices.

Mark laughed and tightened his arms around Rose. "Does Cleo mind you're such a prude?"

"She minds about a lot of things," Sly said. "Which is why I'm here. She hates me."

Mark's smile fell. He loosened his hold on Rose. "Oh, man. Sorry."

"I want your advice," Sly said.

"Good idea," Mark said. "Rose is really good with people."

Rose turned to her husband. "I think he meant you, sweetie."

"Yeah, right," Mark said with a snort. "Because I'm so good with women."

Lowering her voice, Rose put a hand on Mark's jaw. "Oh, you're good, baby."

Mark flushed as pink as a highlighter. Sly looked away, wondering if he could bear to watch another second of these two loving each other when he was dying inside.

"Wow, it's really late," Rose said, pushing away from Mark. "I have to get going. If you can't fix my laptop by tonight, you'd better buy me a new one. Target's open late. Nothing fancy—"

Mark rose to his full height, which was considerable. "*If* I can't fix the thing, which of course I can, I'm not going to buy some off-the-shelf POS at Target. Give me some credit."

Going up on tiptoes, Rose kissed him on the chin. "I credit you with the sense to make sure I have a working laptop by the time I have to write that proposal tonight." She turned to go, catching Sly's eye on her way across the room. "I'm sure Cleo will give you another chance, Sylly. You're a great guy."

"Thanks."

She slung a red purse and a floral laptop bag over her shoulder. "Let me know if there's anything I can do in the campaign."

"Campaign?" Mark asked.

"To win Cleo back, of course," she said.

Sly smiled appreciatively at her. She was a hell of a woman. "Will do," he said. "Thanks."

With a wave, she went out the door and let it slam behind her.

Mark turned to him. "Is that really why you're here?"

"Maybe. I don't know. Yes. How about coffee?"

"Here?"

"If you don't mind," Sly said.

"You know me. I like staying home. Come on." Mark wandered into the kitchen, a gleaming showcase in marble and stainless steel that had cost Sly more than the sum total of every car he'd ever owned. As an investment, however, it had worked. Mark had paid him more for the house than Sly had put into it.

While Sly watched in silence, Mark ground the beans, measured them into a French press, then went over to an electric

Japanese hot-water kettle and, after checking the temperature with an instant-read thermometer, poured the water and pushed down the plunger.

The entire process was slow, deliberate, and exact—with impeccable results. Very Mark-ish. Sly accepted his mug with genuine eagerness and found a perch on a barstool at the counter.

"You make a damn good cup of coffee," Sly said, sipping it. "It's like watching a Nobel chemist in a laboratory."

Mark reached under a low cabinet and pulled out a bag of Cheetos. "Don't tell Rose about these," he said as he ripped them open. "She says they're bad for me."

"Lips are sealed."

Mark held up a puffy morsel and rolled it between his fingers. After a moment, he popped it into his mouth. "You were just kidding about wanting my romantic advice, right?"

"Not at all. Who better to ask than the man who married Rose? I mean, come on. That was quite a score."

Eyes narrowing, Mark stopped chewing. "Admit it. You've always had a thing for her."

"Amazingly enough, no. I was just thinking about how I should have stolen her out from under you when I had the chance, but didn't want to because—I'm just figuring this out now—I'd already met Cleo."

"Thank God," Mark said, looking mournfully into the Cheetos bag. "I shudder to think what would've happened to me if you'd stolen Rose."

Sly felt like he had some idea. It was what was happening to him right now. "Dude. It was you she wanted. From the start."

"Only because you were too obsessed with work to make any moves."

"No, because she was too obsessed with you to ever look at me twice, even if I'd tried," Sly said. "Which is why I'm here. You're the genius. Tell me how I get Cleo to feel that way about me."

"How could I possibly know that?"

"You've got to know something I don't."

Mark smiled. "I know a crap-ton more than you. But not about women."

"I think you know more than you think you know."

Licking his fingers, Mark pondered the ceiling, the smile clinging to his lips along with the orange dust. "I like this. The famously hot Sylly Minguez seeking my sexual counsel."

"Hey. Not sexual. Got that covered. The other stuff."

"There's other stuff?"

Sly waved his hands around the house. "The part where you end up like this together."

Mark's mouth fell open. "You want to settle down?"

He hadn't thought so until a few hours ago. "Maybe."

"Is that how you portrayed your feelings to the object of your affections?"

Sly flinched. "Maybe."

"You dumbass."

"Don't rub it in."

"You're really hurting right now, aren't you?" Mark asked.

"I'm dying."

"You don't look like it. You look the same as you always do, kind of cheerfully smug and invincible."

Sly looked around. "Is it too late to call Rose back home so I can talk to her instead?"

"My point is, you need to show her how you feel."

"She won't see me."

"Maybe I can help you with that," Mark said. "But you have to have a plan. Go at this like you do with work."

"Got it. Like work. Good idea." Sly took out his phone. "I'll start an Evernote notebook."

"Christ. If you must."

Typing with his thumbs, Sly recorded his first few ideas. "I thought I'd take her to dinner. That worked in Vegas."

"Too late. Sounds like she hates you too much for eating right now."

"Then what?"

"When I was in the shits with Rose, I had to trap her at my cabin in Tahoe during a blizzard."

Sly looked out the window. It hadn't snowed in the Sierra for over a year. "Fucking drought."

"How about—" Mark's phone began chiming in his pocket. He held up a finger and looked at the screen. "Hold on, it's my mother. Hello?"

Sly took advantage of the break to gulp down the perfect coffee and type a note into his phone: *1. Trap.*

"You're what?" Mark asked.

Looking up from his phone, Sly saw an arrested expression on his friend's face.

"Yes, he told me," Mark went on. "But—"

Sly watched him, wondering what Trixie was saying.

Suddenly Mark's gaze landed on Sly. "He's right here, actually. In my kitchen."

They stared at each other, one of them having no idea what the phone conversation was about.

"Tomorrow?" Mark pointed at Sly. "You free tomorrow?"

"For what?"

"He's free," Mark said into the phone.

Presumably, Trixie continued to say something, because Mark stared off into space with the phone at his ear.

"Let me talk to her," Sly said. If Trixie was scheming again, he wanted in on it.

"We'll come over at six," Mark said. "Should we bring something? Beer or food or whatever?... Sure, she'll love that... Yes, he's here too."

"Who?" Sly ran a hand through his hair in frustration.

Mark pointed at Mouse, then looked away, listening again. "I'll tell him. Tell your husband I look forward to meeting him." Shaking his head, he put his phone in his pocket.

"Tell me," Sly said.

"Liam and Bev's house, tomorrow at six. Cleo thinks it's a piano lesson. You can talk to her then."

"How—"

"I don't know how she does it," Mark said. "But we might as well be glad that she does."

31

HOLDING HER OVERNIGHT bag, Cleo unlocked the door to her apartment. It was Saturday morning. Because Trixie had said she would be home well before noon, Cleo had packed up and moved out by nine. Now she was home, finally home.

Home smelled stale. She dumped her bag on the couch and walked around opening windows. All three of them. She was glad to be out of Trixie's house for social reasons, but she'd miss the space and the view.

Nice of Bev to dog-sit for a few hours until Trixie got home. The dogs would be all right left alone on the sun porch, but they really preferred company, especially Zeus.

She could relate. But she wouldn't mope. Living alone had its perks, and even if she got lonely, she was used to it by now.

After a few trips back to the car, all her things were back where they belonged. Her clothes, her music, her toothbrush, her mangled heart.

She sat down and tried to lose herself at the piano. After an hour, she gave up composing and opened her computer. She checked her sales on iTunes, compared income to expenses, bought some new shoes.

Finally, it was twelve thirty. Time to teach, something to keep her busy. She set off for her piano lessons with grim determination. Halfway through teaching her first pupil, she realized she hadn't eaten anything since gulping down half a banana in Trixie's kitchen. That got her remembering the last good meal she'd eaten—a week earlier, listening to Sinatra at Sly's side.

Her student, a nine-year-old girl with enviably long fingers, stopped playing "Greensleeves" and said, "I can hear your stomach growling."

"Think of it as a cello accompaniment."

"It's really loud," the girl said. "And you look funny. Are you OK?"

"I'm fine. Thanks for asking. Let's hear that again, all right?"

On her way to her second lesson, she got a chicken sandwich at the Jack-in-the-Box drive-thru, not caring that she hated everything on the menu, just shoving it into her mouth to make the hunger pangs stop.

On her way to her third lesson, she got a call from that pupil's mother, canceling for the week.

"Stomach flu," the woman said, but Cleo figured her son hadn't practiced again. Any eleven-year-old who got gastroenteritis as often as that kid did would be hospitalized by now. It had been so long since he'd been available for a lesson, Cleo couldn't even remember what he looked like.

Now it was two hours until her lesson with Bev. She thought about canceling on account of a recently acquired stomach ailment. She could say it was going around. Rubbing her stomach, she looked at herself in the rearview mirror. She definitely felt sick, but it wasn't the kind of thing you caught from an eleven-year-old boy. A thirty-five-year-old man with bedroom eyes and a dimpled chin, yes.

She'd caught that one bad.

So she went home and took a second shower, got dressed in tight black clothes and leather boots that made her feel sexy and angry and powerful, swallowed a handful of Tums, brushed her teeth, tweezed her eyebrows, and got back into her car to return to the leafy upper altitudes of Oakland.

Because she wasn't an idiot. She knew who was going to be there. Bev hadn't rescheduled her piano lesson because of the baby's gym class. Trixie was behind it.

Cleo strode out of the apartment building to her car and flung herself inside. Keeping busy hadn't helped. She couldn't stop thinking about Sly. Even when she wasn't thinking about him, she was feeling him. Her skin remembered what it felt like to be close to him. Her nose dwelled over his scent. Her tongue trailed over her teeth the same way his had done, slow and confident.

He'd adopted a dog.

He'd then he'd bought a Volvo for his dog.

"I hope they're very happy together," she muttered, coating her lips with another swipe of fuchsia lip gloss.

Starting a family with a human woman was light years away from where he was right now. By the time he was ready for anything like that, with anyone, she'd be dead.

And he hadn't come close to groveling. Blaming his phone for not talking to her—please. He wasn't the one. She had to forget him and move on.

Blasting Philip Glass over the speakers as if he were the hottest new pop star, she drove to Bev and Liam's house. When she pulled into the driveway, she noted it was suspiciously empty. Had Trixie been crafty enough to make everyone park at the end of the street so Cleo wouldn't get suspicious?

Probably.

Squinting down the road as she walked to the front door, Cleo ignored her pounding heart and told herself she could handle this. She could handle anything. They were bound to see each other sometime. They were friends who'd slept together, nothing more. Nothing more to him, anyway. Her feelings were her own business. If he didn't want to be pressured into a relationship he wasn't ready for, he wouldn't remind her of what they'd done, what she'd admitted feeling for him.

She pushed the doorbell. Almost instantly, Bev opened the door. Her dark hair was pulled back into a high ponytail but hung off-center as if someone had been pulling on it. She gave Cleo a quick smile, then turned away to catch a crawling baby who was dragging a large Birkenstock sandal.

"No you don't, Merry. Uncle Markie was looking for that. He can't walk around in one shoe." Bev shot Cleo a smile. "Come on in. You'd better keep your boots on. My daughter has a fetish."

"I can relate," Cleo said, scanning the living room for other people. Her pulse was still overreacting to the journey from the apartment to the front door. She'd expected something other than a couch covered with stuffed animals and a floor littered with plastic blocks. Cocktails, strippers, Elvis—not sure, just something Trixie had worked up.

Bev shoved her feet into some clogs by the front door. "I've still got to bring Merry over to Trixie's. Really quick. Sorry I'm running late. Liam was in LA and I was up with the baby. When she's not stealing shoes, she's breaking out of her crib and playing piano at three in the morning."

Cleo smiled down at Merry, who was busy squatting below her, clutching her boots with both chubby hands and pulling with all she had. "Maybe she could get a job at a nightclub. Bring in some extra funds."

"Great idea." Bev scooped up Merry and hauled her to the front door. "I'll be right back, OK?"

Merry's head pivoted to hold her gaze on Cleo's feet as her mother carried her out of sight.

The door shut behind them, leaving Cleo alone with the toys, laundry, and solo Birkenstock. Pulling sheet music out of her messenger bag, she turned toward the piano.

Sly stood next to the bench, hands in his pockets, staring at her with dark, piercing eyes.

"Don't go," he said.

32

ADRENALINE SURGED THROUGH Cleo's veins. "I knew it! I knew you'd be here. I knew it."

He didn't move. "Yet you came."

"I knew she'd do something to get me up here. I left early enough this morning so I could avoid her, but when Bev asked for a lesson at six tonight, such a coincidence since it was the same day Trixie and Hugo came back from wherever they were after Vegas, I just knew—"

She spun away from him and headed for the door. Being alone with him wasn't what she'd expected. A dinner party, a family BBQ, a group. Not him alone.

"Don't go. Cleo, please. Hear me out."

She opened the door. "Where's the new Volvo?"

"Down the street."

"Thought so," she said.

He came after her. "I'm sorry about Thursday. And everything else."

"Everything?"

"No. I didn't mean that." He reached over her head and pushed the door shut.

She could smell his cologne. A scent memory from their

lovemaking in Las Vegas nearly knocked her over. "You're kidnapping me?"

He braced both hands over her head and crowded her against the door. "Yes."

Her heart was pounding in her throat, blocking her airways. To avoid his gaze, which would see too much, all the longing and the doubt, she squeezed her eyes shut.

Which only heightened her sense of smell.

"Are you listening?" he asked.

She shook her head. Impossibly, she imagined she could hear him smile.

"I bought a new phone," he said.

"I don't care."

"I know." His breath was soft on her cheek. "I screwed up."

"It's not your fault you don't want the same things I do. It's good to get it out in the open before we take this too far."

"Are you going to conduct this entire conversation with your eyes closed?"

She nodded.

Now she knew she could hear him smiling. Something about his breathing changed as it moved through curved lips. "You know what I think?" he asked. "I think you're the one who's afraid of where this might go."

"Now you're just getting desperate," she said.

"You bet I am. Desperate to have you."

Her heart thudded in her chest. She'd make a run for it but her knees were weak. She'd probably fall down and then he'd really have her where he wanted her.

Damned if she wasn't tempted.

"I'm not afraid of... you know," she said.

"Love?"

"I told you that I thought my mom was right all along."

"You're saying you love me?" he asked.

She pinched her lips together and reminded herself about groveling.

He whispered in her ear, sending shockwaves down her spine. "I think you do love me. That's why you're here."

"Big deal. I've told you that before."

"This is different." His lips grazed her temple.

"Is it?" Her voice sounded too high. "Why, just because we slept together?"

"Because we both wanted it so bad. For so long." Brushing her hair to one side, he dropped kisses along her neck and pressed his pelvis into hers. The door was as hard as he was. "And still do."

"I want more than sex."

"Sure you do."

"I do." Opening her eyes, she put her palms on his broad chest and pushed.

He held himself at arm's length, leaning into her hands, staring at her. "So do I."

"You want sex and TV and beer and good times," she said.

"Don't you?"

"I want more than that."

"You're trying to scare me away," he said. "It's not going to work."

"I'm serious, Sly. I want it all. I want all the things you don't."

"I've been thinking. Marrying you wouldn't be so bad."

"Oh, thank you. I'm overwhelmed."

"And it would be interesting to see what our kids looked like. DNA from so many continents. I wonder if any would be as blond as you."

Tears were burning in her eyes. "Don't joke. Don't."

He caught her face in his hands. "I'm not joking." His mocking smile vanished. "I've never let myself think about it before. Once I did, I couldn't stop thinking about it."

"You're thirty-five. Pretty late for it to cross your mind." She broke away from him and stumbled across the room. *Wouldn't be so bad*, she thought as she picked up her bag. "I'm sure it'll pass."

"You're trying to make this about me," he said. "But you're the one who's afraid. You got hurt before. It's natural you want to avoid getting hurt again. Which is why I'm going to be patient."

Sheet music fell out of her open bag. Hands shaking, she scooped up the booklets and shoved them back inside.

Was he right? Was she panicking?

Had he really imagined their children's faces?

While she dropped more sheet music to the floor, the door flew open and Liam strode in with a garment bag over his shoulder. Trixie's oldest son and Bev's husband was taller than Sly. Blond, good-looking, intimidating. A former Olympian, Cleo had heard.

Liam flung his bag onto a chair and turned on Sly. "Just the man I want to see."

"Liam." Sly held out his hand. "Nice to see you again. Bev let me in—"

Liam ignored his outstretched hand. "You were there. In Vegas."

"We both were," she said quickly.

Liam kept his gaze on Sly. "Last week, your uncle and my mother got married. To each other, in fact."

Cleo moved to Sly's side so they could present a unified front. "Don't worry. They're not serious."

One of Liam's golden eyebrows rose. "Not serious?"

"We think it was just a ruse to get us together," she said.

Liam's second eyebrow shot up. "Is that what you think?"

"It was an old Taco Bell," Sly said. "There was Elvis. Playing a ukulele."

Liam flinched. "Have you seen them?"

"Not since Las Vegas," Sly said.

"I was just over at my mother's house," Liam said. "Bev told me to go over there from the airport instead of here, saying her piano teacher needed a few minutes alone with Sylly Minguez."

They didn't say anything. Cleo could feel her face heating.

"You know who really needed a few minutes alone?" Liam bent over, picked up a pair of blocks, and fit them together. "My mother and her new husband."

Sly smiled. "Hugo's over there?"

"Oh, he's over there. And so's his recliner, flat-screen TV, and impressive collection of *Star Wars* memorabilia."

She and Sly exchanged smiles.

"That was fast," Sly muttered.

"You knew," Liam continued, his voice flat. "You were at this *wedding*."

"We were indeed," Sly said. "Elvis too."

"You think this is funny?"

"I think it's great," Sly said. "And so should you. Hugo is a good guy. Your mom seems to think so too. They deserve to be happy."

"This isn't about being happy," Liam said. "It's about sneaking around. Did you tell your family about the wedding?"

"Not right away," Sly said.

"But you told them."

"They already knew," Sly said.

"I didn't," Liam said. "I would've liked to. Did you tell Mark?"

Perhaps out of loyalty to their friendship, Sly didn't answer.

Cleo didn't have the same restrictions. "He's the one who convinced us it was fake."

"Once we got back home, it didn't seem real," Sly added.

Liam set the blocks on top of the piano. "Is your uncle the type of man to go through an actual wedding ceremony for the hell of it?"

Sly cleared his throat. "No."

"Neither is my mother," Liam said. "You wouldn't know that, but Mark should. The woman is obsessed with matrimony. It's like her religion. She'd never lie about something so important to her."

They stood there in silence, an awkward trio with sheet music and plastic blocks littering their feet.

"She says I would've blamed you," Liam said. "My mother. She wanted to tell me herself when they got home."

Cleo and Sly remained quiet. *Ten points for Trixie*, she thought.

"Come on," Liam said, nodding toward the door. "She's opened the champagne. We can't let them drink it all by themselves."

33

RELUCTANTLY, SLY FOLLOWED Liam and Cleo out the door. He wasn't thrilled to join Trixie and Hugo's wedding celebration right now. He'd been so close. Just a few more minutes and she would've caved. She'd be on her way to his place where he could seal the deal. Or begin sealing. It might take hours. *Days.*

Directly behind her, he watched her fair hair sway back and forth as she moved, remembering how silky it felt under his fingers. He'd always appreciated her hair, even before he'd been ready to admit how much he appreciated the rest of her.

She was still fighting it. Maybe the celebratory atmosphere would make his case better than he ever could.

"April and Zack are already here," Liam said, striding down the steps to the driveway. "With their dog. It's quite a zoo in there right now."

"Is Mouse there too?" Cleo asked.

"I'm sure there are," Liam said.

Cleo laughed, giving Sly hope.

"Not that kind," Sly said. "Mouse is my dog. He's with Bella right now."

"Too bad," she said softly.

"It is?" Sly asked.

She glanced at him. "Cool dog. I didn't really get to see him before."

"You will." He held his breath, waiting for her to disagree. She didn't say a word.

So close. One toast and they were out of there. He'd properly congratulate Hugo later.

It was already dark outside, but unusually clear. No fog to block the three-quarter moon glowing over the roof of Trixie's house or the shimmering lights of the East Bay cities below. November brought the first really cold nights of the year, but that was good for climbing into bed.

A red Mini pulled up just as they were crossing the driveway between the two houses. Rose climbed out and gave them all a curious look.

"Turns out Trixie's really married," Sly told her.

"I knew it!" Rose spun around and bent over to shout into the car. "I told you it was real!"

Liam threw up his hands. "Did everyone know but me?"

Mark got out of the Mini and slammed the door. "I thought Mom was fooling around."

"Don't remind me." Liam marched up to the house and pulled open the front door. "Come on, let's meet the guy."

"He's a good guy," Sly said.

"Better be," Liam said.

They filed inside and were attacked instantly by Trixie's three tiny dogs and a larger, quieter dog with three legs.

Trixie rushed over with a champagne flute in each hand. "Oh, Liam, you interrupted them. I told you not to go over there."

Liam whacked Sly's shoulder. "He looked like he needed a moment to regroup."

Trixie shoved a glass into Sly's hand. "Buck up. She'll come around."

"Hello," Cleo said. "Right here."

"I know, dear, that's why I'm holding this glass for you." Trixie gave her the other one.

Hugo joined them with two more glasses. "We got a chocolate cake at Safeway. It's in the kitchen." He handed both glasses to Liam. "Come on, the ice cream's melting."

Putting their arms around each other, Trixie and Hugo wandered back into the kitchen.

"Nice," Bev said, taking one of the glasses from Liam. "It's like a birthday party. Oh, careful Sly. Look out below."

Sly looked down and saw baby Merry crawling around Cleo's feet, patting her boots with two chubby hands.

Sipping her drink, Cleo shot Sly a small smile. "She has a shoe fetish. Isn't that cute?"

"You're cute," Sly said, pitching his voice low. "Irresistible, even."

Cleo held his gaze. Pink spots bloomed on her cheeks.

Moving between them, Liam lifted up Merry and planted a raspberry on her belly. "Leave the shoesies alone when people are wearing them, Mer-bear. Your fingers will get squished."

"We'll get cake," Bev said, clapping her hands. "Cake."

"Ooh," Merry said. Was she trying to say shoe? Could a one-year-old baby do that?

Bev and Liam followed the others to the kitchen.

"Ooh," Merry repeated over her daddy's shoulder.

Sly turned to Cleo. "Let's get a piece of cake, shall we? I should give a toast."

"Tough crowd."

"I've had worse." Sly stole a kiss. Her lips tasted like champagne. When she didn't slap him or run away, he kissed her again. "I like your shoes too."

She blinked and stepped away. "Somebody said there was chocolate."

Feeling more than a little hopeful, he caught her arm in his and walked through the living and dining rooms to the kitchen. Although it was a big room, the Johnson family and its matrimonial satellites were a growing group. Mark and Liam's little sister, April, was there with her boyfriend, Zack. Sly had hired him briefly that spring, but it hadn't stuck. His relationship with April seemed far more lasting. He'd heard they were engaged.

Bev shoved two plates laden with chocolate cake and ice cream at them. "Everyone should start eating."

"That's my girl," Liam said, smiling at her over the fork in his mouth.

"Well, they should," Bev said. "The ice cream's melting."

"While everyone does that," Hugo said, "I just want to say how much I appreciate you welcoming me into your family like this."

There was only a split second of silence. Then Liam said, "As long as my mom's happy, I'm happy."

Trixie burst into tears. "Oh, I knew it would be OK." She flung her arms around her oldest son and hugged him so hard he yelped. When she withdrew, he had chocolate smeared over his white dress shirt.

Hugo blotted her tears with a paper towel. "I told you."

"It's Mark I'm worried about," Trixie said, looking around. She found him sitting on the floor with the three-legged dog in his lap. "Are you OK?"

Mark drained his champagne. "I'm kind of annoyed. But I'll get over it."

"It's annoying I've brought another man into your father's

home?" Trixie asked.

"No, it's annoying I was…" He frowned. "Wrong. I hate being wrong."

"You didn't have all the data," Rose said, stroking unkempt hair off his forehead. "Garbage in, garbage out."

"*I* didn't need any extra data," Liam said.

Mark looked mournfully into his wife's eyes. "He's never going to let me live this down."

"What data did you need, honey?" Trixie asked.

Leaning on Rose, Mark got to his feet. He gestured at Hugo. "I'd never seen you two together."

Sly looked at his uncle, flushed and beaming. He saw the way Trixie stood next to him so that at least one body part was always in contact.

"But now that you have?" Trixie put both arms around Hugo and rested her cheek on his flannel-shirted chest.

"Now I know I've got a new stepfather," Mark said. "Not that I had an old one. Right?"

Trixie smiled up at Hugo. "He's the first."

"And the last," Hugo said.

"Unless you die," she said, still smiling.

More than one person sucked in a shocked breath.

"Well, I am a widow, for Christ's sake," Trixie said. "I'm just being realistic."

After everyone had some cake and champagne and shook Hugo's hand or hugged Trixie, the initial discomfort seemed to fade. Conversation turned to Merry and grandchildren, Rose and Mark's wedding earlier that year, April and Zack's recent engagement, and the family's plans for Thanksgiving.

Conscious of being an outsider, Cleo moved to the back of

the group, near the doorway to the dining room, where she could shovel more chocolate cake into her mouth. As soon as the moment was right, she was going to slip away.

"How about a toast," Sly declared, tapping a spoon against a glass. He was standing in the middle of the group, a relaxed smile on his face.

Cleo ate another bite of cake but was too distracted to taste it. He was always so confident. Anytime, anyplace. Always at ease, always sure of himself. Almost as much of an outsider as she was, but right there in the middle of things, commanding attention and getting things done.

He raised his voice to address the group that was now circled around him. "I haven't prepared anything to say, given the circumstances, so I'll have to speak from my heart. I do have a heart, by the way." He grinned as the group laughed. His gaze met Cleo's and held it. "Not that I can claim to be an expert on love. Not this kind of love. Some people are naturals and seem to be born with an infinite capacity for giving and sharing and caring."

She swallowed.

"The rest of us," he continued, "are selfish bastards." His grin returned along with the laughter.

"Speak for yourself," Mark called out.

"Oh, I do, I do," Sly said. "Which is exactly what Hugo and Trixie said back there in Vegas. I'm not a big fan of Elvis, but he did a pretty good job of capturing the moment in words. Don't be cruel, love me tender. Or whatever. Like I said, I'm not a fan."

"You're rambling," Mark said.

"Hey, you're next, geek boy," Sly said. "Because, as I said, I have a heart, or I did before I gave it away. Some of us are late bloomers. Some of us are slow to figure things out. But we get there in the end. And if we're lucky, we get the chance to make it stick. Make it forever. All those years of getting it wrong have made us experts on what to do to get it right. And we're afraid of going back. It's highly motivating, is what I'm saying."

"What *are* you saying?" Mark asked.

"Let's see if you like it when you get interrupted at my wedding, Mark," Sly said.

"You're getting married?" April asked. "When did this happen?"

34

CLEO COULDN'T TAKE it anymore. She dropped her empty plate on the counter and ducked out of the room.

It didn't feel real. It was like a play, and she was exiting stage left. Just a few days ago, Sly had run away at the thought of marriage. Now he was announcing their mythical engagement in front of his family and friends.

Her body felt weightless, insubstantial. She floated through the living room and out the front door. She floated down the steps to the driveway and across the pavement to her car parked next door.

There she put her hand on the hood and drew in a breath, feeling as if she'd run a marathon at ten thousand feet.

"Hold it!"

She looked back at Trixie's house, not recognizing the voice. To her amazement, she saw Sly barreling down the steps three at a time, arms waving.

What was the matter with him?

He ran across the driveway, tripped over a rosemary hedge, and tumbled to his knees into the mulch. Before he was even on his feet, he gasped "Cleo!" and lurched forward and fell again. "Please."

She continued to stare. Although she did have her hand on the hood of her car, she hadn't intended on driving away just yet. Her plan had been to enjoy the fresh air and ponder the infinite sky while she waited for him to come out of the house so she could tell him she loved him.

But maybe he didn't need to know that. She kind of liked seeing him all riled up. Desperation looked good on him. It went nicely with his dimpled chin and bedroom eyes.

Sure, it was evil, but she'd make it up to him.

"Yes?" she asked, staying where she was.

He got to his feet and brushed the bark chips off his knees. "Don't go. Please, for God's sake. We have a chance to really make something here. You and me. Don't you see? It's real. It's never happened to me before. I didn't realize what it was until it was almost too late. Don't make it too late. I love you, Cleo. I love you like crazy. I think I've loved you for a really long time. I was just too stupid to admit it." He approached her slowly, one hand out in front of him as if he were soothing an unbroken filly.

She overcame the urge to neigh. "How long, do you think? That you've loved me?"

"I don't know, a long time. At least since that time you got me to sneak into the Claremont with you to use the hot tub."

Her insides went gooey on her. "That was ages ago," she whispered. "I thought you'd forgotten about that."

"Hardly. It's the first time I saw you... almost naked. And then you went into the water." His nostrils flared.

The Claremont was a ritzy hotel and spa in Berkeley that catered to rich vacationers and the business elite. That day had been the one-year anniversary of her divorce, and she'd needed a distraction.

"It was one of the best days of my life," he said. "But now I know that's because you were in it."

Her heart skipped. Oh, he did good grovel. She couldn't keep up the tough act much longer. "And you got to see me all wet and slippery."

Nodding, holding her gaze, he took a step closer. "I felt guilty about... dwelling over... that day as often as I did."

"Dwelling?"

He was directly in front of her, inches away. "Fantasizing."

"Why didn't you do anything?"

"Why didn't you?"

"I—" Because she'd never let herself believe it was possible. "I had no idea you felt that way."

"So you fantasized about me, too?" Smiling faintly, he brushed his knuckles across her cheek. Shivers ran down her back.

She'd walked right into that one. "No." When he tensed, she put her hand over his wrist. "I didn't let myself."

"I'm a guy. I let myself. Sometimes more than once on the same day." He pressed the back of his hand against her cheek. "You're blushing again."

She was. Like crazy. But she was also laughing.

With a sigh, she wrapped her arms around his neck. "Kiss me."

Lowering his head, he returned the embrace and slanted his mouth over hers. Gentle and then hard, demanding. She slipped her tongue between his teeth and savored the feel and taste of him. His hands moved down her back and held her firmly against him. The kiss deepened. She ran her fingers through his hair—for days she'd been afraid she'd done that for the last time—and pushed him against the side of her car.

"As much as I'd like to," he said, nibbling her eyebrow, "we can't do this here."

"Why not?"

"Because, sexy temptress, the things I'm going to do to you aren't intended for a general audience."

Running her tongue along his jaw, she twirled a lock of his hair around her index finger. "What kind of things?"

He moved a hand between her legs. "Good things."

Her brain flickered and went dark. She was done thinking for a while. "Sounds good."

"Get your car later. Come on." He clasped her hand and pulled her with him down the driveway to the street. "Mine is parked just a few houses down. A neighbor let me put it there."

"Because of Trixie?" she asked, jogging after him.

"Because of Trixie."

"She's really something," she said.

He stopped and twirled her into his arms. Moonlight lit up his face. "You're the something. My something," he said softly. "My everything."

Her word was only a breath. "Oh."

"I meant what I said at the house. I want to marry you and have babies and watch TV with the babies and maybe even learn how to play the piano."

Was this really happening?

Shaking his head, he stroked her shoulder. "I'm going too fast. I'm scaring you. Forget I said anything."

Belatedly, she found her voice. "Are you kidding? I'm trying to memorize every word. I'm afraid I'll get it wrong when I tell my mom."

He recoiled in mock alarm. "The future mother-in-law."

"Stop that. When you ask me to marry you, *if* you do, make it really obvious that's what you're doing. Or if it's me, I'll do the same. Otherwise it doesn't feel serious. It's like we're just joking around."

He caught her up again in his arms and kissed her so hard she forgot her name.

An immeasurable amount of time later, he asked, "Did that feel serious?"

A siren wailed in the distance. The night breeze, picking up force, blew a strand of hair out of his eyes.

"Oh, yeah," she said.

35

HOLDING HANDS, SLY and Cleo hurried to the next driveway, where his new red Volvo sat under an oleander bush. He opened the door for her, kissed her on the lips and the nose and the forehead, then again on the lips. They lingered for a moment and then finally broke away and jogged around to the driver's seat.

After he'd started the car, he entwined his fingers in hers again and drove one-handed all the way through the narrow hairpin curves down to the flats, which would've made her nervous— their wheels came within inches of open air a few times—if she weren't intoxicated with love, lust, and joy.

She'd been to his apartment many times, but he'd never greeted her at the door before with an openmouthed kiss as he unbuttoned his shirt. Then again, she'd never kicked off her boots and torn off her clothes before reaching the living room either. And she was pretty sure he'd never stroked her naked ass in the doorway to his bedroom while she moaned his name, unbuttoned his pants, and pushed down his boxers.

"Let's move in together," he said, kissing her collarbone. "Tomorrow works for me. I'll clear my schedule."

A phone rang somewhere. Her purse. They both ignored it.

"Your place is almost as small as mine," she said. "Not sure that'll work."

"Size is your only objection?"

Grinning, she reached between his legs. "Who's objecting?"

"Good," he said, his voice tight. He sucked her left nipple into his mouth. "We'll move into the house near Trixie."

"You have a house near Trixie?"

"I've always liked that area." His breath was hot on her breast. "Not as much as this area, of course." He caressed her ass. "Or this one."

The phone paused ringing only for a moment before starting up again. Not appreciating the interruption, she pulled away from him. "Give me a second. I'll turn it off."

He reached for her. "Leave it. Just ignore it."

"It's distracting."

"You're distracting." Hooking an arm around her waist, he rotated her back into his arms, kissing her in the doorway as the phone continued ringing.

Oh, it was good. He was good. She sank against him and ran her fingers through his hair. Eventually the ringing stopped. His knee pushed between her legs and she straddled his hard, strong thigh. The bed was on the other side of the small bedroom, under the window, but even that short distance seemed too far. He was ready, she was ready—

The phone started ringing again. Determined to deal with it this time, she pulled out of Sly's arms and jogged to her purse on the floor near the front door with her abandoned clothes.

"I'm never going to get tired of looking at you," he said behind her. "Coming or going."

She shot him a saucy smile over her shoulder, then glanced at her screen as she felt for the power button. "Figures," she said. "It's my mother."

He snatched the phone out of her hands. "Let me."

The mischievous look on his face made her nervous. "Don't you dare," she said, lunging for it.

But he was already holding it to his head. "Hello, Dr. Lundquist. How are you doing?"

Desperately, Cleo tried to get the phone out of his hand, but he was too nimble and twisted out of range.

"Why yes, she's right here, actually," he said. "But she's a little busy. Can she call you back later?"

Cleo punched him in the shoulder. Her mom was probably imagining the worst. Or the best. Either was annoying.

"We're at my place. One of my places. I own a few properties, because of my long and stellar career in high tech, but I'm thinking it's time to settle down." He caught Cleo's gaze and grinned.

She felt the blood drain out of her face. First the Johnsons, now her mother. On the phone. While she was standing there without any clothes on.

She punched him again. And then kissed him on the cheek. Because her emotions were mixed.

His tone suddenly became serious. "Better late than never," he said, staring at her with those dark eyes.

There was a long pause.

"You were right." He reached out and gently stroked his thumb over her cheek. "All along."

Biting her lip, Cleo closed her eyes and imagined the conversation she'd have with her mother tomorrow. *Are you* sure *he cares about you? Really, really sure? You're not just fooling yourself because you want it so badly?*

"Thanks," he said. "Sounds good." He hung up and set the phone on a hall table before turning to her with a smile.

"Aren't you funny?" She turned and marched into the bedroom. "You can make it up to me with your tongue."

Faster than she thought possible, he caught up to her and tackled her onto the bed. "I can do that." Nuzzling her neck, he nibbled, sucked, and breathed into her ear. "Cleo."

She stared at the ceiling. "I'm putting a password on my phone."

"You should," he said.

"'Time to settle down,'" she said, quoting him.

"That's right. She thought it was a great idea."

"She said that?"

Caressing her hips, he dropped kisses along her collarbone. "You feel tense. Did it really bother you? Me talking to her?"

"I know what she's going to say. She's probably making notes right now, preparing for her session with me in the morning."

"Really?" He rested on his side next to her, propping himself up on an elbow. His warm hand rested on her belly, no longer exploring. "You might be surprised."

She pitched her voice low and soft, the way her mother did when she was in full-therapist mode. "Are you sure he cares about you the way you'd like him to care about you? Are you projecting the depth of your feelings on him?"

He brushed the hair out of her eyes. "That's not what she said."

"Of course not. She was talking to *you*."

"Would you like to know what she said? Or are you enjoying your dark fantasy too much to hear the truth?"

"She told you I'd always loved you. You admitted that it took you a while to figure it out."

"Nope," he said.

"Nope? Please. That's her mantra."

"With you, maybe, but not with me," he said. "I've never talked to her, just the two of us."

"Fine. What did she say?"

"Oh, sure. Now you want to know."

She crossed her arms over her chest, pushing his hand to one side. "I've changed my mind. I'd rather watch TV tonight."

He laughed and wrapped an arm over both of hers, kissing her hair. "We'll do that after. If we've got any energy."

Staying angry was impossible. He smelled too good. "All right, you win. What did she say?"

"I don't know. Now I'm feeling kind of vulnerable." He rolled onto his back and let out a loud, exaggerated sigh.

"Oh, for God's sake."

"Maybe if you held me, I could manage it," he said.

She flung an arm over his chest.

"Closer," he said.

She added a breast and a thigh. "Better?"

"Very therapeutic," he said, sliding his hand over her backside and stealing a kiss.

"You said, 'You were right. All along.' If that wasn't about me, then what? Stock tips?"

"You're so funny." He traced her eyebrow with a fingertip. "I've never wanted to be with a woman—with anyone—as much as I want to be with you."

It was hard to concentrate on the topic at hand when he derailed the conversation like that. She softened into his embrace.

"But I was slow to figure it out," he said. "Like I told your mother. But she'd always known I had to be in love with you."

Three long seconds later, she blinked. "What?"

"That's when I told her she'd been right all along." He held her face in both hands and gazed into her eyes. "I've loved you a long time. I love you now. And I'm going to keep on loving you. Like it or not."

Her heart shut down for a moment, then rebooted with a vengeance. "She thought—she said—she knew—"

"Why are you surprised? You're always saying she's a mind reader."

"But not about you, not—she's never thought that—she's never said anything like that—"

"Maybe she didn't think you were ready," he said. "That you needed more time to get over the divorce."

"Me? I'm ready. It's you who needed to be ready."

He lifted himself on top of her and looked into her eyes. "I'm ready."

"I can feel how you're ready," she said with a grin.

"Listen to me. I think your mother saw the obvious. Why else would I spend so much time with you for so many years? Either I was gay or I was waiting for you to wake up and throw yourself at me."

She traced the dimple on his chin with the tips of her fingers. "Good thing you got tired of waiting and made the first move," she said.

"Good thing you made a few moves of your own."

"I'm ready to make a few more of those as soon as possible," she said.

"I'll give you what you want. Because I love you." He pressed his mouth to hers. The playful kiss turned into a deep, slow exploration. After a long minute, he lifted his face and gazed into her eyes. "I do love you, Cleo."

"I love you too, Sly."

"You mean that in a hot, sexy kind of way, right?" he asked. "Because I'm not talking about watching TV."

"Very hot and sexy. But let's be real—we're also going to watch a lot of TV."

"Not now though," he said roughly, kissing her chin, her throat, her shoulder, her lips while his hands explored her body.

She smiled. "Not now."

Epilogue

FOUR MONTHS LATER, Cleo and Sly stood in the driveway of a yellow house with an oversized blue door. That door was currently propped open by a cardboard box filled with sheet music. Other boxes, large and small, lined the tile foyer, spilling into the living room, kitchen, and master bedroom.

On the floor between all the boxes lay a dotted path of homemade peanut-butter-and-bacon dog biscuits. It trailed between the backseat of the red Volvo in the driveway to an extra-jumbo memory-foam dog bed resting in the living room. Next to the grand piano, which Sly had bought from a hotel in Carmel.

"You know you want those cookies," Sly said to Mouse, who sprawled across the backseat with his head turned to one side, resting his chin on an enormous paw.

Wiggling past Sly, Cleo waved a fragment of cookie under the dog's nose. "Mmm," she said. But the plum-sized black nose didn't even twitch.

"Give it up, buddy." Sly stroked Mouse's ears. "This is our new home now. We're not going back to the condo."

"The tile floor is nice and cool," Cleo said, waving the cookie again. "You'll love it. We know how you hate to be hot."

Mouse let out a sigh. Flecks of drool dripped onto his paw.

Cleo echoed his sigh and dropped the cookie onto the driveway next to the others. They'd tried blasting opera first, but that hadn't worked either. "Maybe we should call Hugo for advice."

"He'll just laugh," Sly said. "He doesn't take anything seriously anymore."

"Marriage seems to agree with him."

"He probably wouldn't even answer his work phone if I called him."

"It is Sunday," she said.

"He used to work Sundays."

"Like I said, marriage agrees with him." Cleo put her arm around Sly and turned him around to face her. "Having second thoughts?"

"About the house? Or about marriage?"

She swatted him on the shoulder. "The house. Too late to back out of the wedding. My mother would kill both of us."

"All right then. We'll have to go through with it." He cast a martyred look at the darkening sky. It had been a long day, even with professional movers helping. Both of them were old enough to have amassed an unreasonable amount of possessions. Caught up in the fun of being together, they hadn't done a very good job of editing down their things before the moving van had arrived. Over the next few days and weeks, they would begin the process of eliminating the duplicates. For instance: as much as they both liked smoothies, they wouldn't need two blenders.

Sly's arms tightened around Cleo. "How about we order pizza tonight?"

"Does Hector's deliver way up here? It's quite a drive from El Cerrito." Their yellow house was in Oakland, up in the hills near Trixie and Hugo, tucked between redwoods and blooming

California lilac.

"Would I ever buy a house that was too far away for Hector's delivery?" Stroking the curve of her waist, he dragged his lips across her hairline, kissing and nibbling. "Please."

"Sorry to doubt you." She stretched up against him and rested her cheek against his. His end-of-day stubble was her favorite. And his scent, just him, after the commercial products had worn off. She didn't have to hold back anymore. She could get as close as she wanted, love him as much as she liked.

They stopped talking for a few minutes, busy with other things. After a while, she pulled back and gazed into his eyes. They were dark and dreamy, filled with love.

"Let's go in," she said. "We'll leave the doors open. He'll come in when he's ready."

Sly slid his hand down her arm and caught her fingers in his. "Some guys just need a little time to figure things out."

She smiled and squeezed his hand. "Not just guys."

They got lost in another kiss before Cleo finally put her hand over his mouth. "Let's order that pizza and continue this later."

He stole a final kiss, then said, "Right. Later. Let's tell Mouse about the plan."

It was then they noticed the backseat was empty. And as their gaze searched the ground for the missing cookies, they found a dark, furry silhouette watching them from the house's doorway.

Waiting for them to come inside.

Author Note

Thank you for reading *This Changes Everything*.

Would you like to get an email when I release a new book? Sign up for my mailing list at www.gretchengalway.com. You'll also hear about sales and special goodies!

All the best,

Gretchen Galway

About the Author

GRETCHEN GALWAY is a *USA Today* bestselling author who writes romantic comedies because love is too painful to survive without laughing. Raised in the American Midwest, she now lives in California with her husband and two kids.

Facebook: www.facebook.com/AuthorGretchenGalway

Twitter: www.twitter.com/GretchenGalway

Website: www.gretchengalway.com

www.ingramcontent.com/pod-product-compliance
Lightning Source LLC
Chambersburg PA
CBHW061519210726
48287CB00006B/1745